W9-BWA-458

Praise for *Murder in Lascaux*, the first Nora Barnes and Toby Sandler Mystery:

"With a colorful mélange of art, French history, food, and a surprising perp, this tale will keep readers entertained (and entice them to visit southwestern France)."

Booklist

"Draine and Hinden have produced a debut novel that many readers will hope is the first of a series."

France Today

"A suspenseful tale intermingled with sumptuous descriptions of art, food, and the French landscape."

Madison Magazine

"A brisk and brainy whodunit. . . . The book feels like the seamless work of a single author."

The Capital Times

Terrace Books, a trade imprint of the University of Wisconsin Press, takes its name from the Memorial Union Terrace, located at the University of Wisconsin–Madison. Since its inception in 1907, the Wisconsin Union has provided a venue for students, faculty, staff, and alumni to debate art, music, politics, and the issues of the day. It is a place where theater, music, drama, literature, dance, outdoor activities, and major speakers are made available to the campus and the community. To learn more about the Union, visit www.union.wisc.edu.

The Body in Bodega Bay

Betsy Draine and Michael Hinden

Terrace Books
A trade imprint of the University of Wisconsin Press

Terrace Books
A trade imprint of the University of Wisconsin Press
1930 Monroe Street, 3rd Floor
Madison, Wisconsin 53711-2059
uwpress.wisc.edu

3 Henrietta Street
London WC2E 8LU, England
eurospanbookstore.com

Printed in the United States of America

Library of Congress Cataloging-in-Publication Data

Draine, Betsy, 1945–, author.
The body in Bodega Bay: a Nora Barnes and Toby Sandler mystery /
Betsy Draine and Michael Hinden.
pages cm
ISBN 978-0-299-29790-9 (cloth: alk. paper)
ISBN 978-0-299-29793-0 (e-book)
1. Murder—California—Bodega Bay—Fiction.
2. Bodega Bay (Calif.)—Fiction.
I. Hinden, Michael, author. II. Title.
PS3604.R343B63 2014
813′.6—dc23
2013033798

For our nephews and nieces, with love:

Josh

Ryan

Caroline

Susie

And in loving memory of:

Danny

Brigitte

The Body in Bodega Bay

1

I'LL BE DAMNED. There's a body on the boat."

We were sitting in The Tides having crab cakes for lunch when the news came in over Captain Andy's CB radio. He relayed the information from the table next to us. Andy's a commercial fisherman who works out of Bodega Bay. His mooring is opposite our house.

"That," said Toby, "explains the commotion in the harbor."

For months, a sailboat had been wedged in shallow water out by the mudflats, a good distance from either shore. From our dockside table we could see a launch make its way to the grounded boat. It stopped about fifty yards short of the sailboat, and two men emerged. They wore the familiar brown uniform of the Sonoma County sheriffs, but they had on waders—the right footgear for walking the muddy distance to the boat.

The gossip in town was that the old boat, a decrepit nineteen-footer with a single mast, belonged to a bankrupt real-estate speculator from the city. Around here that means San Francisco. For a very long time, he hadn't paid his mooring fees, and he hadn't been seen, either. One night in a storm, his boat broke free and was driven by wind into the shallows of the harbor, where it sank into the mud and tilted to one side. Since then, no one had been willing to pay for the derelict's removal, so there it has remained.

"Do they know who it is?" asked Toby, as we both stood to get a better look. Everyone in The Tides was pushing toward the windows, which wrap around the restaurant on three sides, with views over the water.

"Naw. But it isn't an accident—the guy was stabbed," Andy replied, pushing back his chair and joining us at the window. "It's a hell of a thing to happen in Bodega Bay."

Bodega Bay (population 950) is just sixty miles north of San Francisco on the Pacific Coast Highway, better known as Highway 1. We think it's one of the prettiest sites on the coast. True, it straddles the San Andreas Fault, but that didn't stop us from buying a small house overlooking the marina.

My name is Nora Barnes. I teach art history at Sonoma College in Santa Rosa, a short commute from the bay. My husband, Toby Sandler, runs an art and antiques gallery in Duncans Mills, which is up the coast and a few miles inland on Highway 116. We chose Bodega Bay because it's on the water, rural, about equidistant from our jobs, almost affordable by California standards, and—until now—peaceful. Nothing much has happened here since 1962, when Alfred Hitchcock came to town to film *The Birds*. Framed photos of the actors pass for décor at The Tides, where some of the scenes were shot, though the restaurant is a reconstruction of the original, which burned down after the movie was made. These days our little village is home to a dwindling fishing fleet, a swanky golf course, a few restaurants and motels, and us.

"A hell of a thing," repeated Andy.

We could hear sirens wailing outside, as sheriffs' cars veered into the parking lot. The morning had been foggy, but the sky had cleared by eleven and now the sun glinted on the water as we peered out toward the harbor. Officers were walking onto the wharf behind the restaurant. One was gesturing toward the boat. Another was talking into some device in his hand as a small crowd began to gather, mainly tourists who had come up from the city for the weekend.

"They're waiting for the deputy sheriff before they can bring the body out," reported Andy, who was monitoring communications on the police band. That would be Dan Ellis. Dan is married to my friend Colleen, and both are members of our Gourmet Club, four couples who meet for dinner every other month. Dan is Bodega Bay's resident deputy, attached to the sheriff's office in Santa Rosa.

Maybe it was telepathy, but no sooner did I think of Dan than Toby's cell phone rang. He put it on speaker so I could hear.

"Toby? It's Dan. Where are you right now?"

"We're at The Tides watching what's going on in the harbor. Your men are all over that boat that's been stuck in the flats. What's it about?"

"Stay right there. I just turned onto Highway 1. I'll be there in a minute. I may need you."

"Need me for what?"

"Just wait for me at the entrance." He rang off.

"He's on his way," said Toby.

"Yeah, I heard, but what's it got to do with you?"

"I don't know, but he sounded worried."

Andy complained, "That's it. It's gone dead on me." He scowled at the CB in disgust. Reception is weak on this stretch of the coast. Neither radios nor cell phones can be counted on, especially after dark, in the fog, or when there's cloud cover. It's a pain.

Toby caught the eye of our waitress, called for the bill, left some cash on the table, and signaled to me with a tilt of his head toward the entrance.

"A hell of a thing," Andy muttered with finality, tucking the CB into the pocket of his hooded sweatshirt. He nodded at us and headed toward the bar, which had a door out to the docks.

We waited for Dan at the front door, facing the parking lot. In a few minutes, he pulled up in a white SUV, tires screeching. "Toby, Nora, glad you're here," he greeted us, with more warmth than usual. He's generally pretty terse. Dan's in his midthirties, our age, large and powerfully built, authoritative, the kind of person you're inclined to listen to. He was dressed for work in his sheriff's uniform—dark brown pants and a tan shirt—to which he'd pinned his badge.

"Dan," said Toby, "what's this all about?"

"I hope I'm wrong, but I may need you to identify a body. A couple of teenagers rowed out to that abandoned boat last night. My guess is they were looking for a place to make out. Anyhow, they found a body in the cabin. They didn't call it in until an hour ago because they were scared of getting into trouble. One of my guys out there thinks he recognizes the dead man. It could be that new partner of yours."

Toby froze. "Charlie?"

"Won't know until you get a look at him. There's no wallet or ID on the body. And my guy may be wrong. Can you wait here? First I need to see things for myself and make sure no one contaminates the scene. The medical examiner is already on board, and there's an ambulance on the way. Once we get him in the van, I'd like you to take a look. Okay?"

"Whatever I can do," said Toby, his voice hoarse with alarm.

"Why don't you go back inside and have a cup of coffee? You'll know when we're ready." Dan had been looking steadily at Toby. Now he turned toward me and said with a grim smile, "Sorry to ruin your lunch, you two. I'll be back."

We turned around and went back to our table, which still hadn't been cleared. Half a crab cake was hidden under a wimple of napkin on my plate, along with a few stiff fries. I retrieved one from a pool of ketchup and waited for Toby to say something.

"What would Charlie have been doing out on that boat?" he asked, frowning.

"Let's see who it is before we start worrying. We don't know yet if it's him. I hope it's not."

"Me, too," said Toby, peering at the scene unfolding in the harbor.

A motorboat bearing Dan and two others was making its way toward the tilted sailboat, first bearing north through a marked channel, then swinging round to reach the stranded vessel. The tide was now high enough for them to pull a little closer than the first launch had done. We watched as Dan clomped through the mud, climbed over the rail, and disappeared into the cabin. Across the harbor on the far shore opposite the restaurant, a crowd was gathering at the marina to follow the action.

Charlie Halloran—was it possible? And what would he, or anyone else for that matter, be doing on a boat stuck out there in the harbor? As I thought about Charlie, I realized how little I knew about him. It was only a short time that he and Toby had been working together. Until a few months ago, Charlie was running a gallery with a partner in Guerneville, but they had come to a parting of ways. Toby's business wasn't going very well—is still dragging, due to the financial downturn—so as a favor to Charlie, whom he knew through the trade, Toby took him in—that is, offered to share space with him until things sorted out. There was plenty of room. Toby hadn't been buying much, and his showroom was half-empty. Strictly speaking, I suppose they weren't fully partners. Each continued to buy and sell his own stock, but they pooled resources on a few purchases, and they were sharing the rent. Toby's line is antique furniture and, since he married me, the occasional painting. Charlie's wares are more eclectic, including jewelry, prints, and collectibles, but some furniture too. As Toby says, you never know what he might bring into the shop.

Charlie wasn't a close friend, at least not yet—I had been meaning to invite him over to dinner—but Toby enjoyed his company. "You know, I've really started to like him," he said. "Charlie's smart, knows the trade. He's easy to have around. I sure hope there's been a mistake."

Worry lines creased Toby's forehead as he stared out the window. In the strong light, I noticed he was looking haggard, though still to me as handsome as ever, with his chiseled features and dark brown hair. Toby has a sunny disposition, but lately I've missed his usual high spirits. The recession has taken its toll not only on his business but on his parents' financial health, and he's been brooding about it. Recently his father suffered major losses in an investment firm that collapsed, putting his parents' retirement in jeopardy. That's given Toby insight into my side of the family, as my parents' income has always been modest. My dad works for the post office and my mom clerks part time in a gift shop in Rockport, a seaside town north of Boston. The fact that I went to college, then grad school, and then landed a job as an academic was a huge source of pride in my family. I sometimes tease Toby about his upscale breeding, and he comes back at me with a crack about my peasant stock. We hadn't been doing that lately. I missed it.

The waitress finally came by to clear the table. We ordered coffee and waited in silence. Perhaps half an hour went by. Then, as we kept our eyes on the scene across the harbor, two officers emerged from the cabin of the stranded boat and hefted a sagging body bag over the railing, lowering it into the arms of two others, who hauled it to the launch. The engine kicked up spray as the boat started moving in our direction. A few minutes later, Dan climbed out of the cabin, lowered himself into the shallows, and waded toward his motorboat. He looked up and signaled Toby with a wave. We moved toward the bar and headed out to the dock.

It was windy outside. Officers formed a cordon blocking onlookers as the body was carried from the dock and quickly transferred to an ambulance stationed in the parking lot. Dan was right behind his men, ushering Toby with him into the ambulance. It only took a minute before Toby climbed out again on shaky legs. "It's Charlie, all right," he said, wincing.

"Oh, honey, I'm sorry," I said. I moved toward him and put my arms around his shoulders. He was stiff with shock.

Dan emerged from the ambulance and joined us. "I've got a bunch of questions for you, but this isn't the spot. We need some privacy. I was thinking of your place."

"Fine," I said, consulting Toby with a glance. We were only ten minutes away on the other side of the harbor, on the hill above the marina. I could make out our house from here. From our deck we had often looked out at the beached sailboat and wondered about its owner. "We'll meet you there."

We kept a sad silence as Toby drove through the center of town, if you could call it that, with just a gas station, a convenience store, a few roadside shops and eateries, and an older neighborhood of fishermen's cabins set uphill from Highway 1. At the kite shop, we turned left and, hitting the shoreline, turned right onto Bay Flat Road, which loops around the harbor, splitting off from the shore road just before the marina. The shore road takes you out to Bodega Head. Bay Flat Road mounts to a little bluff, which holds a cluster of wood-framed houses. If there's a middle-income neighborhood in Bodega Bay, this is it. The houses here are larger than the rickety bungalows on the east side of the harbor but much more modest than the posh condos that dot the Bodega Harbour Golf Course. Our cedar-sided ranch house sits high up against a sandy dune whipped by long grasses and looks over the marina, out across the harbor toward the golf course on the eastern shore. In the summer you noticed how green the course was in contrast to the dry, brown hills surrounding it, but now in the wet months at the end of winter, all of Bodega Bay looked gloriously green.

Twenty minutes later, we sat in our living room with Dan across from us. A formal element had entered into our usually casual relationship. Dan had seated himself in the low leather reading chair with its back to the glass doors, which give out onto a small deck with a wide view of the harbor. That put us on the couch, with the light on our faces. Dan could see us well, but I found it hard to see his expressions.

"First of all," said Dan, "I need to know about Charlie's next of kin. Wife, children, and so on." He took a sip from the mug of coffee I'd made for him.

Toby had composed himself on the short drive home. "Charlie wasn't married," he said in a matter-of-fact tone. Dan started scribbling in his notepad.

"Was he seeing anyone?" he asked.

"I don't think so," said Toby. "Charlie was gay and comfortable with that. But there wasn't anyone special in his life right now, as far as

I know. No children either. He has a brother somewhere in the state, but I don't know his address."

"Do you know his name?"

"Jim, I think."

"We'll find him. Parents alive?"

"That I don't know."

"All right. What about enemies? Do you know of anyone who wanted to hurt Charlie?"

"No," said Toby, "but . . . well, you probably should talk to his ex-partner, Tom Keogh."

"Romantic or business partner?"

"Both. I think their business broke up when the relationship soured." Toby gave Dan the location of their shop, just off the main street in the center of Guerneville.

"Are you saying there was bad blood between them?"

"Some—but no, I shouldn't say that," said Toby, backtracking. "That's more than I know. They were arguing about the business, but lots of partners quarrel without killing each other. I just meant that Keogh knows more about Charlie than I do, not that I suspect him of a crime like this."

"I'll check him out. How well do you know this Keogh?"

"We've met over the years, but we've never done business together. I don't know him well at all."

"When was the last time you saw Charlie alive?"

"He was fine Friday at the shop."

"What time was that?"

"About five, when I was getting ready to leave. Charlie was going to watch the shop over the weekend."

Dan jotted down the information. That meant that Charlie was killed sometime after closing Friday and this morning, which was Sunday.

"So when you saw him Friday, did he seem nervous, worried about anything?"

"No, just the opposite. He was in an upbeat mood, seemed excited about some stuff he'd bought at auction the week before. I remember he bragged about some movie memorabilia that he picked up for a song. Not 'bragged.' You know what I mean. He was happy about what he'd bought."

"Did he say anything about plans for the evening? Say, meeting anyone, or going out somewhere?"

"He did mention something about a customer."

"Was he expecting to meet someone after you left?"

"That wasn't clear. Maybe. Or maybe he meant Saturday."

"Did he say anything else about this customer?"

"No, I didn't ask. It was more like a possibility that somebody might be by, not a definite appointment."

Dan drummed his fingers on the coffee table. "Tell me, how well off was Charlie? Did he carry much cash?"

"Hardly. He was just scraping by. That's why I offered to share space with him." Toby explained the terms of his business agreement with Charlie. Dan continued to take notes.

"What kinds of things did he bring into the gallery? Was there anything really valuable?"

"Nothing worth big money as far as I know," said Toby.

"All the same, if you haven't been up there since Friday, you better check to see if anything's been taken."

"Are you saying robbery was the motive?" Judging from Toby's expression, that thought hadn't occurred to him.

"At this point, we can't rule it out. Charlie's wallet is missing, but that could be a smokescreen. I'm not even sure he was killed on the boat. The medical examiner says he was stabbed through the heart, but if so, there should have been more blood than there was at the scene. That means he might have been killed somewhere else and his body dumped on the boat. We'll see what forensics tells us. Meanwhile, better make sure nothing's missing from your gallery."

"I will," said Toby. "But if Charlie wasn't killed on the boat, why would anyone go to the trouble of hauling his body out there?"

"Good question," replied Dan. "I can think of a couple of possibilities." He ticked them off on his fingers. "One, to send a message, the point being to make sure the body was discovered. Everybody knows the kids go out there at night. Do you suppose Charlie had any connections to the mob?"

"I can't imagine that," said Toby, incredulous.

"We'll look into it. Okay, two, as a plant, to incriminate a third party, namely the owner of the boat. But we've already tracked the guy down, and he has a tight alibi. He's been in the hospital the past three days. And he's in enough trouble for abandoning the boat."

"That's two," said Toby. "What's your third possibility?"

"Three, and this one I don't like at all, our killer is deranged and the location has a twisted personal meaning for him. But frankly, none of those explanations gets us very far. And if it turns out that your partner was killed on the boat, that raises a different set of questions, starting with, why was Charlie out there in the first place?"

"I haven't the faintest," said Toby, shaking his head.

"Me neither," said Dan, checking his watch. "I've got a report to file. What you can do for me is to get up to Duncans Mills and let me know if anything looks suspicious in the gallery. Tell me if anything's out of kilter or if you can think of anything else I should know about Charlie. In fact, give me a call when you get there. If you don't reach me, contact the sergeant in Investigations. You've got my card. It has my number, and if I don't answer, it'll ring through to Reception. Carol will route you to the sergeant."

"All right," said Toby, standing and shaking hands with Dan. "And you'll keep us posted if you learn anything?"

"You can count on it. This must be hard for you. I'm sorry." Dan put his hand on Toby's upper arm and gave him a manly pat.

"Thanks." Toby gave Dan a grateful look and then led him out. I cleared the mugs from our California Mission coffee table. Toby sank back down on the sofa. I gave him a little breathing space as I puttered around the living room. It was a few minutes after three. Toby switched on the radio to catch the local news. He wanted to see if they had picked up the story. Through the static, it was clear that they had.

"A body was discovered this afternoon in an abandoned boat in Bodega Harbor. The Sonoma County Sheriff's office is treating the boat as a crime scene. No further information is available at this time, pending the notification of next of kin."

Toby clicked off the radio. He wore a pained expression and was nodding his head back and forth, as if denial could restore his equanimity.

"Are you okay?"

"If I said yes, I'd be lying. Charlie was a quiet guy. He didn't say much, but I liked being with him, after all the time I've spent working alone. I'll miss hanging out with him. I'll miss the easy way he had with people who came into the shop. And I'm angry. I'm angry something terrible like this happened to him."

"You have a right to be."

"Maybe this is stupid, but you know what I've been thinking of? That line from *The Maltese Falcon*, when Bogart says, 'When a man's partner is killed, he's supposed to do something about it.' That's how I feel about Charlie. It keeps running through my head."

I sat next to him and took his hand. "It isn't stupid. You love that movie, and you used to do a pretty good Bogart imitation." In fact, we both like watching the classic movies channel, and Toby has a small repertoire of famous actor imitations. He does a few of the most obvious ones: Bela Lugosi, Groucho Marx, Bogie. "Go on," I coaxed him, because I thought it might help.

He curled his lip and tried a nasal whistle, then slumped down. "Not now. I can't. But that line keeps running through my head. Remember when his partner gets shot at the beginning of the movie?"

"Sure I do. The woman, what's her name, did it."

"And by the end Bogie is in love with her, but he turns her in because he's got this code that says when a man's partner is killed, he's got to do something about it. It doesn't matter what he thought of him, or whether the guy was good or bad, he's supposed to do something." There was no hint left now of the imitation. Toby looked determined. "And damn it, I'm going to try."

2

HIGHWAY 1 FROM BODEGA BAY to Jenner is a dazzling stretch of road. The two-lane tarmac spools up and down low, close-cropped hills and winds around treacherous horseshoe bends, while the ocean crashes against the bluffs and throws spume high into the air. At night the drive is dangerous, especially if the fog rolls in, but on a sunny afternoon it's breathtaking. You may pass a cow or two nibbling by a fence or, overlooking the sea, a row of tiny cottages, hardly more than shacks, really. They can't be enlarged, and they're on land that can't be developed thanks to strict state laws designed to preserve the coast. Without those laws, this slice of northern California would look like southern Florida, with high-rise condos and neon signs crowding the shoreline, but along Highway 1 there's nothing to spoil the views. I usually don't talk much in the car so Toby can concentrate on his driving and I can watch the ocean, which I never tire of. We were headed toward the shop, per Dan's instruction.

Just before Jenner, Highway 1 is joined on the right by Highway 116, which follows the Russian River on its way to the sea. After the turn, the drive hugs the river for about four miles until you reach the little town of Duncans Mills. That's right, without an apostrophe. The hamlet was founded in the 1870s by two brothers named Duncan who built a lumber mill there, so by rights it should be Duncan's Mill, or maybe Duncans' Mill, not that it matters. The town was leveled by the great earthquake of 1906, but it came back in the early years of the last century as a tourist destination. It was close to the river and the redwoods and was served by the Northwestern Pacific Railroad, so folks from San Francisco came up on vacation. The railroad and the mill are gone now, but there's a restored depot and an old passenger car on a defunct stretch of track, as well as a cluster of galleries, a craft shop, and a couple of cafés. The wooden buildings are a little ramshackle, and there's even a boardwalk between the shops that gives the place the air of an old cowboy town. The road splits the town in half, with shops and restaurants on either side.

Toby's store, on the left side as you enter from the west, isn't visible from the road. It sits behind the boardwalk stores with an entrance at the rear. It's large enough for a good display of furniture: oak table sets, desks and bookcases, carved bed frames, gilt mirrors, lamps and curios, with a selection of nineteenth-century paintings of modest worth, as well as a wall of framed prints. We drove around to the back and parked in front of the shop entrance. The door was fastened by an old brass lock, but when Toby introduced the key, it wouldn't turn. On closer inspection, the wood around the jamb was loose, and the door stood slightly askew on its bottom hinge.

"It's been jimmied," Toby said with irritation. "Dan was right. We've had a break-in." He pushed open the door.

At first glance, everything seemed orderly. But to Toby's eye there were signs of disarray. "Things have been moved around. Someone's been through this place."

I looked again and saw that here and there a chair had been swiveled away from a table, some drawers had been left open, a back cushion of a

Victorian sofa was turned down, and a rocker was sitting in the middle of an aisle. Someone had done a search. "Is anything missing?" I asked, looking around the large open showroom.

"I can't tell right off the bat." Toby began a systematic tour of the room. His face was taut with concentration as he roamed the floor taking a mental inventory of his stock. After completing a full circle, he came back to where I was standing and said with a puzzled expression, "Nothing of mine that I can tell."

"What about Charlie's things?"

"Ditto. Nothing obvious. The big pieces are all there. But I'll look again." He did a second tour more slowly than the first, this time pausing at the wall of prints, then shaking his head. "Wait a minute." He went over to a large oak desk that Charlie used for keeping his records and stared for a moment at an empty picture hook hanging on the wall above it. "That's what I thought," he said, pointing to the empty space. "There was a Russian icon that he picked up for us at auction last week along with some other stuff. It was hanging above his desk. Now it's gone."

"Was it valuable?" I asked, remembering Dan's question.

"I doubt it. Charlie wanted to do some research before putting it up for sale. To tell you the truth, I didn't pay much attention. It looked kind of dark, needed a cleaning. You know, religious icons aren't my thing."

Or mine. Even though I'm an art historian, icons are out of my bailiwick. My work is on nineteenth-century painting, especially Impressionism and related movements, with an emphasis on women artists. "Can you describe it? What was the subject?"

"An angel with wings. Gold paint in the background. The frame had an odd shape, looked old. That's all I can say about it. Hold on." Toby was rummaging through a pile of printed matter on the desk. "Here's the auction catalog. That should tell us something."

He pulled a glossy catalog out of the stack and opened it to a page that had been marked by a Post-it. The catalog was from Morgan's, a low-end auction house in San Francisco that specializes in catch-all sales under the rubric of "Discovery Days." Morgan's takes consignments that are generally beneath the notice of the high-toned auction houses, and their lots usually sell in the lower price ranges. For that reason the firm is frequented by dealers on the lookout for cheap finds. The lots are mainly furniture and oriental rugs, though now and then an interesting painting or print comes up for sale. Plenty of antique dealers in the Bay Area keep track of Morgan's auctions, but serious art collectors hunt elsewhere for more precious prey. This had been a typical two-day sale for Morgan's, covering a mix of objects ranging from art to carpets, posters, pottery, and what-have-you.

It came as no surprise to me that the icon Charlie had marked for bidding, listed as lot 87 on day 2, had a presale estimate of $1,000 to $1,500. In the heady world of art auctions, that's small potatoes. Next to a color photo of the icon, someone (Charlie presumably) had written "$800," which was either what he planned to be his highest bid or what he paid for it. The brief catalog description read: "A Russian icon on a wooden panel, eighteenth or nineteenth century, showing the Archangel Michael. Originally part of a triptych." Underneath the photo were the work's dimensions: 8" × 4.8". It was small, about the size of a Kindle. It took no great expertise to determine that the painting once belonged to a triptych—a work in three parts in which two side panels, when closed, cover a central panel, and in which all three panels, when open, face the viewer. The panel was shaped like a little door, curved on top, with straight sides. Two grooves on the left side of the little door marked where it once had been attached to a central panel, probably larger in size, so that the two side doors could fold into it. Plainly, this was the right wing of a triptych. Missing were its complements.

A religious icon of uncertain age wouldn't be hugely valuable, I guessed. Nor was the image that impressive. Unless the photo was indistinct, the surface of the painting was clouded with grime. I was looking at a frontal view of a slender, winged figure in armor bearing a raised sword in his right hand and holding an empty scabbard in his left. Billowing around him was a cloak in a dull red color. The iconography was correct. Here was a typical pose of the warrior archangel Michael. Yet as a work of art meant to inspire devotion, the image seemed rather dull. The face was flat and without expression, with large eyes peering blankly at the viewer. The drawing was minimally competent, with hardly any modeling; the paint seemed indifferently applied, the colors sallow. The edges of the panel were indented, and there were no background features other than the chipped gilt sky. As I said, I'm no expert on icons, but this one struck me as mediocre. Who would want to steal it, I wondered, let alone kill somebody for it?

Toby had been leafing through some hanging files in a deep drawer on the right side of the desk. He fished out a manila folder. "Here's Charlie's file on the purchase. Maybe it'll tell us something." He emptied its contents on the desktop. There was a bill of sale from Morgan's marked "paid" in the amount of $960, which confirmed a winning bid of $800 plus a 20 percent buyer's fee. As a dealer, Charlie wouldn't have paid sales tax, because he'd bought the work for resale. There was also an envelope containing a few color prints of photos that Charlie had taken to document his acquisition. One was of the back of the panel, which might prove useful in revealing details about the painting. The others were photos of the front, including several close-ups of various parts of the icon. Charlie's photos reinforced my impression from the catalog that the image was coated with grime and that its underlying colors had lost whatever richness they might once have had.

I shared my thoughts with Toby, and we both shook our heads at the possibility that this unprepossessing work might have been the motive for a brutal crime. On the other hand, how likely was it that the break-in at the gallery was unconnected to the murder? As a coincidence, that strained credulity. "Better call Dan," I said.

Toby went to his desk, in the opposite corner from Charlie's. While Toby spoke with Dan, I studied the photos again but gained no additional information. The men spoke for a few minutes. Then Toby said, "He wants to talk to you." He passed me the phone.

"Hi, Dan."

"Hi, Nora. Based on what Toby's been telling me, this icon that's missing wasn't worth that much, and you don't think it's an important work of art. That right?"

"Well, maybe I shouldn't be jumping to conclusions. Russian icons are way out of my area. But Toby told you what Charlie paid for it, and frankly, judging from the photographs, I wasn't surprised by the price. It doesn't strike me as a masterpiece. Of course, we probably should get an expert opinion."

"That's more your department than mine. How would you feel about helping me out on this one? What I need to know is whether the theft and the murder are connected. You've worked with us before. Are you interested? Same terms as usual?"

What Dan meant was that I'd recently worked as a freelance consultant to his department on two cases, one involving art theft and another involving art fraud, helping to clear up questions of value, authenticity, and provenance. The pay wasn't much, but the work was intriguing, a nice real-world break from my usual scholarship.

"Sure. What would you like me to do?"

"Start by talking to the auction house. See what more you can find out about the sale, who set the estimate, whether it was reasonable, who else might have been bidding, who the seller was, that sort of thing. And then see if you can locate someone who'll help us with the value. Maybe there's more to this than meets the eye. You could save me a lot of time running down that angle."

"I'll get started right away."

"Thanks. Do you still have some of my business cards?"

"At home I do, yes." They would be my credentials for my link to the sheriff's office.

"Great. Let me know as soon as you come up with anything. I'll be in touch."

I ended the call and passed the phone back to Toby, who said, "Good. Dan wants us to help."

I thought better of pointing out that Dan had asked me, not us, to lend a hand. Toby needed to be included. I needed Toby to feel better. "I'll start making some calls. Can I use your phone? You know how my cell phone cuts out here," I said.

"Of course. I'll talk to the other shop owners to see whether they heard or saw anything unusual or whether there were any other break-ins over the weekend." Toby headed for the door. He seemed energized now that he had a purpose.

"That's not a bad idea," I said. "I'll stay right here."

My first call was to my kid sister, Angie, who was scheduled to arrive on Thursday for a two-week visit, which had been planned a long time ago. I had the quarter off and wasn't expected back in the classroom until April. My goals for the break were to finish an article I was writing and to clear some time to be with my sister, who was looking forward to a respite from winter in Massachusetts. I had met goal one, but life was messing with goal two. When Angie didn't pick up, I left a message to call me back. I didn't want to disappoint her, but I also wanted to let her know that some of my time might be taken up by an investigation.

Then I called Morgan's Auctions Galleries. When I said the magic words, "helping the sheriff's office," I was put through to a Mr. Harry Spears, who had been the auctioneer for the sale. He agreed to see me at 11:30 the next morning, a good start. My third call was to Alvin Miller, who taught medieval and religious art at Berkeley and who was one of my favorite professors in graduate school. What little I know about religious art I learned from him; he would be an excellent resource. Al considers me a colleague now and insists on a first-name basis. He was free on Tuesday afternoon and suggested a meeting at his house. "Sure, bring Toby along, it'll be nice to see him again," was his reply to my next question. Toby would be pleased. Tomorrow he'd be tied up filing a robbery report and getting his lock repaired, but on Tuesday we could both go to see Al at his home in the Berkeley Hills. Toby wouldn't mind closing his shop if it meant he could participate in the investigation.

The next morning I woke up worried about the drive to San Francisco. In principle, if you take the freeway, it's only an hour and a quarter to the Golden Gate Bridge, but taking into account weekday-morning traffic, I figured on a good two hours to the city. Traffic was worse than I thought. As I waited for an accident to clear ahead, I listened to Michael Krasny's talk show on KQED and hoped that the auctioneer wouldn't be peeved by my late arrival. Finally, traffic started to move again, and I made decent time the rest of the way in.

Morgan's Auctions sits at the foot of Sutter Street in a quiet neighborhood of furniture showrooms and galleries. The building is yellow brick but otherwise nondescript, and the décor is a tad shabby. The message conveyed is: "Look how low our overhead is." Morgan's is a far cry from Sotheby's. I identified myself at the information desk and was directed to an office on the second floor.

The elevator wasn't working that morning, so I climbed the uncarpeted cement stairs, went through a fire door, and made my way down a dim corridor to Harry Spears's office. He was sitting in a swivel chair at a banged-up metal desk, pushing closed its top drawer. Spears greeted me without enthusiasm and without bothering to rise. He was slovenly and heavy set, bearded, dressed in pants that needed cleaning and a blazer that was too tight around his paunch. His tie was wide as a barn, left over from the days of flower power.

I told him who I was and why I was there. I handed him my Sonoma College business card, which labeled me an associate professor of art history, and Dan's card, which identified him as a deputy sheriff on the Santa Rosa force. He laid them on his desk, unimpressed.

"So what can I do for you?" Spears asked. His words were more welcoming than his tone.

"I'm looking into a Russian icon that came up in your Discovery Auction last week, on March 2. The man who bought it has been killed and now it's missing, so it could be part of a murder investigation." I gave him the lot number and showed him the photo in his catalog. "Do you remember the lot?"

"Yeah. It didn't bring much, as I recall." His nose was running. He blew it and tossed the tissue into a wastebasket.

"Eight hundred dollars, according to the bill of sale."

He checked his records. "That's right."

"I'm wondering if it could be worth a lot more."

"If it is, nobody else thought so. There was only the one bid, and since it met the reserve, I had to sell it."

"So the only bid came from Mr. Halloran?"

"If that's his name. I opened asking for a thousand, couldn't get a bid, so I went down to eight hundred, and he raised his paddle. It was a thin house that day, not too many bidders. I was glad to sell it."

"Can you tell me who set the estimate on that lot?"

"I did. I do all the lots."

"And are you an expert on Russian icons?"

He bristled. "Listen, lady. I know something about auction prices. I didn't think it would bring more than a grand, and it didn't."

I allowed a polite smile. "May I ask what you based your estimate on?"

"I ran the database. Looked for comparables in our recent sales and didn't find any. To tell you the truth, we don't sell a lot of icons. There's no market for them here. People go for landscapes, still lifes, marine paintings, pretty stuff. Give me a landscape with a sunny sky and a river in it, and I can run up the bidding. Religious paintings, forget it. Now, this icon looked old, which gave it a certain cachet, if you know what I mean, and the subject, being an angel, gave it a boost. But it wasn't in top condition. If anything, the estimate was optimistic. Maybe at another auction house that specialized in icons or religious objects it could have brought more."

"I see. Would you mind telling me who the seller was? It might be useful if I could talk to him or her."

"That's private information. We don't give it out."

I slid Dan's card toward him across his desk. "You can call Deputy Ellis at that number if you don't want to talk to me. I'm trying to save him from having to come down himself."

He hesitated.

"This is a murder investigation, Mr. Spears. Deputy Ellis has his hands full. He's short staffed. He's asked for my assistance. If he has to make a separate trip because an informant won't cooperate, he'll do it but he won't be pleased." I added, "So far you've been very helpful."

Spears shot me a glance that said, "Don't take me for an idiot." I sat straight-faced, hands folded in my lap. My glance said, "No? Then help me out." We waited a few seconds, and then he snorted and reached for a record book. The consignor was a woman named Rose Cassini who lived in Cazadero, which isn't far from Duncans Mills. I copied down the address and phone number.

"Thank you."

"You're welcome," he said grudgingly. "Now I'll tell you and the sheriff something else, so you won't have any reason to complain. You aren't the only ones who've been asking about this lot."

"Oh?"

"The bidder—Halloran, is that his name?—also wanted to know the name of the consignor. Called me up the day after the sale and wanted to get in touch with her to ask if she had any more items like it that she might want to sell."

"Did you give him the information?"

"I told you, that's against our policy. But I called her and gave her the buyer's number and relayed the message. Said that if she wanted to contact him, that was up to her."

"And did she?"

"You'll have to ask her. I don't know. But that's not all. The next day I get another call from a guy with a heavy accent who wants to know who the buyer was on the lot. Said he was a collector from Russia who had missed the auction and might be interested in making the buyer an offer. Well, I handled that the same way. I called the buyer and delivered the message and gave him the guy's number. And that's all I know."

Dan would be interested in that piece of news. "Do you still have the number?"

"No, I jotted it down somewhere but didn't keep it. Look, we're talking about an eight-hundred-dollar sale. How was I to know it would cause so much trouble?"

How, indeed? "Do you remember anything else about the call?"

He shook his head in the negative.

"What about the voice? Did the man with the accent sound young, old?"

"It was a deep voice. Not too young, not too old." He shrugged.

"Anything else?"

"No, that's it. I've told you everything I know." He reached for another tissue and blew his nose again. This time he balled up the tissue and clenched it.

"All right, Mr. Spears. Thank you for your help. If you think of anything else, please call Deputy Ellis at the number on his card."

"Is that it for now?"

"That's it." I rose to go. Spears withdrew a half-eaten cheese sandwich from the top drawer of his desk and waved me out. The cheese was pretty ripe. I could smell it.

I left a message for Dan, fed the parking meter to give me time for lunch across the street, then headed back across the city to the Golden Gate and 101 north. Toby and I had arranged to meet back at his shop. The fastest way up to Duncans Mills from the city is to take the freeway as far as Cotati and then cut over to 116 going west. The afternoon traffic wasn't half-bad.

"How'd it go?" Toby asked when I got back to the gallery.

I gave him an account of what I'd learned at Morgan's.

Toby grew more alert with each detail. "I wonder if Charlie got in touch with the consignor, or if he ever called this Russian guy."

I wondered too, and hoped that the consignor of the icon would be willing to talk to us. If not, she'd have to talk to Dan. Meanwhile, I asked Toby how things had gone up here.

"No big news. I filed the robbery report, waited for the locksmith, talked to the other shop owners. Nobody else had a break-in. No one heard or saw anything suspicious. Obviously, whoever broke in and stole the icon did it late Friday or Saturday night. This place is a ghost town after the restaurants shut down. I've also been going through Charlie's desk but haven't come up with anything. I'm ready for a break."

"Coffee?"

"Good idea." In his half of the gallery, Toby had a nook set aside for his office, where there was a little refrigerator and a coffee machine. We were sitting on a divan, sipping and collecting our thoughts, when the door opened and in walked Tom Keogh, Charlie's ex-partner. "This could be trouble," Toby grunted under his breath. Toby got up and walked over to offer Tom a handshake. Tom wasn't reciprocating. I decided to sit this one out. I had a ringside view.

"Tom, what can I say? I'm really sorry about Charlie." To me, Toby sounded sincere and compassionate, but Tom didn't take it that way. He looked enraged.

Tom had the hawkish bearing of an aging Irishman. In fact, he reminded me of a photo I'd seen of the playwright Samuel Beckett. He was tall and lean, with a thatch of stiff hair, an aquiline nose, and piercing blue eyes. His fair complexion burned red at this moment, but I could see that in a calmer moment he would be handsome, even compelling. "Shit, Sandler," he spat out bitterly. "Charlie's dead, and you report me to the cops as a suspect. Don't try your sympathy act on me."

"That's not what happened, Tom. I just told Dan he should talk to you. I didn't know Charlie as well as you did. That's all I meant."

"Well, your detective friend gave me a hell of a grilling. He knew we were together—I suppose you told him that. But he talked to me like I was the one who killed him." He sputtered with grief and anger, "I could never hurt Charlie." He swallowed hard, his jaw working.

Toby's eyes shifted to the floor, in embarrassment. His voice was low when he replied. "I know that. Charlie didn't talk much about himself, but he trusted you."

"He trusted me? That's a good one, after all the shit he's pulled. Charlie wasn't exactly an expert on the subject. Trust wasn't his number one priority, was it?"

"Meaning what?" Toby asked defensively. Tom looked away. "Are you saying he did something underhanded by moving to my shop?"

Tom retorted, "Charlie was free to leave whenever he wanted. I didn't keep him locked up."

"Then don't take it out on me." Toby put out his hand, palm up, to ward off a reply. "You know what? We shouldn't be having this conversation now. We're both of us too upset. If you have accusations to make against Charlie, you need to make them to Dan, not me."

"You're the one I need to talk to, Sandler. Look at you. You're sitting on Charlie's inventory—mine, really. It was my money that bought that desk you're leaning on. And that big oak table over there, for starters. When he walked away from me, Charlie owed me thirty thousand dollars. I'm telling you, I'm going to take back what's mine." His chiseled jaw was set defiantly.

Toby looked surprised. "I don't know anything about that, but this is no time to be talking money. We can deal with that later."

"Oh, yeah. You sound just like him. 'We'll talk about the money later.' That was Charlie's favorite refrain. Well, 'later' hadn't come when he moved his stuff in the dead of night from our store to your shop. Later is now." Standing at his full height of over six feet, Tom towered over Toby as he jutted a finger into his chest. Toby rocked on his heels but didn't step back.

"Don't do that again," Toby said in an even voice. That was all he said, but it was enough.

I walked forward and put myself between the two men. "Hold on, guys. This is the last thing Charlie would want, you two fighting over his things. We're all grieving. Let's think about that tonight." And it was nearly night by now. The sun was getting ready to set suddenly, the way it does in late winter. I stepped round to the wall to flip on the lights.

When I turned back, Tom had pivoted away, and his shoulders were wrenching. Was he crying? I heard no sobs. I pulled up a chair for him, one of Charlie's for all I knew. And he sat there shaking for a long time. We waited it out.

Finally, Toby said, "I know you and Charlie were partners a long time. I don't know what happened between you, and it's none of my business, but he never bad-mouthed you to me. I'm not your enemy. I want to help find whoever did this to him."

Tom rubbed his nose with his fist and repeated, "Later, later. That was all I ever heard from him. He never wanted to confront the facts. Never wanted to settle things. Well, he sure as hell left things unsettled between us." He slumped forward in the chair, his long arms dangling between his knees.

"How do you mean?" I asked.

"I mean in every way, but never mind the other stuff. We had a business agreement that he left up in the air. When he couldn't figure out how to pay back that thirty thousand dollars, he just took off. And you gave him a place to go, Sandler. He came to you with stock that he bought with my money, the money I loaned him, over and over, just so he could take advantage of this one unique opportunity, this one super auction, this one client who would slip away tomorrow."

"Look, Tom," Toby said again, "this is no time for us to sort this out. Some of my stuff is mixed up with his, as well. Let's put all that aside for now and just deal with Charlie's death." That caused a heavy silence.

When Tom straightened himself up in the chair, he looked stricken. "You shouldn't be alone right now," I said. "Do you have anyone to stay with?"

He bit his lip and then shook his head. "I'm all right. Annie's coming over." I knew who he meant. Everybody in the Russian River Valley knows Annie, the lovable butterball of a gal who runs the Guerneville Tavern. She has a heart as wide as the river that runs by her bar. She's always there for those in trouble, and that was Tom tonight. He would be in good hands.

Soon enough, we were alone in the shop, looking at each other with fatigue and dismay. "He seems really broken up by Charlie's death," I said.

"He's going to be a pain in the ass, is what it seems," said Toby.

"There's more involved than just business for Tom. Did Charlie ever say anything to you about their relationship?"

"No. He kept his private life to himself, which was fine with me."

"Didn't he say anything at all to you about Tom?"

"Nothing personal. I never said much to him about you, for that matter."

"Oh? Don't men ever talk about their love life to their friends? Women do. All the time."

"Men are different," said Toby.

"No kidding," I said. Why is it men get turned off whenever we want to talk about relationships? Doesn't the subject interest them? Toby once joked that his idea of hell was to be locked in a cell with a TV on twenty-four hours a day with nothing to watch but Oprah Winfrey.

"So what do you say about me?" Toby pursued.

"Hmm?"

"What do you say when you talk about me to your friends?"

"Relax. They're the ones who usually complain. I just say I'm lucky. I married a great guy."

"Come on. What do you say?"

"No, it's true. I do feel lucky." I puckered, and our lips met in a comfort kiss.

"So do I," said Toby. Then a distinctively guilty expression clouded his face, and he looked toward his shoes. "But I have a confession to make."

Uh-oh, I thought. What's coming?

"Tom isn't the only one who loaned Charlie money. I did too."

"You did? How much?"

"I don't know. A few thousand."

"You don't know? What do you mean, you don't know? I thought you were watching every penny around here."

"I am. But I felt sorry for Charlie. Or not exactly that. The guy was just likable."

"So likable that you tossed a wad of money at him and didn't even count it?"

"Don't fly off the handle. It didn't happen that way. It was an investment in our partnership. Charlie needed some cash for Morgan's auction, but he didn't have ready money. So I gave him access to the shop's account. I said he could charge up to five thousand dollars on it. Then we'd figure out how he'd pay me back after he resold the items, or maybe we'd go in together on the purchases. We left it sort of vague."

"'Unsettled' was the term Tom used," I said. "I see what he meant."

"You could say that. For now, the shop, my shop, was buying the items at Morgan's."

A thought occurred to me. "Let me see that bill of sale again," I said, returning to the file drawer in Charlie's desk, if indeed the desk was his. Sure enough, the bill was made out to the shop, a detail that hadn't registered with me before. "So that icon and whatever else Charlie may have bought belongs to you."

"I suppose so. But Tom Keogh won't see it that way. Say, you don't think it really could be worth something, do you?"

"The icon? I wouldn't count on it."

"After all, somebody went to the trouble of stealing it." Toby raised his eyebrows, considering the prospect of a windfall. I'd seen that look on his face before, whenever he thought he was cadging a piece for his shop that he could turn around for a quick profit. When that happened, he usually was disappointed.

"Don't get carried away," I said. "Remember *The Maltese Falcon*? What was that line in it about greediness and dreams?"

Toby made a sound between a snicker and a snort. "'The stuff that dreams are made of,'" he quoted, with a rueful grin.

3

IN EARLY MARCH, daybreak sometimes starts with a streak of rose over the dark Bodega hills. As dawn swells, I like to be seated in the kitchen looking out at our deck, so I can watch the sky shift from orange to pink, with a hint of green, giving way to daylight blue. Sometimes I just sit, soaking in the view. Other days I'm grading papers or answering e-mails but looking up every minute to catch the kaleidoscope of color before it's washed out by the clear light of morning.

On this day, however, in the aftermath of Charlie's murder, I rose late and sat in the living room brooding over a hot mug of tea and following the white sun as it hovered in the distance over Tomales Bay. Toby was sleeping in. He heals best by sleep. I cure what ails me by keeping busy, and now I was sketching out the best possible day. I would make some calls and then get the kitchen ready for a comforting breakfast once Toby was up. He and I were going to spend all day together. We'd made the plan in our exhaustion the previous night. We'd get a soft start to the morning, and then he'd drive with me to Berkeley, to consult with Al Miller.

Before Toby was up, I put in a call to my sister, Angie. Since she lives on Cape Ann north of Boston, she can take a call when it's dawn in

California. About then she's due for her midmorning coffee break at the coolest beauty salon in Gloucester, where she's made her way up from manicurist to top stylist in just three years. I texted her to call me when she was free from clients, and sure enough, she was back to me in five minutes.

"Hi, Angie, we're still on for your visit," I assured her. "But I want to let you know we've had an awful thing happen here. Toby's business partner has been murdered, and I'm helping the sheriff's department look into some art that's missing."

We took some time going over the story, and I accomplished what I'd aimed to do—warning Angie that I might be less available than we'd planned, but making her feel as welcome as ever. It was true what I told her. Toby and I were in need of those special gifts she always brings with her, a light touch and a shot of joy. It makes me happy that Toby delights in Angie's zaniness as much as I do. You see, Angie, who is twelve years younger than I am, is a man-magnet. Since nursery school, she's been attracting the opposite sex and finding that delightful. Unfortunately, her enthusiasm isn't always matched by her discrimination. She's been passionately involved with fellow students, a musician, a writer, a magician, a fashion photographer, a lawyer, a yogi, two grocery store clerks, one of her teachers, and a few first-class swindlers. Each time she's convinced she's found her soul mate.

Last summer, we helped extricate her from a relationship with a bored barista who wanted her to lend him money for a cockeyed business scheme. His idea was to buy a camper and convert it into a van for hauling motorcycles from New England to Florida in the winter. His premise was that bikers would pay to ship their cycles so they wouldn't have to ride them down to Florida themselves—a dubious business plan, as Toby pointed out. There was supposed to be room left over in the camper for Angie and the boyfriend to travel with the motorcycles and thus benefit from a paid winter vacation. Of course, it didn't happen. Angie woke up and smelled the coffee, and the boyfriend's blend was bitter. So just before sinking her trust fund into the camper, she backed out, on her own accord. There may be some in my family who are more startled than amused by Angie's unpredictable antics, but Toby and I are in the fan club, and we were glad she was coming.

"You're going to bring your scissors, right? I haven't had a haircut since the last one you gave me."

"My God, that was Thanksgiving!"

"I know, but I don't have much time for that sort of thing, and you're the only one I trust anyhow. Let's not even talk about how that diva in Santa Rosa scalped me last year."

"Well, if you'd get your hair cut more than once every six months, the stylist wouldn't be so tempted to shear you like a sheep."

She could talk. Born with bones, as my mother used to say. That means the rugged jaw and high cheekbones that characterize the Boston Brahmins and signal "class" in our area of New England. Plus skinny genes, smooth blond hair that can be styled any which way, and, let's face it, gloriously God-given beauty. I am five-five to her five-eleven (though her dating profile says five-nine), size 10 to her size 6, brunette to her blond, short-bobbed to her long-maned, and presentable-looking to her gorgeous. I can deal with that. She can't. She's always trying to make me over into her likeness, or maybe it's some idealized vision of her beloved older sister.

Anyhow, I realized we'd better change the subject before she started in on my list of chronic grooming errors. "You've rented a car with GPS, right?" I asked. "It's a winding road to get here, but it will be really pretty."

"Yeah, the car has one and they're usually fine right up to 'You have arrived at your destination.' What does your place look like?"

"It's the cedar-sided ranch house at the top of the hill, and there's nothing but pebbles and poppies in the front. Yellow ones."

"Sounds nice. I'll call you when I leave the airport." Only two days till the sisters would be reunited. It had been a long time since Thanksgiving.

I made a second call that morning, to Rose Cassini, the woman who had consigned the icon that Charlie bought at the auction. We were discussing a time to meet when Toby emerged from the bedroom. Eavesdropping on the call, he pointed to his chest to say that he was coming along. So I set our arrival for eleven the next day, allowing for Toby's slow mornings.

Two hours and six pieces of French toast later, we were on our way down the coast to meet with Al Miller. Al lives in a cozy Victorian on a crowded street in the Berkeley Hills. It was difficult, as usual, to find a parking space in his neighborhood, and once we did, it was a bit of a hike to his address. As we climbed the familiar wooden stairs to his front porch, I found my thoughts drifting back to my graduate school days. Al always invited his seminar students to his home, and I had happy memories of evenings sitting on his living room floor and joining in earnest debates fueled by generous amounts of wine and cheese. I was in his Giotto seminar, but he also taught a seminar on Russian icons, and though the subject itself wasn't a draw, he had a devoted following of graduate students who prized his irreverence and wit. I remember the laugh he got one day when he was lecturing on Michelangelo's statue of David. Michelangelo posed David in the nude, with a slingshot on his shoulder as he faces off against Goliath. But the great artist made a blunder, claimed Al, because why would David show up on the battlefield without his pants?

Al liked to shock us with his views on religion. He maintained that theology was a form of literary criticism, since its arguments were chiefly about works of fiction (the Bible, the Koran, and so on). And he was fond of saying that if you picked a group of kids at random hanging around a street corner, any one of them could have designed a kinder universe than the one we've got. Yes, Al enjoyed getting a rise out of us.

I once asked him why he had chosen to specialize in early Christian art, given his irreligious views. Would anyone, he replied, expect him to be an animist if he taught Aboriginal art? Half-seriously, he added that his field was less crowded than some others and so he felt he could make a mark in it. In fact, he was an excellent scholar. "But the real reason,

Nora, is that religious art can be just as beautiful as other kinds of art, and beautiful is what art history is about. Everything else is secondary." I've never forgotten that.

Still, he was an odd member of his field. Usually faculty gravitate toward subjects that are in sync with their beliefs. Most professors of medieval art I've known have been believers, while those who teach contemporary art have not. You might ask, what about folks like me, who teach Impressionism? Considering my colleagues, I'd say we're all over the map. As for myself, I had a traditional Catholic upbringing, but while I still attend the occasional Mass and sometimes even take communion, my views on religion are, well, flexible. Toby, now, is the real skeptic in the family. His parents are mainline Protestants, but he jokingly refers to himself as an "Orthodox Reprobate."

Those were some of the stray thoughts running through my mind as Toby and I stood waiting on the porch for the doorbell to be answered. We weren't kept long. Al hadn't changed much in the years since I'd been his student. He was short, slim, and still dapper, with a full head of curly hair now gone silver and a trim white beard that reminded me of Civil War portraits. In class, he used to favor sports jackets and bow ties, but today he greeted us wearing khakis and a bulky hand-knit sweater. His wife, Irma, knitted.

"Come in, come in," he said, beckoning. "I can't wait to hear more about your missing icon. You've got my curiosity up." He gave me a hug and shook Toby's hand. "So good to see you both. Make yourselves at home." He led us into the living room, where a cozy fire crackled in the hearth. Offering us the couch, he pulled up a wooden chair for himself. The room was furnished just as I remembered, with Arts and Crafts–period furniture and oriental carpets, much to Toby's liking.

"How are your courses going, Nora, and your work?" We made small talk as we settled in. "Will you take tea?" A tray with a steaming pot was waiting for us on the coffee table.

"Yes, that would be lovely."

"Now, what's this all about?"

Toby recounted the events surrounding Charlie's death and what was known so far about the missing icon, while Al fussed with the tea cups and pouring. "Charlie bought it at auction for only eight hundred dollars," I added, "but we think it may be more valuable than that." I pulled the auction catalog out of my bag.

Al cast a disdainful glance at it. "Never mind the catalog. If it's Morgan's, the description won't be worth a damn. You mentioned photos. May I see them?" He placed his porcelain cup on its saucer.

Toby took an envelope out of his jacket and pulled out the photos for Al, who spread them out on the coffee table. He set aside the one of the back of the panel and glanced quickly over the others. "The archangel Michael, yes. Commonplace treatment, early modern period. Might be worth something to a believer but not much to a collector. Eight hundred dollars? Fair enough. Disappointed?" He raised his eyebrows.

"I don't know if I am or not," said Toby. "We're trying to figure out if it could have been a motive for murder."

"But wait. That's just what the front tells us, and it's not the front that interests me." Al picked up the photo of the back of the panel. Holding it between thumb and forefinger, he continued: "Do you see these horizontal bands of wood attached to the back? They're supports to keep the panel from warping. The way they were made and the way they're attached, as well as the patina of the wood, tell me that this panel is much older than the painting. How much older I can't say. I might be able to tell if I had the actual panel. But I already know that this image of Michael might be covering something else, and if so, the question is, what? There's no way of telling from a photograph."

"You mean there might be another painting underneath this one?" asked Toby.

"It's possible," Al replied. "In fact it's even likely that there are traces of an older painting underneath. But I can't say anything about its age or condition or quality without examining the physical work."

"But isn't it possible," I asked, "that the maker of this icon found an old panel to work on and that's all we're looking at, a recent painting on an older support?"

"Of course there's a chance of that. But icons in Russia were never regarded as mere works of art. They were objects of devotion. No one ever discarded an old icon just because it had been discolored or damaged. They were conserved and used over and over again by the next generation of artists because the panels themselves were considered sacred." Al finished the last few sips of his tea.

"You see," he continued, "when a painting was no longer legible, another artist would paint over it, sometimes just to bring out the original by highlighting the lines and refreshing the colors, restoring what was in danger of being lost. Yet sometimes the old painting was too far gone, and when that was the case, the artist would start over again on top of the old, maybe even with a new composition."

"How often would that happen?" asked Toby.

"All the time. The drying oil used by the old masters to fix and intensify their colors naturally darkened over the years. And if the icons were hung in churches, which most of them were, the soot from votive candles and incense was absorbed by the varnish, which only made matters worse. After eighty or a hundred years, the original painted surface became impenetrable."

"You mean, the image would completely disappear?" asked Toby.

"That's right. Today we know how to clean the panels to restore their original luster, but in times past the only solution was to repaint the original icon or to paint over it on a new background. That's why some masterpieces of earlier centuries have come down to us in the form of weak copies of the originals."

Toby edged forward on the couch. "So underneath the angel there could be a painting that's centuries older."

"As I said, possibly, but even if that's so, what might be left of it can't be determined without testing."

"But if somebody had a suspicion there was a more valuable painting hidden under the angel, that could be a reason to steal it."

"Perhaps so. Let me show you what I've been talking about. I've prepared a little demonstration for you." Al got up and led us toward the back of the house, where he had set up his study and workshop, talking as we walked. "I've been examining an icon for the Berkeley Art Museum. It was donated by an alumnus. They've asked me to value it and, in response to my suggestion, to clean it, which, as you'll see, it badly needs. I've done some preliminary tests, and now I'm ready for the next step. Unless I miss my guess, you're in for a surprise."

On a workbench in the studio, cushioned by a towel, a rectangular icon rested on its back. The central area of the panel was recessed. The board, including the frame, was carved in one piece. The icon may have been a foot long and almost as wide. At first glance, the central area appeared to be completely black, as if the surface had been expunged. However, when Al held it up at a slant under raking light, I could dimly perceive the outlines of a familiar subject, a three-quarter length portrait of the Virgin and Child.

"The Mother of God of Vladimir," Al announced. The name, he explained, came from the city in which the original was painted in the twelfth century. The icon was said to produce miracles, and so the subject and its treatment were copied again and again on the same panel over the years, down to the present day.

"Although sometimes," Al remarked, "these so-called wonder-working icons backfired."

"How so?" I asked.

"Take the Virgin of Vavarsky Gate, which was a famous wonder-working icon in Moscow. When a plague hit the city during the reign of Catherine the Great, crowds of sick people flocked around the icon to pray for relief. What happened was they just spread the infection. Poor bastards died by the thousands." He shook his head in bemused disapproval.

"You can't blame that on the icon," I pointed out.

"I blame it on wishful thinking and superstition." He raised an eyebrow. "Anyhow, as to this one," he said as he redirected our attention to the panel, "it's an indifferent version of the Vladimir icon, maybe mid-nineteenth century. But let's look at the reverse." He turned it over gently in his hands and pointed to the narrow strips of wood spanning the back and held in position by wooden pegs. "You see these? Before the fourteenth century, the support slats were fastened with pegs like this, and occasionally also reinforced by two additional slats set into the top and bottom outside edge of the panel." He pointed out the vertical slats. "The practice was revived in the eighteenth century, and that's what I think we have here."

The back of Charlie's icon looked different in the photo, and I said so.

"That's right. The carpentry there is typical of the practice dating from the fifteenth century through the end of the seventeenth, when grooves were scraped into the panel and horizontal wedges were forced into them with a hammer."

"So is that how old you think Charlie's icon might be?" asked Toby.

"Quite possibly. Sometimes it's not easy to tell. In the nineteenth century they returned to the wedge-in-groove method, which is why panels made in the eighteenth century tend to stand apart. That's my clue as to this one's age."

"And this coating on the surface was caused by the varnish they used?"

"Yes. Now watch what happens when I apply the lightest dab of sunflower-seed oil." There was a bowl filled with clear oil sitting on the table alongside another bowl containing a darker, thicker liquid, and a row of small instruments lined up waiting to be used: a pair of scissors, tweezers, wads of cotton wool, and a thin scalpel. Al soaked a ball of cotton in the clear oil and very delicately swabbed the icon, using even, vertical strokes from top to bottom and bottom to top. He replaced the cotton ball several times during this operation. As soon as he had finished, I could see the figures in much clearer outline, as though I were looking through a transparent tinted glass.

"Now for the next step." Al used his scissors to cut a small rectangle from a soft flannel cloth and soaked it, holding it by a corner with tweezers, in the bowl of the darker liquid. "The solvent," he explained, "is specially formulated for this purpose. I'll start by applying it here." He gently draped the patch of cloth over a section of the Virgin's robe, flattening it with a piece of glass of the sort commonly found in a frame for a photograph.

"Toby, would you bring over that dictionary, please?" Toby picked up a heavy book that was sitting on a chair and brought it to the table, where Al placed it atop the glass, as a weight. "Perfect. Now we give it a chance to work." After a few minutes, he removed the dictionary and the glass, and, with the tweezers, carefully lifted the patch of cloth from the icon. A good portion of dark gook came up with it. Quickly now, he discarded the dirty cloth and applied a new cotton ball dipped in solvent. The result was astonishing: the remaining elements of black substance were absorbed by the swab and vanished as if by magic. A rectangle of bright color sprang to life.

Al pronounced the procedure a success. "Let's do the rest." Meticulously, he repeated each step of the process, covering the surface of the icon with swatches of cloth soaked in solvent and pressed under glass by the weight of the book.

When each swatch was removed, the surface beneath it was covered with loose swirls and flakes. These were swabbed away by fresh cotton balls dipped in solvent, although here and there traces of varnish still adhered to the surface in the form of sticky moist tendrils. Working carefully, Al scraped away the remaining traces, using the side edge of the scalpel and additional cotton wads. Before long, the image was completely transformed.

Now the Virgin's robe appeared in rich purple, that of the baby Jesus in bright yellow clasped by a green sash. The Virgin stared directly at the viewer, with large, round eyes, her face meant to convey compassion, as she cradled Jesus in her right arm. She pointed to him with her left hand. His hand, in turn, rested on her neck. The colors, though bright, were flat, and the facial expressions, now that they were clear, seemed slightly forced.

"Much better," said Al in a tone of satisfaction. "No masterpiece, but we're not finished yet. We've only taken off the top layer. Now comes the really interesting part." Much to my shock, he began to repeat the entire process, this time spreading a section of solvent-soaked cloth right over the newly cleaned surface. "Underneath we'll probably find another layer of dried oil, and when that's removed, an older painting, and a more interesting one, unless I miss my guess."

We looked on in fascination as Al continued his operation step by step. Gradually, as the newer paint dissolved, another layer of black varnish appeared, partially mixing with the surface pigments. Al treated the section again with solvent and replaced his plate of glass, now smudged and oily, on top, anchored by the weight of the heavy dictionary. "This time we wait a little longer. Do you mind if I smoke?"

"Not at all," I said. Al is one of the few people I know who still smokes, in his case, a pipe. He owns a large collection of handsome pipes in all shapes and sizes, and they anchor him to an earlier time. After all, how many men smoke pipes these days? He walked over to his pipe rack, chose one with a well-chewed stem, scooped some tobacco into it from a pouch, tamped it, and struck a match. He slowly drew a few contented puffs. The aroma that filled the room was pleasantly familiar.

Toby meanwhile was looking closely at the icon under treatment. "When you talk about finding an older painting, how old do you mean? How far back do icons go?"

"To the beginnings of Christianity," said Al, "but I'll spare you the lecture. 'Icon' is the Greek word for image. The veneration of icons began in the eighth century and flourished under the Byzantine Empire, which in turn influenced the Russian tradition." He blew some smoke toward the ceiling. "The 'golden age' of icons dates from the fifteenth and sixteenth centuries, about the same time as the Renaissance in the West. The best examples from that period are worth a fortune."

That didn't jibe with what Harry Spears had said. "Really? The auctioneer at Morgan's told me there isn't much of a market for icons. Was he wrong?"

"I'll say. That may have been true before the fall of the Soviet Union, but these days the new oil billionaires will pay huge sums for old icons, especially rare ones. Collecting is a mark of prestige. Even the Russian mafia is involved. Think about it. There aren't many new Leonardos floating about, but it's still possible to uncover icons from that era that have never been equaled in terms of color or line."

"That's what's always puzzled me," I admitted. "There doesn't seem to be much progression in the tradition. Why is there so little variation in the style of icon painting from one century to the next?" In fact, I had avoided studying icon painting precisely because the tradition struck me as repetitious.

"One reason is that the Church had rules as to what you could or couldn't paint." Al peered into the bowl of his pipe, which apparently had gone out. It was always doing that. He relit it. "Another is that later painters were in such awe of the early masters that they imitated their compositions, so their work tends to follow set patterns. It's the quality that differs. It's true that by the time you reach the nineteenth century, much of the production is mechanical. That's why the excitement lies in peeling back layers of time. When you start cleaning an icon that's really old, say one from the sixteenth century, you may have to remove three or four layers of overpainting before you get down to the authentic work." Al laid his pipe in an ashtray and reached for the dictionary he was using as a weight. "Now, this one here isn't as old as that, but I think it may be ready. Let's see what we have."

Al lifted the soiled glass and started working again with fresh cotton balls dipped in solvent. Once he was satisfied with the result, he gently lifted any remaining flakes of residue by gliding the edge of his scalpel at a low angle to the surface in a delicate movement. He repeated this process until the entire icon had been treated. Then, using clean balls of cotton, he swabbed the surface one final time until it glowed. "There!"

At first I thought we were looking at the same painting freshly renewed, just as the dull hood of a car seems newly painted after a rainstorm. But in another moment I realized that not only were the colors brighter, but the composition had subtly changed. Whereas the previous Virgin stared out at the viewer, cradling Jesus in a presentational pose, the Virgin in this painting looked tenderly into her infant's eyes, her head turned to the side, toward his. Jesus in turn looked into his mother's eyes, his fingers resting trustingly on her shoulder. The facial details of both figures were more convincing, compared to the first painting, and the brushwork more complex, as in the intricate design of the hem of Mary's robe.

"It's a different painting altogether. I believe it's the Mother of God of Feodor," Al exclaimed, with brio. "The original belongs to the Temple of St. Feodor in Kostroma. This version clearly was done in the eighteenth century. You can notice elements of realism as the result of influences filtering in from the West. At the time, the style was controversial. Brighter colors and more detail. Oh, yes, I think the museum will be pleased."

"That's amazing," said Toby. I could tell he was getting into it. "But now how do you know there isn't still another painting underneath the one you've removed?"

"I don't," said Al, evidently content with himself. "There's a remote chance that there's even an earlier image under this one, but the risk of ruining the icon would be too great. Now that I've got an eighteenth-century panel with an eighteenth-century image, it's time to stop."

"Say you didn't stop. How would you know for sure you've gone too far?" Toby persisted.

"Well, if you get down to the gesso—that's the primer—then you're in the crapper, because that means you've gone and wiped out the original image. Goodbye, painting." I was familiar with gesso. It's a white, chalky mixture that artists laid down on raw wood as a primer to create a smooth surface on which to paint. "Once you expose the gesso," Al went on, "there's no going back."

Toby nodded soberly. "But what if you'd found gesso underneath the layer you just removed? What would you tell the museum?"

Al raised his palms and contorted his features into an expression of mock horror, then confided with a grin, "Thank God for tenure."

Toby laughed. "I thought you didn't believe in God."

"It's just a saying. Besides, it never hurts to be polite." Then Al looked at me, as if in warning. "But seriously, folks, it's a delicate business when you're dealing with an older panel, because the question always is when to stop. In this situation I was pretty confident, but yes, there's an element of risk."

"That would be the case with ours, then, if we found it, wouldn't it?" I said.

"Exactly," agreed Al.

Toby picked up the thread. "In our case, something you said earlier has been bothering me. If the same kind of supports were used in the nineteenth century as in the Renaissance, what makes you think our panel is any older than the nineteenth century?"

"I'll show you. Let's take another look at your picture." Toby handed Al the photo showing the reverse of the panel. "See here?" Al asked, tracing his finger along the top horizontal wedge across the back. "This wood is of a lighter color than the rest of the panel, which suggests that these wedges are replacements of the originals. The early icon makers hammered their wedges into place but didn't use glue, and eventually the strips became loose and fell out. You wouldn't expect to find replacements in a panel of more recent construction. So my guess is that your icon dates back at least to the 1600s, if not earlier."

I was thinking hard. "I can see why it's so important to examine the panels. But there was only one photo of the icon in Morgan's auction catalog, and the same was true of their catalog online. I checked. The picture was of the front of the icon, showing the angel. So how could anyone, say a prospective bidder, know what the back was like or that there was any reason to think this particular icon, listed with a low estimate at a secondary auction gallery, was much older and more valuable than its description?"

Al shrugged. "They couldn't."

Toby, who had been staring at the cleaned icon, looked up at me. "You're right. That would explain why there weren't lots of bidders. No one was interested."

"With two exceptions," I pointed out. "Charlie." I waited a beat.

Toby finished my sentence. "And whoever killed him."

4

ROSE CASSINI, the consignor of the icon, had agreed to meet with us the next morning at her home in Cazadero. On the way, we stopped off in Duncans Mills so Toby could hang a "closed" sign on his shop for the second day in a row. Wednesday morning is a slow time for business anyway, we rationalized. That done, we continued east for another few miles on 116.

The road that branches off 116 leading up into the hills to Cazadero is called the Cazadero Highway, but it's a narrow country road, with a speed limit of thirty-five miles per hour. It weaves alongside Austin Creek through dense forest impermeable to the sun. And now it had begun to rain. They say it always rains in Cazadero—it's officially the wettest place in the state. As we drove, mist rose from the pavement, the leaves dripped gloom, and the scent of sodden pine needles thickened the air. If you want to get away from it all and your favorite outfit is a poncho, then Cazadero fills the bill. Otherwise, I wondered, why would anyone choose to live in this sequestered hamlet? It's got a fire department, a post office, two churches, a general store, an auto repair shop, a bakery, and a bar.

"How did she sound on the phone yesterday?" asked Toby as we approached the outskirts of town.

"Upset to think that her icon might have had anything to do with Charlie's death. She never thought it was particularly valuable. She seemed willing enough to talk when I told her we were helping the sheriff."

"Did you mention I was Charlie's partner?"

"Yes, and she said anything she could do to help, she would."

"Let's hope she can. What are we looking for?"

"A small wood-frame house painted red, on the right side of the road just past the Cazadero sign. Slow down. I think that may be it."

Toby eased up and pulled over. The house—a cabin really—was set well back from the street under a stand of pines. A shingle hanging from the roadside mailbox said "Cassini." It had been a long time since the house had been painted. The siding was still recognizably red but faded. Moss clung to the roof. A rusty Dodge from another era sat on a dirt driveway in front of a small garage with a sagging door. The yard grew wild, but a big pot bursting with daffodils brightened the front porch.

Rain lashed the yard as we hurried to the door, which opened just as we gained the stoop. "Come in out of it," Rose said as she waved us inside. "You can hang your things up here." She pointed to a row of pegs next to the entrance. In contrast to the dilapidated exterior, the inside of the house was warm and welcoming. There were hand-loomed mats scattered on the pine floor and brilliant throws and blankets draped over the simple furniture, which consisted of wicker chairs, side tables, and a sofa. An old pine dining table was covered with an inviting tablecloth glimmering with gold threads and many shades of green. As I took things in, a smile rose to my lips, in response to which Rose said simply, "I'm a weaver. Do you like them?"

"Oh yes, they're beautiful! Did you make all these?"

She smiled and nodded. She was used to compliments about her work. "A number of shops around here carry them. It keeps me busy."

We hung our wet things on the pegs and she led us to the table, where a pot of coffee and a platter of brownies awaited.

Rose Cassini was still an attractive woman, though she looked to be in her late sixties, perhaps even a few years older. Like so many other local women of her generation, she retained the style of a flamboyant youth: long hair gone white, which she wore in a thick bun held by a silver clasp; dangling earrings, also silver, matched by a wide silver bracelet; jeans and a shaggy pullover; no makeup. Tall enough to look commanding, she had kept her figure mostly, had full lips, creased cheeks, and dark, inquisitive eyes that searched our faces as we pulled chairs up to the table.

"Help yourself," she said, extending the platter to Toby, then me. "Made them this morning, so they're fresh." She poured each of us a cup of coffee.

"Thanks for agreeing to see us on short notice," I said.

"Listen, I'm glad to have company." Her manner was friendly and frank. "I have to tell you it was quite a shock when you called about this business. I mean the man who was killed. What was his name again?"

"Charlie Halloran," said Toby. "We were partners."

"That's what your wife said. You know, I spoke to him on the phone right after the auction."

Rose had mentioned her conversation with Charlie when we'd agreed to meet, but then we spoke only briefly. "Yes," I said, "I know he asked the auctioneer for your phone number. Can you tell us about it?"

"The auctioneer gave me his name and number and said the man who bought the icon wanted to get in touch with me. I was curious, so I called him."

"Do you remember exactly what he said when you spoke to him, Mrs. Cassini?" I prompted.

"It would be Ms. Cassini, actually. But please call me Rose. Yes, I remember the conversation clearly enough. He was very pleasant, polite. He asked me what I could tell him about the provenance of the icon—you know, where I had gotten it—and whether I would mind telling him whether I was also the consignor of another lot that he had bought, which, it so happened, I was."

The second part of her answer caught me off guard.

"What lot was that?" asked Toby. He was surprised too.

"The storyboards," she said.

We both looked blank.

"You see," Rose continued, "both lots were listed in the catalog as 'the property of a lady'"—she made air quotes with her fingers—"which is the terminology they use in these auctions. I can tell you I got a good laugh out of that. Me, a lady? Anyhow, your friend wanted to know if I was the 'lady' in both cases. I told him yes I was, and then he wanted to know more about the storyboards and whether I had any others I might want to sell and whether I had any other icons I might want to sell, too."

"This is the first we've heard about any storyboards," said Toby. "Can you tell us what they were?"

"The sketches for *The Birds*, you know, the Hitchcock film."

Toby pursued the point. "Charlie bought some sketches for *The Birds* at the same auction? And you were the consignor?"

"That's right."

He raised a finger to his lips. "Come to think of it, he did say something about buying some movie memorabilia. But he wasn't specific. What did they look like?"

"Wait a sec," I interrupted. "I'm going to have to relate all this to the sheriff's department, and I better get it all down." I brought out a pen and notepad and then turned to Rose. "So the first thing Charlie asked you about was the provenance of the icon and the next thing he asked you was whether you were the consignor of some Hitchcock memorabilia?"

"That's right."

"And this was artwork connected with *The Birds*?"

"Right. Back in the early '60s I had a boyfriend named Peter who was an assistant to the art director for Alfred Hitchcock, and these were some of the storyboards that he had drawn while they were working on the film. And as a matter of fact, Peter was also the one who gave me the icon."

I caught Toby's eye. Rose seemed primed to continue, so neither of us made a comment.

"I told all that to your friend, and he seemed really interested in the coincidence that the storyboards and the icon had come from the same person. And I said it also seemed odd to me that one person would bid on both items. He said it wasn't that odd. He explained he was a dealer and sold antiques as well as popular culture stuff. 'Collectibles,' I think he called them. Then he asked if I had any other Russian icons or any more Hitchcock material to sell, and I said no, and he said that was too bad and thanked me and rang off. That was it. I didn't think any more about it until you called."

Toby glanced again in my direction. "Could you describe these storyboards to us?"

"Sure I can. I don't know if you know much about the way Hitchcock worked, but before he ever shot a scene, he had the whole film laid out on panels called storyboards. They were like black-and-white cartoons, scene by scene, giving the camera angles and so on. Sort of like a visual outline to follow. Some had the characters in them, some just the sets, some were close-ups, some were distance shots. Hitchcock had a team of artists working on the storyboards, and my boyfriend Peter was one of them. There were hundreds of drawings for *The Birds*. Peter kept some of the leftovers. I had quite a collection, but most of them got ruined over the years. I was dumb, stored them in the garage, and the roof leaked."

"What about the ones you sent to auction?" I asked.

"Those I kept in the house in a closet. Peter had asked me to keep a special eye on those for some reason. I don't know why. They weren't the most interesting, just set designs, really. Sketches of the farmhouse used in the movie where the family gets attacked by the birds at the end of the film. Shown from different angles and distances. There were three of them. There's an illustration of one in the auction catalog."

I made a mental note to check that out. "Do you remember when it was that Peter asked you to keep an eye on those particular drawings? Was it before or after he gave you the icon?"

"I'm not sure," she replied after a pause, "but it must have been around the same time."

I made a note of that and continued. "I don't know if you feel comfortable talking about your relationship with Peter, but it might be helpful if you could tell us a little more about him."

Rose sighed. She refilled her cup and creased her chin. "It's a long story if you want the whole history."

"That's what we're here for," I said. "I mean, if you don't mind sharing it with us."

She smiled ruefully. "You could say it's the story of my life. All right. I grew up in Bodega Bay and that's where I met Peter when I was eighteen. At a protest meeting. You're from Bodega Bay—does the name Rose Gaffney mean anything to you?"

Yes, it did have a familiar ring, and as Rose filled in the background, I made the connection. When we first moved to town, we heard of a local woman by that name who once owned property out on Bodega Head, near us. In the early '60s she led a campaign against Pacific Gas and Electricity when the company tried to build a nuclear power plant abutting her land. It was Gaffney who organized the protest movement and took them to court. The case dragged on for several years until a geologist discovered that the proposed plant would be sitting directly atop the San Andreas Fault. That put a quick end to the scheme. PG&E had to withdraw, leaving behind a seventy-foot shaft that everyone now calls "The Hole in the Head."

I briefly recounted what I knew about Rose Gaffney.

"Well, she took a shine to me when I was a teenager; I don't know why. Maybe it was because we had the same first name. People say she was gruff and all that, but she had a good heart and she was awfully kind to me. She was just like an aunt. We spent lots of time together, clamming, walking on the beach. She taught me to bake—in fact I made these brownies with her recipe. And she got me interested in crafts. She had a huge collection of Native American artifacts—baskets and blankets and so on. She was the one who got me started on weaving.

"Anyhow, when she began organizing the protests, naturally I came along, and I met Peter at one of them. I fell for him on the spot. And pretty soon the three of us were hanging out together. I think Rose took him under her wing just to encourage our relationship."

Toby began to fidget in his chair. The relationship thing again. That's testosterone for you; the eyes glaze over. I could guess he wanted Rose to get to the part about the icon. Rose noticed it, too. She tilted her head at him. "I'm telling you all this for a reason."

He sat up straighter, chastened.

She took a sip from her cup and resumed. "That would have been the winter of 1962. Peter came up to Bodega Bay in January with some other members of the crew to get ready for the shoot. He was doing preliminary sketches for the storyboards and drawing some of the locals to get the costumes right for the actors. They didn't start the actual filming until the spring. I guess that was the happiest time of my life. Peter was working hard, we were in love, the protests against PG&E were growing, and there were Hollywood types walking all over town. It was all so exciting. And then—everything fell apart. It started with the icon."

Rose paused. "Am I going too fast?"

I shook my head. "Please go on."

"Peter was Russian by descent. Did I mention his last name? It was Federenco. One day he showed up at my house very upset and asked me to hide an heirloom that had caused a fight in his family. That was the icon. He wanted me to hold it for safekeeping until the dispute blew over."

"Did he give you any background on the icon, like where it came from?"

"He was pretty evasive about it. I did piece together that this icon was part of a set he was given by his father, but a cousin had questioned the inheritance and was trying to get it back. From what he told me, the dispute had gone on for years, but a story had just appeared in the newspaper that had stirred things up. He was worried about what this cousin might do. Afraid of him, in fact. Said he was unstable and prone to violence. So would I keep the icon under wraps until things cooled down? He said the cousin didn't know who I was, and I'd be safe. That's how the icon came to me, and that's all I've ever known about it. Because shortly afterward, Peter died. By the way, I didn't tell this whole story to your friend when he called. It was too personal. But I'm telling it to you now."

We sat in silence for a moment.

"I'm very sorry you lost Peter," I said. "What happened?"

"It was just a couple of weeks later. He'd gone home for the weekend to San Francisco. He was with a friend who told me about it. They were getting out of a taxi when a motorcycle came roaring around the corner and clipped Peter while he was standing in the street. He was thrown to the pavement and smashed his head. By the time the ambulance arrived, he was gone. The kid who hit him never went to jail. He was the son of a policeman."

"How awful for you." I placed my hand on Rose's arm.

"And you know, there's something about his last words that still puzzles me. I've always wondered what he meant. According to his friend Terry, just before he died, Peter murmured, 'Tell Rose Gaffney . . .' But he never completed the sentence. Tell Rose Gaffney what? Or was he trying to tell *me* something but because of his head injury he mixed up my name with hers? I'll never know. I'd like to believe he was thinking of me at the end, but. . . ." She shook her head sadly. "That's why I told you about Rose Gaffney."

"I see," said Toby.

There was another pause. "Rose, would you mind answering just a few more questions?" I ventured.

"No, it was all a long time ago. Go ahead."

"Did Peter mention the name of this cousin he was afraid of? Is there any chance you remember it?"

She thought a moment. "The same last name as his, I think. Federenco. I don't remember a first name."

"Okay. And when Peter first told you about the icon, he said it was part of a set? I think that's the word you used. Is it possible that he used another term like 'triptych'? That's an icon made up of three attached panels."

"That sounds right. It always looked to me that the icon he gave me was meant to be connected to another one."

"And did he ever say anything about the other two panels?"

"No, not to me."

Toby asked in turn, "You said that Peter referred to a story in a newspaper that had stirred up an old quarrel in the family. Do you know anything else about it?"

"I'm afraid not. I never saw it."

"What about the newspaper? Did Peter say which paper it was in?"

"I don't recall, but it probably was the *San Francisco Chronicle*. That was the paper he always read. He'd carry it around."

"Then it might be possible for us to track it down," I pointed out. "But we'd need to know the date. Can you help with that?"

She shrugged. "Peter died in May, and he gave me the icon a few weeks earlier, which would have been late April. Late April 1962. Does that help?"

"At least it's a start."

"What ever happened to Terry, the friend who was with Peter when he died? Did you stay in touch with him?" asked Toby.

"Terry? He also did some art work for *The Birds*. Yes, we stayed in touch for a while. Then he went out to New York to work as a set designer for the theater. I'd hear from him every now and again. He died, though, a few years ago. Drugs and alcohol, is what I heard."

"And after Peter died, what about you?" I wondered whether she had anyone in her life. "You never married?"

"Oh, I had my chances. But I never wanted to, after Peter. He was the one, the love of my life. Not that I lacked for male companionship, mind you. At least until I hit sixty." She grunted. "Then it was like somebody turned off a switch. But up until then there was usually someone. Peter was the one, though. Guess that's why I held onto that angel icon all these years—for sentimental reasons, certainly not religious ones."

I must have looked curious.

"What?" Rose asked. "You want to know my religious views?"

"Not unless you want to talk about them."

"You know, I heard a guy on TV last week who had a great theory. He said maybe there are millions of inhabited planets in the universe, and maybe there are different gods for different sectors, you know, like assistants to the Big One. As in any organization, some are capable, some aren't. Maybe the one watching over our sector has Attention Deficit Disorder. That would explain a lot."

Toby chuckled. "Is that what you think?"

"Not really. Let's just say I've worn out a lot of outfits in my time. I've tried them on one after another—Catholic, Buddhist, Quaker, New Age, blah, blah, blah, and now I'm tired. I'll tell you something, though. I've been frightened of the idea of death ever since I was a little girl. I know it's going to happen. But I just never got used to the fear. You know, it's a strange thing. You can get used to an idea but you can't get used to a feeling, no matter how long you've had it. Either you feel it or you don't. I've been thinking a lot about death again since you told me about the murder. And the feeling is back. Well, maybe something I've said today will help the sheriff. I hope so."

Toby smiled. "Thanks, Rose. You've been very, very helpful. We appreciate it."

"We really do." I stood up to leave.

"Is there anything else I can tell you?"

"There's just one thing," I said. "What made you decide to sell the icon now after all these years? And Peter's artwork?"

"Simple. I needed the money. Times are bad. My sales are way down."

Toby got up too. "So how did the storyboards do, if you don't mind my asking?"

"You know what? I cleared twelve hundred dollars on the lot after Morgan's took their cut and only six hundred on the icon. I was expecting a whole lot more. And to think that someone might have been killed on account of it—it doesn't make sense."

"No, it doesn't," I agreed. "It doesn't make sense at all."

That was quite a story," Toby remarked as we headed back to Duncans Mills. The rain had slackened to a drizzle.

"She's quite a woman. It must be a lonely life for her, but she seems to have it together. She's independent. I liked her."

"So did I."

"Even when she slapped your wrist for getting antsy?"

"Even so. Sometimes I do get impatient."

"You're such a man."

"And that's bad?"

"Actually, in the general scheme of things, it's good."

"Thanks. I suppose. What do you make of her story? The pieces don't all seem to fit."

"No," I admitted. "There must be a link between the icon and the Hitchcock memorabilia, but how in the world could Charlie have made a connection? Unless it was just luck that they ended up in his possession."

"If luck was involved, it was bad luck for Charlie. I wonder what he did with those storyboards? I'm going to have to make another search of the shop."

"Fine, and while you're doing that, I'll check the catalog entry on the storyboards and type up my notes for Dan."

We stopped at the Cape Fear Café in Duncans Mills for a quick bite to eat before reopening the gallery. They make a good, old-fashioned BLT. I always ask them to hold the tomatoes, so I suppose the sandwich I order should be called a BL. While we were wolfing down our lunch, Caroline, the woman who owns the gift shop next to Toby, came in.

"Hey, Toby. There was someone asking for you this morning. When he saw you were closed, he seemed disappointed. I told him to stop by again later today, and he said he would."

"Thanks. I'll keep an eye out for him."

"Sure, me too."

"Did he say anything else?" asked Toby.

"No. Just that he'd call again."

"Okay, thanks, Caroline."

Back at the shop, Toby removed the closed sign from his door and started a systematic search of the premises while I scanned Morgan's auction catalog for the lot Charlie bought. It didn't take me long to find it.

> Three preproduction storyboards for
> Alfred Hitchcock's film *The Birds*, 1962.
> Original watercolor and ink drawings.
> Each 12" × 20".
> The Property of a Lady.
> Est. $2,000–$2,500.

Only one of the three was illustrated in the catalog. The sketch showed a side view of a wood-frame house partially hidden by a group of trees. There wasn't much detail. It was years since I'd seen the film, but I vaguely remembered the farmhouse where the family lives and where the final bird attack takes place. At least now we knew what the storyboards looked like.

But that was as close as we got to them. After an hour, Toby threw up his hands. "They're not here. Either Charlie never brought them to the shop, or whoever stole the icon found the storyboards and took them too. They're gone."

Meanwhile, though, I had made a discovery. "Toby, come take a look at the catalog. The storyboards are listed on the first day of the auction, the icon on the second."

"So?"

"That means that Charlie bought the storyboards first and then went back on the second day to bid on the icon. Why? I've checked his files and found the bill of sale. That's the sequence, all right. First he bought the storyboards, then he bought the icon, then he asked the auctioneer how to contact the consignor."

"What does that tell us?"

"I wish I knew. Then, when he speaks to Rose, she tells him that the icon and the storyboards both came from her."

"And a few days later, Charlie turns up dead, and both the icon and the storyboards go missing," Toby summed up. He shook his head. "It still doesn't make sense. I'm going to search the shop one last time."

Toby set out again, prying into drawers and nooks and crannies, and I began working on an e-mail to Dan. I tried to summarize our interview with Rose. I recounted what she had told us about her phone conversation with Charlie, her relationship with Peter Federenco, the circumstances under which he had given her the icon, including Peter's report of a threatening cousin, and what we had discovered so far about a link between the icon and Peter's artwork for *The Birds*.

An hour later I was almost finished when the bell tinkled above the door and a man entered. He was elderly, well dressed in a cashmere sport jacket and slacks, carrying a cane, yet walking briskly. He had close-cropped gray hair and a pencil-thin gray mustache. "Are you Mr. Sandler?" he asked Toby, who was going through a bookcase at the far end of the shop.

"That's me," said Toby, approaching him. "Is there something I can help you with?"

"I came by this morning, but you were closed," said the potential customer in a neutral tone, without accusation.

"I'm sorry for the inconvenience."

"Not a problem," returned the man, "I'm used to dealers who keep odd hours." His eyes made a slow sweep of the gallery.

"So you're a collector," Toby said. "Are you looking for anything in particular?"

"It so happens I am. I'm looking for something very particular." There was a pause. Toby waited for him to continue. "But then my tastes are broad within the general category of my interest."

"Which is?" queried Toby.

"Russian decorative arts—silver, jewelry, Fabergé eggs, pre-Revolutionary objects. And religious art," he added, narrowing his eyelids meaningfully. "I have a small but to me very precious collection of Russian icons."

Toby tensed. "And you've dropped in today because you happened to be passing by?"

"Not exactly. I saw a story on the news last night in San Francisco about the murder of your partner. It mentioned the robbery of your gallery. I'm very sorry. You have my condolences."

"Thank you. So the story made the TV news in San Francisco," said Toby, angling for additional information. "I didn't know that."

"Yes, and there was mention of a Russian icon that might have been the object of the robbery," continued the stranger. "That was the first time I was made aware that any gallery outside the city handled material of that nature, so I drove up for the day to see what else you might have along those lines. Again, I'm very sorry for your loss."

"I see. Then I have to disappoint you. I don't have anything else at the moment that would meet your needs."

"Nothing at all in the category of Russian icons or antiques? Imperial porcelain, perhaps?"

"I'm afraid not. We don't usually carry items of that description. The icon was a one-off find. A chance purchase, you might say."

"Oh. Well in that case, I must be disappointed. May I ask if you were the one who made that purchase?"

"No, my partner did, and as a result, I know very little about it."

"Ah. Out of curiosity, can you describe it? What was the subject, for example?"

"It was an icon of St. Michael, I believe," answered Toby, "but I only glanced at it when my partner brought it to the shop. I know almost nothing at all about Russian art, to tell you the truth. I'm afraid I can't tell you much about it."

"St. Michael, you say? A pity it was stolen. I have a special feeling for St. Michael. I would have liked to see it."

Toby nodded.

"Are there any other galleries in Sonoma County I may have overlooked that carry religious icons or Russian objects of historical interest?"

"Not that I know of," replied Toby. "But it might be worth your while to look around in Guerneville or Graton. Even Sebastopol. You never can tell what might come into a shop from week to week."

"Yes, you're right. You know, I may spend a day or two more in the area. Let me give you my card. In case you do come across any Russian objects that might interest me, would you be so kind as to give me a call?"

"Of course."

"And in the event that the missing icon is recovered, I would be extremely interested in seeing it. As I've said, I have a special reverence for St. Michael, and I won't quibble about price if I find a piece I like." He extended his card to Toby, who slipped it into his shirt pocket without reading it. "Thank you," said the stranger, and with that, he exited the shop, with a quick, polite nod in my direction.

I had felt a growing sense of unease during this conversation. Now Toby walked back to where I was sitting, withdrawing the card from his pocket. As he gazed at it, he stopped abruptly, then looked up.

"What's the matter?" I asked.

Wordlessly, he handed it to me. It was a plain white business card bearing a name, an address in San Francisco, and a phone number. There was nothing particularly interesting about the card except the name.

Andrew Federenco.

5

THE COUSIN? The man Peter feared? I called Rose right away, but the best she could do was confirm that Andrew might have been the cousin's name. Honestly, she couldn't remember. Still, it was enough of a reason to call Dan. He picked up the phone on the first ring. He had just been reading my e-mail, and now with this piece of news, he decided to swing by to see us. He was at the shop within twenty minutes.

"Hey, guys. Thanks for the Cassini notes. Let's review them step by step."

In answer to his methodical questions, we walked Dan through our interview with Rose, relating her conversation with Charlie and her tales about the past. We concluded with Andrew Federenco's recent visit. Toby handed over Federenco's card, and Dan studied it. "Address and phone number, that helps," he said. "I'll have somebody get on it right away. Good job, you two."

We thanked him. Dan was now following several lines in the investigation. He'd discovered that Charlie had been a regular at a high-stakes poker game run by a gambler named Arnold Kohler, who moved the game around from place to place in the county. It was rumored that

Charlie owed him a bundle. Kohler's alibi for the night of the murder was strong, but he was known to have unsavory associates. Dan was also looking into Tom Keogh's affairs.

Toby mentioned that Tom had come to the shop and complained about his interrogation.

"Upset, was he?" Dan said, with a shrug of dismissal. "That's too bad."

"Is he a suspect?" I asked.

"At this stage of the investigation, he's a person of interest. We don't have any evidence to hold him, but he did have a motive. You were right about there being bad blood between the two of them," he said, looking at Toby. "Tom was jealous of Charlie playing around, and that's why they broke up. In fact, Tom threw him out of the house."

"I guess I heard that from Annie when I stopped in for a beer," said Toby.

"According to friends, they had a couple of loud fights in public about Charlie's infidelities before Charlie packed up and left. Tom admitted that much, though of course he denies having anything to do with Charlie's murder. Plus, he claims to have an alibi for that night, which we're still checking out."

"Charlie owed him some money, too," Toby added. "Did Tom mention that?"

"He didn't volunteer it, but it came out during the questioning."

None of this felt right to me. "Tom Keogh didn't kill Charlie. He seems really broken up by Charlie's death."

"That doesn't mean he didn't do it. I've seen other cases of jealousy leading to violence, and it's not uncommon afterward for the attacker to feel remorse. In fact, that's fairly typical in a crime of passion."

Toby looked annoyed. "Aren't you jumping to conclusions?"

"No, I'm just speculating. Now I've asked you this before. Can either of you tell me what Charlie was doing on a lonely stretch of road leading out to Bodega Head at one or two o'clock in the morning?"

We couldn't.

"Because that's where he was murdered, on land, not on that boat. We've marked out a crime scene on Westshore Road between the marina and the turnoff to the housing for the marine lab."

Dan's reference was to a desolate stretch of road that runs along the harbor from the marina leading out to Bodega Head. There's a research center out there for the study of marine life, run by the University of California–Davis. But aside from a driveway to a few small dormitories that provide housing for the lab workers, there's nothing along the shore but scrub brush and a few stands of cypress.

"We found an area of matted grass with scattered blood traces near the water," Dan continued. "There was a struggle there. And there's a clamdigger's rowboat tied to a tree, which is what I think the killer used to transport the body. I'm guessing that he didn't intend to kill Charlie on that spot, but when it happened, he improvised disposing of the body by using the rowboat to haul him out to the grounded sailboat. Could be he figured that nobody would find the body for a while if it was stashed in the cabin. It was a moonless night and high tide around the time Charlie was killed, which made it easy enough for the killer to move the body without anyone seeing or hearing anything."

"What about the people from the marine lab dorms?" I asked.

"We've talked to all of them who were there that night. No one heard or saw a thing—didn't expect anyone would, unless one of them happened to be out for a stroll. But we've got bloodstains on the rowboat, and I'm betting they'll match the stains found in the grass. And there's something else you should know. Someone broke into Charlie's apartment on the night he was murdered. Threw stuff around. In anger, maybe? That would fit a crime of passion. So I'm thinking, what if Charlie was on his way out to Bodega Head to hook up with some guy for a nocturnal tryst, and what if Tom caught him at it, followed him, say, and flew into a jealous rage? Let's say he didn't mean to, but he killed him, panicked, hid the body on the boat, and then trashed Charlie's apartment. It's a plausible scenario."

I shook my head. "I don't know, Dan. If Tom killed Charlie and trashed his apartment in anger, are you saying he's the same one who ransacked Toby's gallery? That won't wash. Whoever went through the gallery did a careful search. Things weren't tossed around in anger. The person who did it was looking for something, not just vandalizing property. Maybe when Charlie's killer didn't find what he was looking for in one place, he went looking for it in the other—isn't that a more likely scenario?"

Dan grinned. "You know, I can walk and chew gum at the same time. If theft was the motive for Charlie's murder, that opens a different line for the investigation. That's why I'd like you to follow up on Rose Cassini's story about the boyfriend who gave her the icon and this cousin of his who was involved in a family feud. Didn't she say that an article appeared in a newspaper that spooked the boyfriend into giving her the icon for safekeeping? Let's find out what that was about. Is there any chance you could dig up that story for me? I've got enough on my hands. That kind of research is more in your line of work than mine."

I had already thought of doing a newspaper search. "Sure thing. I can start going through the archives of the *Chronicle* tomorrow."

"Good. You look for that story and I'll look for"—he glanced down at the card in his hand—"Mr. Andrew Federenco. Plus I'm still talking to Arnold Kohler. Then we'll compare notes."

"Dan? One more thing," said Toby.

"Yes?"

"What about Charlie's next of kin? Does his family know?"

"There's just the brother. I've been in touch with him. He's asking when the body can be released for a funeral. I think that can happen in another day or two."

"I'd like to know about the funeral," said Toby. "I want to be there."

"I'll keep you posted. You liked Charlie, didn't you?"

"Yeah, I did."

Dan got up to go but paused and turned in the doorway. "I'm not finished with Tom Keogh yet, either."

The public library on 3rd and E Street is a wonder for a city the size of Santa Rosa. I was there when it opened the next morning, and when I inquired about back issues of the *San Francisco Chronicle*, I was told that the library housed an extensive archive. Recent issues were available in digitized form, but issues dating from the '60s were stored on microfilm. A chatty librarian led me to the area where the files were stored, around the corner from the information desk. These occupied a good part of a wall, offering pull-out trays arranged by date, each containing a fairly sizeable spool of film. Two huge gray microfilm readers, antediluvian machines, were at the patrons' disposal.

I had used microfilm before, so I was comfortable with the process. The spools of film are cylindrical in shape and designed to fit over a little spindle that holds them in place. You thread the film under a glass screen and attach it to another spindle on the opposite side. Then you simply turn a crank, and the magnified images flit across the screen. To stop, you stop cranking. To go faster, you crank faster. There are no electronics involved at all—only a projector bulb that occasionally needs replacing. The technology is antiquated but still quite serviceable.

But what was it I was looking for? According to Rose, Peter Federenco had spotted a story in the newspaper, presumably the *Chronicle*, that had stirred the pot of an old family quarrel about an icon. What would be the nature of that story? Would it be about the family, about a court case, about Russian immigrants, about—what exactly? The only way to proceed was to scroll through the headlines of each day's paper, hoping that something would catch my eye. That might seem an impossible task, except that Rose had given me boundary dates that limited the search. The period in question, she recalled, would have been around April or May 1962. Scanning two months' worth of newspaper headlines would be manageable.

Make it three months, starting with March, I said to myself, selecting the appropriate tray from the files and threading the first spool onto the machine. As I cranked, the headlines flew by with remarkable speed, and I found it hard to resist pausing to read various tidbits that had nothing to do with my search but drew me in simply because they came from a bygone era. Even the ads were fun to read. They seemed so understated, given the kind we're blasted with today. I stopped to read a couple of stories that covered the protests against the nuclear power plant proposed for Bodega Bay, and another on Alfred Hitchcock's coming to town to film *The Birds*. One of the stories on the protests contained a profile of their leader, Rose Gaffney, the woman who had taken a kindly interest in Rose Cassini. According to a neighbor, Gaffney "was a wonderful friend but a wretched enemy, so you always made sure she was a friend." The irascible Gaffney was quoted in the story as saying that Bodega Bay "was a village of 350 souls and a few heels." She must have been quite a character.

Otherwise, the contents of the *Chronicle* for March offered no sign of the clue I was looking for. It wasn't until I was midway through the spool for April that a headline flickered in the corner of my eye, prompting me to stop and rewind the film. The word "Russian" leaped from the page, so I backtracked until I found it again. The story was part of a series to mark the 150th anniversary of the founding of Fort Ross, a Russian trading post that was established in 1812 about twelve miles north of Jenner. The Russian presence left its mark in local place names like Sebastopol, Moscow Road, and the Russian River. In 1962 the site of the fort was designated a National Historic Landmark, and to celebrate the event, the Museum of Russian Culture in San Francisco sponsored a monthlong festival. The *Chronicle* ran a series of Sunday features on the festival, which included music, dramatizations, and lectures.

I read each of the stories, but it was the last article in the series that riveted my attention. It was titled "Hidden Treasures of Russian California":

Just when you think you've heard it all, here's a tale that may send local descendants of Russian immigrants straight to the family attic.

According to Professor Ivan Roskovitch, who spoke on Saturday at the Museum of Russian Culture, a hunt for objects from pre-Revolutionary Russia may turn up hidden gems. He regrets that today many younger Russian Americans have lost touch with their ancestral heritage. As a result, they may not appreciate the significance of the many heirlooms that their forefathers brought with them from the old country.

As examples, Professor Roskovitch mentioned the silver samovars and gilded icons that used to be given pride of place in immigrant homes but today are at odds with modern tastes. Roskovitch made a plea to his audience to dust off any neglected heirlooms and to donate to the museum those that were no longer wanted.

To spur this statewide treasure hunt, he spun a tale as marvelous as any fabled pot of gold. For if legend can be trusted, one of the most important icons in the history of Russia, missing for centuries, may have found its way to California among the belongings of Russian immigrants. The key word, of course, is legend, because it isn't known for sure whether this wondrous work ever existed.

However, the story goes that Andrei Rublev, the most famous of all icon painters, was so pleased with his masterpiece, *The Holy Trinity*, made in 1427 for the Cathedral of the Trinity–St. Sergey Monastery, that he painted a smaller version for himself in the form of a portable triptych that he could take with him on his travels.

As Professor Roskovitch tells the tale, no one knows what became of this famous work. According to one version of the story, Rublev's images were later painted over and hidden by another artist. Some think they were spirited out of the country. Even so, there were rumors of the triptych being seen here and there in Russia until the 1860s, but never later. One variant of the legend has it that the icons were transported to America by a Russian family who never recognized their value. "Who knows?" concluded the professor. "They may be sitting in a trunk in San Francisco as we speak."

Asked what Rublev's icons would be worth today if they turned up in someone's home, Professor Roskovitch replied, "They would be priceless."

Was this the story that had sparked the Federenco quarrel? It seemed a likely candidate. To make sure, I marked my place by date and hurriedly read through the remainder of the newspapers for April and May of 1962. There were no other relevant stories, so I returned to "Hidden Treasures of Russian California" and read it once again. Yes, it was possible. What if two sides of the Federenco family had been arguing for years over an inheritance, more specifically, a religious object, and what if it became known at a later date that this heirloom might—just might—be far more valuable than anyone had thought? Wouldn't that have been enough to fan the embers of their quarrel? A phrase that Dan used came to mind again. At least it was a plausible scenario.

I knew almost nothing about Andrei Rublev. As I've said, Russian icons are far from my area of expertise. It was enough for me to know that his works were sought after. My more immediate interest was the Federenco feud. How could I learn more about the family? On a hunch, I called the Russian Cultural Center in San Francisco. In response to my question, a knowledgeable receptionist suggested a check of the Fort Ross library, which contains material related to the settlement as well as to Russian immigration in the state. Better yet, she added, the catalog of the library is accessible online. Why not try a search? She provided the website address. I thanked her, opened my laptop, and logged on.

All I had to do was type "Federenco" in the search box and click Enter. Immediately I was rewarded with a tantalizing hit. In fact, there were two entries in the database. The first was a listing for Euvgeny Federenco (1814–77) in the original Fort Ross records. He arrived at the fort in 1836 at the age of twenty-two and returned to Russia in 1841, when the fort was abandoned. His trade was listed as carpenter. The second entry was even more intriguing. Andreyev Federenco (1844–1907), his son, emigrated from Russia to California in 1870 and dictated a memoir to his daughter two years before he died. The typescript, dated 1905, was bound in a folder and available to scholars. A brief description of its contents indicated that it contained anecdotes of life at the fort told by the father to the son, as well as the son's description of his own immigrant experience. Was it worth a trip to Fort Ross? I thought so. Today was Thursday. Angie was arriving by plane later today, and a trip to Fort Ross on the weekend would make a perfect excursion for us. With that resolved, I hurried to pack up my notes.

When I got back to the car, I checked my cell phone and saw there was a message from Angie. She'd landed, was picking up her car, and thought she would reach us by three. Though I like to greet a houseguest with a home-cooked meal, I was too wrapped up in my discoveries to shop or cook. So I made a reservation at River's End, on the coast just where the Russian River spills into the sea. The tables look over rock-strewn water into the sunset. Happily, the food stands up to the setting. Then I dialed Fort Ross and made an appointment to use their library on Saturday.

Once home, I dashed around making the place ready for my sister. I put a bottle of Pimm's Cup on ice. This fall, during a salon internship in London, Angie took up the official drink of polo players as a tribute to her most elegant and handsome male client. I moved some family photos from my study to the guest room. Angie likes to sleep under the loving gaze of our Irish grandmother, Molly Barnes. And I checked that there were Angie-approved toiletries in the bathroom. Since London, she uses only Pears soap. High maintenance, but I love fussing over my sister.

A half hour later I woke from a nap on the couch when I heard the ding of the doorbell. There stood Angie, smiling broadly, her silky blond hair bouncing and curling around her heart-shaped face. That's the face I've cherished since I was a preteen lovingly bottle-feeding my tiny little sister.

We spent the next hour assessing each other physically the way sisters do, arranging Angie's luggage in the guest bedroom, and giving

Angie a look around our home, of which I am unduly proud, since it's mainly Toby who's furnished the place. We shared an initial Pimm's Cup, hers neat, mine cut with lemonade, the way the ladies do it in London, Angie says. I thought the first thing she would ask me about would be the case I was working on, but she insisted on getting the haircut out of the way.

"So, should I give you about the same cut that I did on Turkey Day?"

"Fine. Except I like that it got longer."

"Hair tends to do that, especially when left neglected."

"Yes, I know you told me to deep-condition. We can do that tomorrow. Today just cut a little off. I like the longer length because I don't have to do anything with it. It just hangs there."

"Exactly. My darling sister, as we age, things start to just hang there. Jowls just hang there. Wiggly chins just hang there. The last thing we need is for our hair to just hang there and call attention to all the other parts that are doing the same."

"So what are you saying, that I need a facelift?"

She laughed. "A good cut with a little more complexity would give you all the lift you need. Even my nuns know that."

"Your nuns?"

"Dad's nuns. You know."

"You mean the sisters at Grace Quarry?"

"That's right. I've been cutting their hair since I got back from London. Dad got me into it. You know how he's always had a sweet spot for those sisters."

"Well, he would, wouldn't he?" They practically raised him during that spell when his mother was ill. "But they all must be ancient now. What are they doing getting your air-lift haircuts?"

"The sisters have gone rogue. The bishop was bothering them about giving out communion and having Buddhist speakers. So they staked their claim."

"What do you mean?"

"Grace Quarry was a gift to them from the Graces, the lady author and her Beacon Hill husband. You remember them. They were nice to Granddad—hired him as a chauffeur when he sold his garage."

"Sure, I remember when we used to swim at the quarry when we were kids. I asked Dad why there was an echo out there when we talked. He told me the story of Echo, the nymph who could only repeat what others had said. Dad claimed that Echo lived at the far end of the quarry, behind the trees."

"That's just like Dad." Angie smiled. "Well," she continued, "when the Graces died, they left the property outright to the order. Now all these years later, when the nuns got feisty and the bishop threatened to shut them down, they declared themselves free of the church—went ecumenical."

"Gee, didn't the bishop raise hell?"

"I'll say he did, but he couldn't touch them. The order is independent of the Vatican."

"I didn't know that."

"Yes, and they're doing great. There are a dozen sisters there, some Catholic, some Anglican, and a bunch of young nuns from the Philippines who visit and study. Plus the lay sisters who have gathered round. There's a whole young community there."

"And you do their hair?"

"Why not? Even a nun likes to look half-decent. Unlike some people I know."

"Stop ragging on me. Give me the cut you think I should have."

"Bless you. This will be fun. You know, your hair's not half-bad. I know you say it's thin. But it's not. It's fine. But thick. You have Helen Mirren hair."

"Oh, God. She's decades older than I am."

"But still sexy. You should feel lucky that I even put you in the same category."

"The point being?"

"Helen Mirren is not gifted in the hair department. But she knows that she needs help, and she gets it. And the result is: she is Helen Mirren, sex goddess for the golden years."

"You win. Cut away."

An hour later, I looked ready for our dinner at the River's End. But would Toby notice?

"How about a second Pimm's Cup?" I proposed, in approval of Angie's work.

"We have a long night ahead," Angie replied. "Let's wait for Toby." Upon which, he burst through the door.

"Angie, you look terrific. And what have you done to your sister?"

"You like?" I ventured.

"You bet," he answered on cue.

And we were on for a happy evening. While we were freshening up, I gave Toby a quick rundown on my day's work in the library, but we agreed to leave all that aside for tonight and to enjoy our dinner out.

We left quickly, so that we'd have light for Angie's first drive up the coast. We wanted to be seated at our table looking out at Goat's Rock when the sun set. That's the whole point of River's End. Water, sunset, and a great meal. We weren't disappointed. On the drive up, Angie admired the views, as the road skirted one dramatic beach after another—the long sandy sweep of Coleman Beach, with its surging white surf, then Arched Rock Beach, which always reminds me of Monet's paintings at Etretat, then hidden coves that made the road veer in and out at sharp angles. We'd had a good share of ocean drama by the time we reached River's End, which in spite of the turbulence caused by the entrance of the Russian River to the sea, always breathes peace.

Before taking our table, we walked around the deck, watching the sky gather color for the sunset and pointing out the shoreline features to Angie—Goat's Rock, the array of birds that nest there, and the sandbar where seals play with their pups. We'd timed it right, just as the color wheel in the sky put on its full show. On this stretch of coast, late winter holds the most spectacular sunrises and sunsets. That's the secret that year-round beach residents keep from the summer people. Angie and I reminisced about our youth, recalling the sunrises we used to watch from the sea wall behind Grammy Molly's beach house in Hull at the other end of the country, looking out at the Atlantic.

By then it was time to move inside. The entrance to the restaurant, which is done in rustic redwood décor, passes through a narrow space adjacent to the bar, and there, listing slightly on a stool, sat Tom Keogh. He was perched between two men I didn't recognize, sloshing a swizzle stick in a tall drink. His eyes were glassy when he looked up and saw us. "Toby Sandler," he said in a challenging tone. "I want my stuff back."

Toby nodded hello, smiled, said nothing. Meanwhile a hostess approached with menus and led us to our table. Tom got up and followed us. He stood swaying next to the table as we were seated. "That stuff is mine, and I want it back," he repeated. The hostess shot him a disapproving glance, and several heads turned at the tables near us.

Toby replied in a calm but firm voice, "This isn't the place to discuss it, Tom. I said we'd work something out. We will."

Tom stood there for a moment looking confused. Toby said, "We'd like to enjoy our dinner, Tom. We'll talk soon."

"Is that right?" Tom said, slurring the words. He placed a hand on Toby's shoulder and drew his face up close. But by now his two companions had risen from their stools, and one of them grasped Tom by the elbow. "It's okay," he said to us, as he coaxed Tom to turn around. "C'mon, Tom, it's time for us to go."

"Wanna have another drink," said Tom.

"At home, Tom. We'll have one at home. C'mon." His two friends began to lead Tom away. "Sorry about that," said the one who hadn't yet spoken.

"It's all right," said Toby. "Be sure he gets home safely."

"We will." They propelled Tom unsteadily toward the door and left.

Angie wanted to know what that had been all about. I explained who Tom was and what he had recently gone through.

"He's a complete mess," said Toby.

"He's not a bad sort, really," I said. "Let's put it behind us and enjoy our dinner. And the view."

We did. A chilled bottle of sauvignon blanc smoothed the way for the "crab dégustation," a four-course dinner devoted to various preparations of the delectable crustacean, a specialty of the house at this time of year when the local catch is at its peak. A second round of wine by the glass went down as easily as the bottle, and the meal flowed along agreeably.

Over dessert we began to plan the next day. I proposed that we go to Whole Foods in Sebastopol to get the supplies we would need for our Gourmet Club. Angie surprised me by saying that she hadn't flown all the way across the country just to see Whole Foods. She could do that in Gloucester. "The point of Whole Foods is that they're all alike, wherever you go. They're the McDonald's of health food."

"Oh, come on, Angie. I'm talking local culture here. You should see this place. Outside, there's an accordion player dressed like a French marionette. And sitting next to him is an old man with a long white beard and a hat with a pot of daffodils on top of it, and his fat bulldog is sitting there with a smaller version of the same hat. It's some kind of happening, every time I go there. And that's just the outside. The produce is like nothing you've ever seen in New England—watercress with leaves as big as quarters, and fresh out of the stream."

"I believe you," Angie said apologetically. "But I have something else going."

"You haven't found a boyfriend here already, have you?" I blurted out my fear under the influence of several glasses of wine on top of the Pimm's Cup.

"Of course not." Angie pouted. Toby hunched around to nudge me with his elbow. He knows what I think about Angie's tumultuous romances. And he knows I go overboard with protective feelings.

"Sorry, sweetie," I apologized. "I'm just disappointed. I was looking forward to your company tomorrow. What's up?"

She looked a little uneasy, and her glance at Toby made me guess that she hadn't planned to discuss this in front of him. But she soldiered on. "Well, you know this case you're working on about the missing icon of the angel Michael? I told one of the sisters at Grace Quarry about it, and the next day she said that it was providential I was coming out here this week, because she had a dream about me. In this dream I was talking to the angel Michael and he had something important to say to me, but Sister Theresa couldn't hear what it was. You know how I've always felt about angels."

Since she was a toddler, Angie has loved anything to do with angels—statues, pictures, trinkets, stories. When she was about four she used to talk with angels. When I'd take her for a walk in the Millbrook Meadow, she'd stop at a certain tree and talk to an angel she said lived there. She used to make me walk ahead a bit and leave her alone so they could talk freely. It was sweet.

"Well," she continued, "I went online and found out there's a really talented angel reader in this area and this woman might be able to help me understand what Michael was trying to tell me in the dream."

"What's an angel reader?" Toby interjected. I could sense Angie checking out whether Toby was just humoring her. He seemed serious enough, though we both know what a skeptic Toby is in matters spiritual.

She seemed to feel safe enough with Toby, so she continued. "An angel reader helps a person listen to her angel guide."

"Her angel guide?" I asked. Having been brought up on Grammy's Irish lore of fairies and angels, this was less alien territory for me.

"You know how the nuns taught us. Everybody has a guardian angel. Some have more than one. When we're young, we hear them clearly, and they show us right from wrong. But as we get older, we get so we can't hear them, and then we're on our own. But they're still there and still trying to guide us. We can learn to sense what they want us to do. And some gifted people can actually hear them. Those are the angel readers."

I remembered how Sister Mary Joseph always told us to make room on the side of our desk chair for our guardian angel to sit. She would remind us all day.

"So you want to go looking for an angel reader tomorrow morning?" Toby asked.

"I'm not looking for her. I've found her. I've been reading her website and e-mailing her. I have an appointment for tomorrow at ten."

"Near here?"

"She's in Graton. I have a GPS, but I was hoping you'd go over the map with me, so I'd know where I'm going."

"It isn't far," said Toby. "I can show you on the map. But"—he couldn't resist—"do you honestly believe, now that you're grown up, that everyone has a guardian angel?"

"I do."

"Even me?"

"Oh, yes," said Angie. "Everyone has one. Including you."

"What kind of hours do they work?" Toby asked with a straight face.

"They're with a person all the time," said Angie.

I shot him a cautionary look. He received the message and refrained from further comment.

With that settled for the moment, we paid for our meal and started for home. I was glad Toby was driving. Negotiating that winding coast road at night was not my idea of a calming activity at day's end. But, with his usual expertise at the wheel, he got us home safely. The sisters were tired—Angie from her travels and I from my busy day. But we had an unwelcome jolt in store for us. When I reached the front door and put my key in the lock, the door opened at the first pressure. There were no lights on. When I fumbled for the hall light and got it on, we saw the living room in a jumble. All the drawers were open. Toby's appointment desk, our linen chest, the cupboard by the dining table—all open, with half the contents spilling onto the floor. I moved to light the kitchen, the bedrooms, the bathroom, and I saw disorder everywhere. Closet doors were ajar, and items had been swept aside so that the back of each space could be examined. Drawers had been scoured. Our home had been violated. All the sweetness of the evening had gone bitter.

Toby took a turn around the living room, hands thrust deep into his pockets. His face bore an ironic frown. "Just my luck," he said at last, as he surveyed the mess. "It looks like my guardian angel took the night off."

6

NOT A THING WAS TAKEN, not a blessed thing. Drawers and closets had been tossed, but the upset was just a quick turnover of the contents, in search of something that hadn't been found. The woman officer Dan sent over was especially impressed that a thick envelope of twenty-dollar bills and my jewelry box with some gold items in it were touched only enough to check for the absence of something else. The intruder had not lingered a second over things a normal thief would pocket.

After documenting the break-in with photos and notes, Officer Carla Moore and her sidekick Sue joined us in cleaning up the mess. I believe it was sheer neighborliness, but Carla insisted that she often got an insight during the process of putting a room back together. Not this time. But it sure made getting up the next morning a less daunting prospect.

We each had a different reason for getting up early. Angie wanted to work on a writing exercise for her angel reader. Toby was busy trying to estimate the worth of the items Charlie had brought into the shop. And my mind was on the dinner party we were committed to having that night, in spite of all our troubles. Dan and his wife, Colleen, were members of our Gourmet Club, so I knew I'd be seeing him that evening and that we'd talk about the case. For now, I tried to push aside thoughts of the break-in and to concentrate on getting ready for our company. I needed to double-check my grocery list and get into town. So, I made coffee, put out cereal muffins and yogurt, and tried to take solace in the fact that my family was together, each of us quietly having breakfast and doing our own thing. I left before Toby and Angie did, getting a promise to see her after lunch and him before dinner.

I missed Angie as I performed the necessary errands. I had been looking forward to showing off the funky little shops where I was greeted by name and given the best pickings, whether for stone-baked sourdough at the Freestone Bakery, or for sweet-cream butter at Mary's Dairy, or for fresh duck at Willy's poultry farm. Everyone at the shops asked after Toby. Since Toby is the real cook in the family, he's the one who has forged relationships with local food producers. Toby started the Gourmet Club, and he usually takes charge of our contribution. This time, though, he suggested that my term off from teaching would be a good time for me to take the lead. So we had created the menu together, and I had committed to doing the cooking that could be done before the guests arrived. He'd do the rest.

You could say I'm a middling cook, and that would be generous. One thing that keeps me in the middle is my time limit. I say it should never take longer to prepare a meal than to eat it. With really good friends, I'm content to eat and drink and talk for three hours, but not more. So that's my limit on food prep and cooking: three hours. Lucky for me, Sonoma County caters to lazy gourmands as well as gourmet cooks, so I can pick up pre-made duck stock and any kind of crust and pretend it's my own. When I'm chef de cuisine, you get the speedy version.

My last stop was at Whole Foods in Sebastopol, where nobody knows me but where they always have what I need. As I was pushing my shopping cart out the door, I suddenly froze. A man in the parking lot was staring at me intently. He was standing next to an expensive-looking car and casually resting one arm on the roof. He was tall enough to do that easily. In his other hand he held a cell phone pressed against his ear. I'm not that glamorous that strangers stop and stare at me in the street, and besides, a woman can tell the difference between casual male interest and something else. This was something else, though I wasn't sure what. The guy wore jeans, had shaggy, movie star–length hair, and sported a stubble beard. That was a style these days but one I didn't care for. I say either grow a beard or don't, but why look like you just rolled out of bed?

As soon as our eyes met, he folded his phone, opened the door of his car, and got in. "Creep," I said to myself as I loaded my bags into the trunk. I made a determined effort to forget about him and to concentrate on our upcoming dinner.

It was noon when I walked in the door. I was cutting it close. The recipe in my trusty edition of *The Cuisine of California* called for the duck to marinate for six to twelve hours in the fridge. It was one-thirty by the time I had unpacked the groceries, assembled the marinade, made the decision to double the amount of black currant syrup (to make up for the lost marinating time), washed and dried the halves of duck, and dunked the duck in the purple goop. I set the bowl aside, hoping it might hurry things along if I didn't refrigerate the duck for a while, say till Angie got home.

I figured I'd better get the prep work done on the rice pilaf so that Angie and I would have time to talk. I can get pretty sloppy with the cooking if I'm trying to carry on a conversation at the same time. So I plumped the dried currants in hot water and brandy, toasted the pine nuts, sautéed the onions, and rinsed the wild rice. These procedures were slowed by the disorganized state of the post-break-in drawers. Still, my timing was good. I could hear Angie at the door.

Two cups of tea later, I remembered to turn the duck in the marinade and stash it in the fridge. Angie and I were hot in discussion of her visit to the angel specialist. I don't think I've ever seen her so full of conviction.

"So, tell me about her. Who is she?" I asked.

"She's wonderful." Angie was bubbling with enthusiasm. "Her name is Sophie Redmond, and she runs the bakery in Graton. She lives above it. That's where she gives her readings."

So the angel reader had a day job. I knew the little bakery. It had a reputation for good croissants and morning buns, but since it was a bit of a drive, I didn't shop there unless I was passing through Graton. "Okay, I'm interested. Start from the beginning. You go upstairs, and what happens?"

"Well, on the first visit, naturally, she needs to get to know you. She asked a lot of questions, what my affinities were and so forth, what issues I had, what help did I need from my guardian angels, you know, really basic things."

"Angels in the plural? You have more than one?"

"Everybody does. Like people, angels have specialties. So depending on what your problems are, she can help you get in tune with the angel who is best equipped to help you."

"Is that so? What kinds of specialties do they have?"

"Okay, there are the healing angels, the romance angels, the moving angels who will help you find a perfect home, the angels of abundance who guide you in careers, and I can't remember all the others now. But they're always near you and trying to communicate, even if people don't realize it. That could be what's happening when people hear a ringing in their ears. The ringing could be your guardian angel trying to get through."

"Now that you mention it, I do hear a ringing in my ears from time to time."

"There you are," said Angie. "That could be your guardian angel."

My doctor thought it was tinnitus. "So what happened next, or did the angel reader only ask you questions?"

"Oh, no, next comes the important part when she teaches you the relaxation techniques that help you open your mind to receive the communications from the angels who are near you." Angie demonstrated some deep-breathing exercises and postures that weren't far removed from the yoga routine I did when I wasn't too slothful. One maneuver, though, was eccentric. "You place the middle finger of your left hand on the highest point you can reach on the back of your head. Go ahead—try it."

I did.

"Then you imagine a bolt of electricity passing through your head and ending at the tip of the middle finger of your right hand, like an electrical circuit. It's a way to clear a pathway through your mind so you can be receptive."

I gave it a try.

"Next," Angie demonstrated, "cup your right hand behind your right ear and your left hand behind your left ear"—she showed me and I followed instructions—"and imagine the electricity passing through your right hand's middle finger. Then move both of your hands toward the highest point on the back of your head and concentrate. That's the area of the brain that is most receptive to awareness. Keep moving your hands in little circles and keep concentrating until you see a white light. Do you see it?"

"Not yet. Do you?"

"Yes, I do see it," said Angie.

I massaged my head. "Nope."

"It's something you have to practice before it works," Angie said. "That's the exercise we did today. She's going to show me other exercises next time. And then we began the personalized reading, which is different for everyone. Sophie says my special guardian angel is Michael. He offers spiritual guidance to help you find your way in life. And not only that, Nora, but from what I've told her, Sophie says that Michael is your guardian angel too, and that you need to be attentive to his messages."

"Really? How does she know that? She's never met me. Well, maybe I bought a baguette from her, but we weren't introduced."

"Sophie knows what she's talking about. And she agrees with Sister Theresa. The archangel Michael has something to tell you, and me too.

But he hasn't been able to communicate with us because we haven't asked him to help us."

"You mean, he won't help unless he's been invited?"

"Absolutely not. You can be as skeptical as you like, but it will just keep him away. Sophie told me that one of the first principles of working with the angels is that you have to ask for the angel's aid. He won't come to you otherwise."

"I see. And what makes your Sophie think that we should be asking for Michael's intervention?"

Angie's pretty eyebrows rose in protest to my tone.

"First," she said, "you've lost his picture, that icon. That's a direct connection. Second, Michael is the angel who guards your personal safety. He's the defender. You've had a murder, a robbery, and a house invasion. You need protection."

She had a point there. "And what about you?"

Angie looked uneasy. "That's completely different. It's not relevant."

"Well, it is to me. If Sophie is claiming that you need Michael as much as I do, I want to know what her reasoning is and why you believe she's right."

Angie fumbled with her teacup. Then she raised her eyes to mine. "Can you keep a sister-secret?"

"Sure. What's up?"

With a pained look, Angie admitted, "I haven't been very happy since I came back to the salon from London. The training was fun, and I know I'm doing skilled work now, but it doesn't feel right."

"Are you thinking of moving to another salon?"

"The salon isn't the problem. Barb is the best boss ever, and Carol totally cracks me up. But I may need to leave anyhow. And that's where the angel Michael comes in. You can look it up for yourself. Michael is the defender. But he's also the angel who can help you find your life's purpose. That's what I need help on—being sure I'm doing the work I was meant to do."

Nothing could be more important, so we kept talking about Angie's choices till the tea was cold. Then we worked together setting the table, laying a fire, putting out the wines, and setting up the barbecue for the duck. Suddenly, Angie clapped her forehead.

"What's the matter?" I asked.

"I just remembered. Sophie gave me a homework assignment. I almost forgot it. We're supposed to clear our minds of psychic negativity in order to keep the receptive channels open. One way to do that is to write down the name of anyone who's abused you or caused negative feelings in your relationships. That's got to be Hank."

Hank was the boyfriend who had tried to swindle Angie out of her small inheritance with his scheme of buying a Winnebago to ferry motorcycles from Boston to Florida. Good riddance to him—anything that put distance between them had my blessing. I found a pen and paper for Angie.

"Here's what I have to do. Write his name on a sheet of paper, put it in a plastic container, then place the container in the freezer compartment of the refrigerator."

I dug out a plastic container and watched as Angie followed this prescription.

"The key is to keep the container in the freezer for a minimum of three months."

"I can do that," I said.

"Even after I'm gone?"

"I promise." I moved packages around to find a corner for the container bearing the offending name. I stacked some frozen peas on top of it and a bag of breakfast sausages on top of that.

"I can already feel a sense of release!" Angie exclaimed.

I'll make that six months, I said to myself, just to be safe.

"And now you," Angie urged. "Who are you going to deep-freeze?"

That would be Charlie's killer, but I didn't have a name. I wasn't going to ice-cube Tom Keogh, because my heart said he didn't do it.

The only other names I had were Andrew Federenco and Arnold Kohler, and I didn't know yet whether either was involved. Dan should be arriving with more information from his interview. For now, I just wrote "Charlie's killer," folded the paper a couple of times, put it in a Ziploc bag, and buried it in the freezer next to Angie's container.

By the time twilight fell, all the chores were done, and we had shared enough nonsense and confidences. We were ready for Toby's company. After a day at the gallery, he was head chef for the evening. I was counting on him to take charge of the double-cooking of the ducks, first roasted in the oven, then grilled on the barbecue. The recipe looked good on paper, but I wouldn't trust myself with the execution. So we were relieved when he came in, proffering a sunny bunch of daffodils. Early March is the daffodil moment in Sonoma County. I set Angie to arranging the flowers to go on the table, while I poured all of us a glass of white wine.

Angie started singing her favorite song and Dad's, "I'm gonna love you like nobody's loved you, come rain or come shine . . . ," as she washed the stems of the flowers, trimmed them under cold running water as Mom taught us, and arranged them in the vase I brought her. "I just love daffodils—the way their trumpets pop out from underneath their frilly skirts."

"Hey, you're good," I said. "How did you make that bunch of simple daffs look like a still-life painting?"

"The artist's touch, my dear. There's not much difference between cutting flowers and cutting hair." She gave me the fetching smile that has gotten her into mischief with so many men.

Toby spoke up. "How about giving me some room, girls? A man needs his space to cook a decent duck."

In the dining room, I gave Angie the scoop on the Gourmet Club we were hosting. It started out as a way for three basketball buddies—Toby, Dan, and Ken—to keep their friendship going through the non-hoop season. Periodically they would get together and make spaghetti. It turned into a tradition, and the guys had a decade of bachelor pasta parties until the women came along and were added to the club. One by one, the girls became wives and the menu became more diverse. Now we're somewhat self-mockingly called the Gourmet Club, and we meet six times a year.

Dan's sheriff's work keeps him perennially on call, so Colleen takes responsibility for the Ellis family's assignment. She's a busy real-estate agent, but she loves making desserts and presenting them with all the frills you see in the cooking magazines. For tonight, we gave her a recipe for frozen vanilla mousse with blackberry sauce, and I knew she'd do something special with it. The third couple, Ken and Gloria, run an art gallery in Sebastopol, and they cook together as well. They were coming with a starter of baked goat cheese and watercress, as well as an orange and fennel salad to follow the duck.

Dan, as expected, arrived before the others, and I sat down with him while Toby bustled around in the kitchen.

"We don't have any leads on your break-in last night," he admitted. "Whoever did it probably is the same guy who broke into the gallery and Charlie's apartment."

"Looking for Charlie's icon," I added.

"Could be."

"But at least you agree he was looking for something particular, not just trashing the premises."

"Looks that way, yeah," Dan concurred.

"And that pours cold water on your theory that Tom Keogh killed Charlie out of jealousy and trashed his apartment out of anger, doesn't it? I mean, now that our home has been a target, doesn't that suggest a different scenario?"

"It might, though it won't hurt to see if Tom's got an alibi for last night."

"We ran into him last night at River's End," I said. "He was pretty drunk. Some friends took him home."

"What time was that?"

"Around dinner time, about six."

"And afterward?"

"I assume he went home to sleep it off."

"What time did you leave the restaurant?"

"It may have been close to nine," I said.

"So he could have gone over to your house while you were at dinner."

"Do you think so?" I said. I doubted it.

"I'll look into it. And the same goes for Andrew Federenco."

"You've talked to him?"

"Not about last night. But yes, I tracked him down yesterday, which wasn't hard to do, since he gave you his cell-phone number. He does have an alibi for the night of Charlie's murder, but there are reasons to keep him in the picture. He's been staying at the motel in Jenner. I ran him through our computers and found an old arrest record, which may or may not mean anything. He had a couple of scrapes with the law years ago when he was a young guy in his twenties—assault and battery, malicious mayhem, petty stuff. He got in with a rough crowd. But that was forty-some-odd years ago, and since then he's cleaned up his act. He's a retired businessman and a pillar of the Russian Orthodox Church in San Francisco. The fact that he gave you his name and number suggests that he doesn't think he has anything to hide."

"What about Rose Cassini's story about the cousin of her boyfriend who threatened him in order to get back a family icon?"

"I ran that story by him. He granted some of it was true. In fact, he was open about the quarrel. Swears he never threatened his cousin Peter, though, and it would be difficult to prove he did. In any case, Federenco claims that Peter's side of the family had no right to the icon, which went missing when Peter died in 1962. He's been looking for it ever since. Not because it may be valuable. He says he doubts it is. But because it has sentimental value to the family. Of course, there's no reason to believe him on that point."

"So why is he here?"

"He says he never knew that Peter had a girlfriend. But when he heard about Charlie's murder and the description of an icon that may have been stolen in connection with it, he thought he might pick up the trail he lost in '62. So he's been staying in Jenner and checking out all the art and antiques galleries in the area, asking about icons. I told him to go home and stay out of our way but to keep himself available for further questioning."

"And that's it?"

"So far. We haven't come up with anything solid against Kohler, the poker king, and Tom Keogh's been firm in his denials."

A little while later, Ken and Gloria arrived, and while Gloria went into the kitchen to help Toby, Ken joined our discussion in the living room. Ken's a sweet, roly-poly guy with salt-and-pepper hair and a messy moustache. Apparently, he already knew the basic details of the case through conversations with Toby. "I was going to tell you about this Federenco guy myself," he said to Dan. "He came into my gallery too, asking lots of questions about icons, which raised my suspicions. And he left his card, just like with Toby." Ken had no additional information about Federenco. But what he said next sent a chill down my spine.

"Funny thing. He wasn't the only one nosing around. Another guy came into the gallery today also asking about icons. A big, tough-looking customer with long hair and a pushy manner. Reminded me of a wrestler. He hadn't shaved for a few days, and he had an accent, maybe Russian. He was hard to understand. He almost gave me a heart attack. Came up behind me without my hearing him and—boom!—there he was, in my face."

"That's the same creep who was staring at me this morning in the parking lot of Whole Foods!"

Dan sat up, alert. "Tell me about it." I did. There wasn't that much more to tell.

Dan turned to Ken. "Did you get a name, any information from him?"

Ken shook his head. "Sorry."

"What did he want to know?"

"Whether I had any icons for sale or knew of any other local gallery that might. Whether any had come through the shop lately. He was gruff, only asked a couple of questions, then he turned and left. No 'thank you' or other pleasantries."

"Dan," I said, "the auctioneer at Morgan's told me a man with a Russian accent called him the day after the auction, asking for information about Charlie—that is, wanting to know who bought the icon and how to reach him. The auctioneer relayed his name and number to Charlie. It has to be the same guy."

"It's interesting that this guy hasn't been to Toby's gallery asking for information." Dan pursed his lips.

"I wonder why?" asked Ken.

"My guess is because he's already searched it."

Now I was truly alarmed. "He must be the one who broke into the gallery. And our house as well."

Dan turned to Ken. "If he comes in again, see if you can get a name or number where he can be reached. Tell him you may be able to help him find what he's looking for. Make something up."

"Definitely. I'm sorry I didn't come up with something at the time."

"What else can you remember about him? Age? Height? What was he wearing?"

"Thirties or forties, I'd say. Over six feet tall, husky but solid build. He was wearing a brown leather jacket." That description matched my recollection of the man in the parking lot, though he wasn't wearing a jacket at the time. "Oh, and one other thing," Ken added. "He had a gold tooth up front."

Dan got out his notepad. "Did either of you see what kind of car he was driving?'

"I did," I said. "A black sedan, new-looking. An Audi, I think, but I'm not sure."

"Okay," said Dan, jotting a note. "Big guy in his thirties or forties, speaks with an accent, long hair, has a gold tooth, last seen wearing a leather jacket and driving a late-model sedan, color black. Shouldn't be hard to spot if he's still around. I'll put out a bulletin on him in the morning: wanted for questioning."

"I'm glad you said in the morning." The mock-stern voice belonged to Colleen, who had just come through the front door, balancing a tray crowded with bowls of dessert fixings. "You're not still talking shop, I hope," she huffed. "You're off duty, for crying out loud. We're here to make a dinner! Give me a hand, will you?"

"Yes, dear," Dan cringed with pseudo-meekness, as if he were a henpecked husband in a '50s sitcom. He shot Ken a wink. It wasn't the first time I'd heard Dan and Colleen go through this routine.

"All right, then," said Colleen, calling a halt to their spousal game. She was an attractive redhead with an infectious smile. Her cheeks were pink, which meant the wind was up again outside. With Dan's help, she settled her tray on the sideboard and slipped out of her coat. Then she joined Gloria and Toby in the kitchen. "Mmm! That duck smells good."

Toby's main course was in fact a triumph. At the table there was no more talk about the Russian. The wine flowed freely, and I felt myself beginning to relax. It pleased me that Angie seemed to be enjoying herself too, though she was among people she didn't know. She followed the chitchat with interest and even joined in when the conversation took a philosophical turn. That's often a feature of our dinners, thanks to Ken, who's a great reader and whose tastes include physics and astronomy. Sometimes Toby is the only member of our group who goes along with Ken on these excursions, but this time Angie added her convictions to the mix.

"So, I'm reading this new book on the cosmos," Ken began. "And it starts out with a terrific question, which is, why is there something rather than nothing?"

"What kind of question is that?" protested Colleen.

"It's a real question," said Ken. "Obviously the universe exists. But why does it exist instead of nothing? Well, the author argues that there may have been nothing to begin with, but from a physics point of view, nothing is unstable, so it had to give rise to something, namely the universe."

Colleen pursed her lips. The only sound was the scraping of silverware. "But I have a simpler explanation," Ken went on.

"I hope so," said Colleen.

"Okay," said Ken. "So why does the universe exist instead of nothing?"

"I'll tell you why," Angie piped up. "It exists because God created it."

Ken looked a bit crestfallen. "All that does is take the question back a step. Why does God exist instead of nothing? Where did God come from?"

"That's simple. He's always existed," said Angie.

"That's possible," conceded Ken. "But here's my solution. If you assume there was nothing to begin with, then, yes, there had to be a cause for something to exist. But why assume that there was nothing to begin with? Isn't it a fifty-fifty proposition that something might have existed all along?" He turned to Angie. "You don't even have to invoke God. The something could just as easily have been a set of physical laws, or quantum fluctuations, or who knows what, that gave rise to the universe."

"In other words," said Toby, "your answer to the question of why is there something rather than nothing is, why not?"

"That's the gist of it," Ken beamed.

"Hmm," said Colleen. Angie crinkled her brow. We ate for a while without talking. It seemed to be a conversation stopper.

"Okay," Ken said. "Here's another puzzle."

"Ken," warned Gloria in a cautionary tone.

"I know, honey. Just one more. Here's the question: how old is time?"

Toby raised his fork. "I think I know the answer to that one." Toby reads *Scientific American.*

"Please," said Gloria, exasperated. "I agree with Colleen. It's another trick question." Gloria, who in contrast to her soft-bodied husband is skinny and high-strung, propped her chin in one hand, elbow on the table. Dan was shaking his head, too. He didn't see much point in these flights of fancy.

"Toby thinks he knows the answer. Okay, tell her." Ken waved a finger at his wife.

"Well," Toby began, "if everything in the universe, including space and time, started with the Big Bang, then space has been expanding ever since and so has time."

"Right," said Ken. "And astronomers can date the Big Bang as occurring 13.8 billion years ago, so that's how old time is. It's 13.8 billion years old, the same age as the universe."

"That's ridiculous," said Angie. "Time is forever."

"Is it?" asked Ken.

"It's logical. If the Big Bang happened whenever it did, there was a time before it happened."

"Maybe not," Toby replied in a let's-be-reasonable tone of voice. "If time came into existence with the Big Bang, then the question of what existed before time isn't meaningful."

"Right-o," said Ken, pouring himself another glass of wine.

Angie pushed her chair back from the table. "So you're saying that the Big Bang was the start of everything, is that right?" Ken and Toby nodded in the affirmative. "And all this stuff happened after it?" She raised her arms palms upward, taking in the room, the house, Bodega Bay, the planet, and the stars. "Well, how can you have an after without a before?" That stymied them. Sensing an advantage, Angie pressed on. "So there must have been a time before the Big Bang." She folded her arms.

"Well . . . ," Ken began.

"She's got you there," said Gloria.

"We can't really say if there was a before," Ken limped along.

"Of course there was a before," said Angie. "If you can imagine 13.8 billion years ago, then you can imagine 13.9 billion years ago, can't you? So wasn't that before?"

Ken looked down at his plate. "Maybe there was another universe before this one that expanded and contracted and then expanded again. More like a Big Bounce. So maybe time began . . . a second time." He foundered.

"I don't see why it has to be so complicated," said Angie. "Why don't you just admit that time is forever? Just as God is forever, which he obviously is. And if the universe started 13.8 billion years ago, all that means is that's when God created it. That's the time he picked. He could have picked an earlier time or a later time, but God picked that time. What's the problem?"

Ken scratched his ear, looking perplexed. Toby's cheeks creased into a broad smile.

"Pass the bread, please," said Angie, mentally dusting off her hands.

7

THE FOGHORN WOKE ME. I lay in the dark, counting the seconds between its eerie notes: ten, as usual, never varying. Finally, I fumbled for my clock and saw it was just past five. The call of the foghorn wasn't necessarily bad news for my day's plan. In fact, it's a constant feature, day and night, all year long, because of the dangerous rocks off Bodega Head. But last night's news had forecast morning fog, and it's not wise to take the winding road up to Fort Ross in that kind of weather. I might have to cancel my research at the fort's library. With this worry nagging at me, there would be no more sleep. I gently rose and crept into the kitchen.

Before dawn on this stretch of the coast, and especially in fog, there's no radio reception, so I couldn't get the weather report that way. I made a cup of tea and fired up my computer. The Internet would give me an hour-by-hour forecast, which was necessary for planning the trip. In addition, the computer could deliver data by zip code, which we definitely would need. Conditions in San Francisco can generally predict temperature and rain in our bay, which is only sixty miles from the city and similarly exposed to the sea. But getting to Fort Ross entails climbing mountains and negotiating a tortuous road. Conditions there could be very different from the city and even from Bodega Bay—clear when we are foggy, foggy when we are clear. It took me a while, but I figured out that the fog would lift from the mountain by ten. That should allow time to get to the fort, do the work, and get home safely.

I switched to my e-mail and kept looking out the deck window to track the light, which hung like a white curtain, blocking a view of the harbor. The horn kept calling. Some may find its one note comforting, the ultimate lullaby, like a heartbeat, slowed nearly to coma. I find it alarming, which is what it's intended to be. It must be my Portuguese sailor's blood welling up to sense danger on the rocks—my mother's ancestors were Gloucester fishermen, immigrants from Portugal a century ago. Luckily, there's a series of sand dunes between us and the horn, so its sound is muted at our house. Angie and Toby slept blissfully through its muffled calls, until I filled the air with the aroma of coffee and pancakes.

Over breakfast, we talked about the wisdom of our excursion. Looking out the window, Toby argued for postponement, but when he saw how disappointed I was, he volunteered to do the driving and skip an afternoon at the gallery, provided we would start home early. With that as the plan, I sent them off to get dressed while I packed a lunch in the cooler, since there's no restaurant at the fort, or anywhere near it.

It's always tough to get Toby out the door, so I wasn't surprised that we didn't start till 11:00. The sky was still white, but the landscape by now was visible. Nonetheless, the usually bright views of the ocean from Route 1 were dulled by the cloudy weather. Steel-gray waves crashed onto black rocks and brown beaches, producing a dirty gloom. A few intrepid tourists wrapped in rainwear walked the shore, intent on proving that their Saturday had not been ruined by a little weather.

At Goat Rock, in Jenner, farther up the coast, we hit the first mist cloud. We were in and out of it in a few seconds. That was just the remnant of the morning fog. A sign appeared, announcing that it was twelve miles from Jenner to Fort Ross, a short distance as the crow flies, but Toby and I knew that the way consisted of a steep, perilous climb along ocean cliffs on a veritable corniche. Suddenly a hawk swooped across our windshield, and I watched it sail past the cliff and over the steely sea. On our left there was a photographer standing at the side of the road trying to catch a view of the fog over the Jenner rocks. A white car far ahead of us was disappearing into mist.

I tried not to fret as our Nissan Altima began its steep climb. For a while we were the only car on the road, until a pickup truck loomed up behind us, flashing its lights. There's no passing on this road. Instead, there are turnouts, and etiquette requires that slower drivers pull off whenever someone comes up behind. Fortunately, at the height of the grade, the road swerved inland to cross the hill at its crest. Toby clicked his turn signal, slowed, and took the first turnout. The pickup shot by, driven by a young guy, of course, and it soon disappeared. Toby shook his head and eased back onto the road. I began to breathe more calmly. A few minutes later another car appeared behind us, but the driver thought better of passing and dropped back to a safe distance. As the road twisted and turned, we gradually lost sight of him.

Now we were greeted by a series of exclamatory signs. First, "Rough Road." That was an understatement. Then, "Rock slide area next 8 miles." Sure enough, the road there had been shored up by a retaining wall with wooden scaffolding that looked like it was starting to buckle. I was about to say something about it when Angie saw a big yellow diamond of a sign, stamped with the image of a black cow. She couldn't help but laugh. Where would a stray cow come from, with a sea cliff on the left and a retaining wall on the right? Actually, there are cattle ranches nearby, and it's not unusual to see a cow or two grazing on the wrong side of their fence—as if there weren't enough road hazards. "Oh, boy," said Angie, "I'm glad I'm not driving." That made two of us.

Toby continued carefully, hugging the right side of the road to allow as much room as possible for traffic that might be coming the other way. They would be on the ocean side, a steep, curvy descent bordered only by a low wall. We would be facing that on the way back.

It was a relief when we finally spotted Fort Ross spread out below us on a broad swath of green. The encampment tops a bluff overlooking a sheltered cove, which at one time harbored the small boats of native peoples and Russian settlers. The bluff is wide enough to house the reconstructed stockade and its redwood buildings, surrounded by acres of farmland. As the road circled down toward the site, it flattened out, and as we approached the fort, the tall stockade walls made a striking impression. At this lower elevation, most of the fog had burned off, and by now the sun was high. The fort looked inviting and prosperous, with a superb view of the sea.

That's how it must have looked in the 1830s, after two decades of colonization by the Russian-American Company. By that date, about a hundred Russians and as many Native Alaskans and local Pomos, along with their children, filled the compound and spilled over into villages outside the stockade. The Russians' hunting and farming barely sustained them, but they maintained a healthy trade in the thick furs of sea otters. If not for competition with the Hudson Bay Company operating farther north, they might have stayed indefinitely, but by 1841 they were negotiating to sell the property. All Russian nationals were ordered home. The property changed hands several times until it was acquired by the California Historical Landmarks Committee and eventually incorporated into the national parks system.

We drove through a grassy field to the visitor center, parked, and walked up to the entrance along a short path bordered by orange poppies and purple phlox. At the information desk inside I inquired about my appointment, while Toby and Angie set out to peruse the exhibits. Our plan was to meet again in an hour for a picnic lunch, after which they'd continue touring the fort while I worked in the library.

The tiny library was tucked away behind the information desk. The older woman who managed the desk doubled as the librarian. She checked my name against a register, then led me behind the counter and through a door that wasn't accessible to the general public. "It's been a busy day for us," she joked. "You're the second person who's come in."

The little room was efficiently organized. A table with chairs filled the central space, surrounded by floor-to-ceiling bookcases. The shelves were crammed with books and cardboard file boxes packed with records, architectural drawings, photographs, and documents. I looked around for a card catalog but found that the holdings were listed in several plastic binders stacked on the table. "Are you looking for a particular item?" the librarian asked.

I briefly explained my mission.

"You might check this one first," she said, extending a thin, green-covered binder marked "Oral Histories." "If it's not listed in there, try this one," she added, tapping a thicker white-covered binder next to it. "It has everything alphabetized by authors' names. Just holler if you've got a question. Materials don't circulate, but you're allowed to photocopy things if you want to. There's a coin-operated machine in the hall."

"Thank you," I said, setting right to work. It didn't take long to locate what I wanted in the first catalog binder: "Federenco, Andreyev (1844–1907). 'My Life.' Category: Oral History. Typescript prepared by Natasha Veronsky (daughter), 1905. Annotated." A catalog number followed.

The slim oral-history folders, with catalog numbers on their spines, were grouped together on four shelves of one bookcase, so finding it should have been easy, but the file wasn't there when I looked—or rather, it wasn't in its proper place. There was a small sign on display on the table that stated: "Please do not return items to the shelves. Leave them here for the librarian." That's the policy in most libraries, and in most cases users ignore it. Aiming to be helpful, people constantly re-shelve books they have consulted, but as often as not they misplace them, creating havoc in the system and causing trouble for the next user. Fortunately, this collection was small enough to scan, and soon I found the errant work, which some absentminded do-gooder had returned to the bookcase one shelf above its rightful place. Withdrawing it, I made a mental note to follow the rules when I was finished.

"My Life" by Andreyev Federenco was a fragile, sixty-six-page typescript on paper now brown and brittle, fastened by a large clip and protected by a transparent plastic sheath, which in turn was placed inside a manila folder. As I delicately untied the ribbon that secured it, my excitement mounted. On top of the typescript was a cover letter dated July 12, 1972, marking the occasion of the document's donation to the Fort Ross Interpretive Association. The letter was signed by Andrew Federenco, then a member of the Citizens Advisory Committee for Fort Ross State Historic Park. The letter expressed the family's wish to commemorate their ties to the first Russian colony in California. It went on to explain that the donor's great-great-grandfather, Euvgeny Federenco, had lived and worked at the fort in the 1830s, then returned to Russia when the fort was abandoned in 1841. The accompanying memoir had been dictated by his son, Andreyev Federenco. Andreyev, who was born in Russia in 1844, had immigrated to California in 1870, retracing his father's footsteps, and this memoir, it was hoped, would be of interest to historians, not only for Andreyev's account but also for his recollections of the stories told to him by his father about the life and times of the fort.

Andrew had attached to his letter a genealogy in the form of a family tree. The line of descent ran from Euvgeny (1814–77) to Andreyev (1844–1907); from Andreyev to a son, Vladimir (1873–1951), and a daughter, Natasha (1878–1942). Natasha had no children. The line continued from Vladimir through two sons, Feodor (1904–64) and Boris (1907–60). In turn, Feodor and Boris each had a son. Naturally, they were cousins: Andrew, born in 1946, and Peter, born in 1933. I knew that Peter, who died in 1962, had acquired the triptych and that Andrew wanted it. Whether the manuscript now in my hands could shed further light on their quarrel was my question.

Soon I was immersed in Andreyev's memoir. As a boy he loved the romantic stories his father had told him about Fort Ross and the near-magical land of California, where there was no winter. These tales—about daily chores, logging, fur trapping, hunting, trading with the Aleuts and Pomo Indians—were exactly what gave the manuscript its historical interest, but they offered no insight to my search. Until, that is, the father mentioned to the boy that he received the gratitude of the entire fort when he lent the family triptych, which had traveled with him, for display at the little Chapel of St. Nicholas. To my frustration, there were no added details here. Instead, the narrative turned to Andreyev's story—how the boy resolved to immigrate to America when he came of age, how he courted a girl from a nearby village and convinced her to accompany him as his wife, how the couple struggled during their first year in San Francisco, how he earned his living as an upholsterer, learned the language, started a small business making umbrellas, and began a family.

An hour flew by. I was halfway through the memoir, and it was time for lunch. I left the manuscript on the table open to the last page I had read, gathered my things, and headed for the entrance, where Toby, Angie, and I had agreed to meet. Angie was standing there, looking eager to talk. She gave me a hug and directed me out to a picnic bench, where Toby had laid out our provisions: apples, peanut butter and jelly sandwiches, and cans of ginger ale. "I can't believe you," Angie said. "You packed us Grandma Silva's picnic." That was what Mom's mom used to make for us when we wanted to eat lunch on the rocks by Gloucester harbor. All that was missing was the waxed paper around the sandwich.

Reverting to childhood, we gobbled the lunch quickly and began sharing our discoveries as we sipped on the ginger ale. I told Toby and Angie about the memoir, and they had news for me.

"We had a woman guide, and she knows everything about this place," said Angie. "I got friendly with her because I was the only one answering her questions. You know, like, which fur is softer, otter or mink. It's otter! I learned that when I modeled furs for Filene's."

"Did the guide mention anything related to my search?" I was looking at Toby, but it was Angie who replied.

"Could be. I noticed two things. First, about this guy you're researching. I asked her whether a Russian who came over to work at the fort would have been able to remain around here after the fort was closed. She said no. Everybody who was sent over had to go back. No exceptions. So if Peter's ancestor was here with the colony, he would have had to go back to Russia and then return later to start his family in California."

"That's right," I replied. "Euvgeny served at the fort and then went home. It was his son who came to America, decades later. So what the guide said fits."

"Well, then there's what she said when we were in the chapel. She showed us the candleholders, up close to the wall, and the marks where there used to be shelves for the icons. The originals are all lost now, but they have a new one up, to give an idea of the effect."

"What's the subject?" I asked.

"A kind of stiff head and torso of Christ, with an open book," Toby replied. "Lots of gold around him."

"If we have time, I'd like to see it, even though it's bound to be recent."

"The guide said this odd thing about it," said Angie. "She pointed out the shiny gold and said that the old icons would have been darkened by the candle smoke. They might have been so dark that the worshipers couldn't make out the image. And then she said that in spite of that, word of mouth says that one of the icons was a triptych with a Virgin Mother who could get God to forgive any sin, however awful."

That squared with the memoir I was reading.

"I don't know if I want people's sins, however awful, to be forgiven just because they prayed to the right image," observed Toby.

Angie laughed. "You can tell you didn't go to catechism class with the Barnes kids."

"What do you think I missed?" he said, teasing her.

"Humility," Angie replied. "There but for the grace of God go I."

Toby shook his head. "Everybody says that, but if you believe in free will, aren't we all responsible for what we do?"

"Of course, but don't you believe in grace?" asked Angie.

"For everybody, no matter what they do?"

Angie gave Toby an indulgent look. "You're mixing up grace and mercy—completely different things. We need a little catechism lesson here," she offered.

I intervened. "No talking religion at the table, children. It's bad for the digestion."

Toby laughed and then said, "You ought to get back to your work anyhow, Nora. This air is beginning to feel wet. I'm thinking we should head south as soon as we can."

"Can I take another hour?"

"Just. Angie and I will clear up here and then we'll walk down the hill to the cove. We'll meet you at the counter at three-thirty."

"Have fun."

As I headed back toward the information desk, I was startled to catch a rearview glimpse of a man who had come around the counter from the wrong side and who was now walking away. The attendant must have stepped out for a moment. A large man with a mop of hair, he brusquely strode toward the back exit without giving me a chance to see his face. He didn't have to. I was pretty sure I knew who he was. Had he just come from the library where I'd left the manuscript open on the table? Or was my imagination working overtime? There are plenty of tall men with longish hair in Sonoma County, I told myself. And how could I be sure he had been in the library?

Disquieted, I scanned the hall for the librarian, but she seemed to have gone. I approached the library's door and tried to calm my nerves. At first nothing seemed amiss. The manuscript was still open to the page where I'd stopped reading. But there was a slight alteration in the room. The chair I'd been using was pushed up neatly against the table, as were the others, which hadn't been moved from their original positions. I remembered pulling mine back when I got up and leaving it like that. Was my memory at fault, or had someone returned the chair to its proper place while I was out? My first impulse was to run back outside to find Toby, but since time was limited, I needed to complete my task. So steeling myself, I sat down and returned to the manuscript.

It wasn't easy to concentrate. My mind wandered as I skimmed the rest of the memoir, which covered the latter half of Andreyev's life. In these pages he told of expanding his umbrella business into a factory, which wasn't of great interest. He related incidents concerning relatives back in the old country. And he expressed the hope that his children would remain faithful to the religion of the Eastern Orthodox Church. It was only here, toward the end of the document, that I found a passage that reclaimed my attention, as Andreyev dictated to his daughter a benediction for future generations.

> Our Holy Mother Church has always played a major role in my life. May it continue to do so for my children and theirs and for their children as long as our family lives on. May they always honor the saints. May they respect our priests. May they remember the poor and be charitable. May they honor our holy icons, and may these continue to pass from eldest son to eldest son, as is our custom. For our icons are our family's most precious possessions. Cherish and protect them. I speak especially of our venerable triptych, which shows the Mother of God and the archangels Michael and Gabriel. My father called it the work of a great maker. Whether that is true I cannot say, yet it has traveled twice across the ocean, once with him and once with me, and it has brought health and good fortune to our families. So, children, treasure it. I can leave no greater gift.

That one passage made the trip worthwhile. We were tracking part of that triptych, the panel depicting the angel Michael. But what had become of the other two panels? And why had the Michael icon ended up in the hands of Peter Federenco, who then entrusted it to Rose Cassini? I flipped back to the family tree. Assuming the genealogy to be accurate, there was no ambiguity as to the line of descent through eldest sons in the Federenco family. It went from Euvgeny to Andreyev to Vladimir to Feodor. True, Feodor had a brother, Boris, but Feodor was three years older. Had he inherited the family icons, as was his due, they should have gone to Andrew, his son. But instead, they went to Peter, who was Boris's son. So what had happened?

By now it was nearly time to meet Toby and Angie. I went to the copier and duplicated Andrew's cover letter, the family tree, and several other pages, then returned the manuscript to its folder and left it, as instructed, on the table. On my way out, I thanked the librarian, who had returned to her post at the gift shop counter. "By the way," I said, "I was wondering if anyone else was using the library this afternoon."

"I don't think so," she returned. "Why?"

"Oh, just a small thing. I think someone moved my chair while I was outside having lunch. Or was that you?"

"It wasn't me. Why, are you missing anything?"

"No, everything was there. Just wondering if my mind was playing tricks with me. It's not important."

"I did step away for a couple of minutes to use the ladies' room. You sure everything's okay?"

"Oh, yes. No problem. And I did find what I was looking for. Thanks again."

Toby and Angie were at the entrance on schedule. Outside, the lowering sky looked ominous. "Do you still want to check out the chapel?" Toby asked. "There's weather coming in. It might be better to get on the road."

"I agree. Let's get going." On the way to the parking lot I explained my suspicion of having been spied on in the library. I asked if either of them had noticed a tall man with long hair while they were touring the grounds. They hadn't.

Toby frowned. "Let's say it was the same guy from Whole Foods. How could he know we would be here?" He paused. "Unless he followed us."

"Come on, let's get out of here," I urged. Already waves of fog shimmied along the ground, and the air was clammy with a soft drizzle. I was worried about the drive home.

We started our climb up the steep bluff above the fort as the fog grew worse. The higher we climbed, the thicker it became. Well before we reached the summit, the road disappeared and we were enveloped in a murky cloud. Toby slowed to a crawl, using his fog lamps and straining to see. He was following the red glow of the taillights ahead of him to anticipate curves, but he was wary of getting too close to the car in front of us. Behind us someone was following our taillights for the same purpose. In another few minutes, the car in front vanished. It was only because the road flattened out that we knew we had reached the summit.

It was then that the car behind us picked up speed, coming uncomfortably close and causing Toby to snarl, "That idiot is using his brights." That meant he wasn't local. Anyone who's used to driving on the coast knows that high beams don't cut through the fog but reflect it, making things worse for the driver as well as the guy ahead. Toby tapped his brake lights but whoever was behind us didn't get the message. Instead he edged closer. Toby cursed and adjusted his rearview mirror. He slowed even more. I turned around to look. The lights behind us were growing larger as the car came on.

"What the hell does he want to do, pass me? Is he crazy?" I could make out a lone driver in a dark-colored car. Toby beat out a light tattoo on his brakes. There was no room to pull over, so that was all he could do. Gradually the lights behind us fell back.

We continued in tandem for a mile or so, with the distance between us holding steady until the road began its spiral downward at a steep incline aggravated by hairpin turns. That's when the drive is most dangerous for a car going south, for there's only a light guardrail serving as the bulwark between you and a plunge to the sea. Toby shifted the automatic to its low gear. Again we slowed. I turned around again. The driver behind us was drawing close. I turned back to face ahead and saw that a sign indicated a turnoff in a quarter of a mile. "Toby, how about letting him get by? It's not a race."

"That's fine with me," growled Toby. He put his turn signal on, and I leaned forward in my seat, peering through the obscurity to discern the turnoff. We continued for what seemed longer than a quarter of a mile. Had we missed it? I could feel Toby's tension.

"There it is up ahead," I pointed out when the turnoff finally appeared out of the gloom.

"I see it," Toby grunted. I heard the sound of gravel under our tires as we pulled off the road into a semicircular parking area. On a clear day this might be a scenic lookout, but nothing was visible now beyond the rolling fog, not even the railing.

"Thanks, Toby. You're doing a great job," said Angie.

He acknowledged the commendation with a terse nod. "I'm going to wait here a minute. I want him to get far ahead of us." I thought that was a good idea. Toby isn't a macho driver, and I'm grateful for that. After a pause, we set out again. Thin needles of rain hit the windshield, the fog as thick as ever. It was getting harder to see. We inched along until a mile went by and then another. The road swerved, dipped, and started climbing again.

"What the hell—?" shouted Toby. I turned. The high beams of the dark-colored car were right behind us again, and he was pushing, pushing.

"I think it's the same guy," I said. "How can that be?"

I'll tell you how," said Toby angrily. "After I let him pass, he took the next turnout and waited for us. He waited for us to go by. The bastard's chasing us!"

"I'm scared," cried Angie. Then she called out, "Archangel Michael, protect this vehicle and everyone in it!"

"Roger that," muttered Toby under his breath.

I was terrified. I remembered that there had been a car that drew up behind us at one point on the drive up. Then someone had sniffed around the library while I was at lunch. Now this. "What does he want?"

"To drive us off the road," said Toby grimly, clutching the steering wheel and increasing his speed.

"Be careful!" I warned. "You're going too fast."

"I don't have a choice." We crested the hill and headed down again. The car rocked as we careened around a curve, the pursuing vehicle hard on our tail.

"Hold on," said Toby. He braked. Swerved. Stepped on the gas again. Braked. Accelerated into a curve as the road rose upward for a stretch. But in front of us the highway vanished—it veered sharply to the left. We took it on two wheels. Now we were descending again, but we weren't gaining ground. The other car was right behind us, grazing our bumper. In another moment it would hit us.

But that moment never came. For a split second, Toby took his eyes off the road to check his rearview mirror, and in that fraction of a second, a dark form appeared without warning in the middle of his lane.

"Stop!" screamed Angie.

Toby cursed, slammed on the brakes, and jerked the steering wheel instinctively to the left, skidding toward the rock face that bordered the oncoming lane. Fortunately, no one was in that lane, or we would have crashed head-on. The driver behind us wasn't so lucky. There was a thud, audible even through the closed windows. The high beams of the other car swung crazily, pitched at a high angle, and as I looked back in horror, two dark silhouettes lifted improbably into the air and disappeared over the guardrail.

Toby pulled back into our lane and parked against the rail. We jumped out and ran to look. Even at this height, through the dripping fog, we could make out the flames of a burning vehicle on the rocks below. Angie clutched my arm tightly as we stared down at it in stunned silence.

8

AS SOON AS HE REACHED THE RAILING, Toby pulled his cell phone from his pocket to call the sheriff and cursed when there was no connection. Angie and I reached into the car to get our phones and turn on the emergency lights. But neither of our phones worked, either. We had zero bars. The highway was deserted in both directions, so we had no choice except to drive on to the River's End in Jenner, which was still a few miles away. From there we called Dan, who told us to report the accident to the Highway Patrol, because they were in charge of crash investigations. He promised to talk to them directly.

We spent the next hour at the restaurant, waiting for the Highway Patrol investigators, answering their questions, and watching them examine and photograph our car. Then they asked us to accompany them to the crash site and to walk through our recollection of how the wreck occurred. Emergency vehicles were on the scene when we arrived. The officers pressed us on what speed we'd been going, and they made Toby go over his driving moves from the moment he realized the other car was on our tail. He was calmer in his replies than I would have been.

I was steamed that they were treating him as if the crash were his fault. It was a relief, at least, that they let us go home before they brought up the body from the site.

None of us slept well that night. In the morning, Dan called. According to his colleagues, he said, accidents with cows aren't uncommon on that stretch of road, but he had his suspicions about the chase based on what we'd told him. He was coordinating with the Highway Patrol and would let us know when they identified the dead driver, whose body was badly burned. I felt better knowing Dan was on the investigative team. Toby opened his shop in the afternoon and suggested that Angie and I go shopping to take our minds off the crash. So she got to see our funky Whole Foods after all, but neither of us was in the mood to enjoy it.

After we came in from marketing, I rooted in the hall closet for an art puzzle that I thought we could work on to keep the inner horrors under control. But I was so nerved up that the box fell to the floor, spilling all five hundred pieces. Angie pulled me up by the arm, walked me over to the couch, and put her hands on my shoulders. "You are going to sit still till you absorb this," she said firmly. "You've been dithering all day, making up errands and pastimes, apologizing to me right and left, and theorizing your head off about what happened yesterday." She lightened the pressure on my shoulders but kept her palms there. "Nora, only two things are important. First, we almost died yesterday. Second, we didn't."

"I know," I said defensively.

"But you don't. Not inside. Just think about those two things while I get you a cup of tea. Then we can talk if you want to." She disappeared into the kitchen.

The center of my chest was aching from tension and confusion. I decided to use my yoga breathing and treat what Angie said as a mantra. Over and over, I said to myself: "First, we almost died." Breathe in. "Second, we didn't." Breathe out. Before Angie came back, tears were escaping from my closed lids.

Angie handed me a mug of hot tea. She didn't talk. I noticed that she'd put a full spoon of sugar in the cup, just the way I like it. I felt grateful for her presence.

"I feel guilty," I confessed. "I almost got us all killed, and you're the two people I love most. And someone did die, not to mention the poor cow."

Angie looked only half-surprised. "How do you figure the crash was your fault?"

"I should have known better. It was dumb to propose going up to Fort Ross on that treacherous road, fog or no fog. I should have realized that creep might be stalking us. And with my little sister in the car. Some big sister I am."

Angie sipped her mug of tea. "Remember what Toby said about how we're each responsible for what we do?"

"Yes, that's just what's bothering me."

"And remember what I said about humility? Think about it. You're pretty big stuff if you're the only one responsible for what happened yesterday. It was my decision to go with you and make it an outing. It was Toby's decision to come with us and do the driving. Then there's whatever decisions the jerk behind us made. You didn't know what was going to happen. How could you?" She took another sip of tea. "Have some humility, Nora."

That took me down a peg. "We need to do something to pull you out of this," she continued. "Something upbeat, something happy."

"You're right." I decided I had had enough. "We should plan something fun for tomorrow. Do you remember what we talked about the other day?"

"You mean, golf?"

"How about it?"

"Sure, as long as we can be a foursome with Colleen and Gloria. They said they'd be patient. I haven't played since high school."

"Then you're perfect for us. We call our group the Feel Good Golfers. Boy, do I need some of that."

"Then why wait until tomorrow? How about a Pimm's Cup and that puzzle?" Angie knows just how to handle me.

The Feel Good Golfers have a standing date for 8 a.m. on the second and fourth Mondays of the month. The Scottish-style links at Bodega Harbour form a big, sweeping course, but we're in obligatory golf carts, so we can fit in eighteen holes before lunch at the clubhouse. In March, in deference to the weather, there's a rain-check system. This Monday we didn't need it. Sunday night's wind had blown away all the weekend's clouds.

We met Colleen and Gloria at the pro shop, as agreed. The night before, Toby and I had fielded phone calls from friends who had heard about the accident. There was a story about it in Sunday's paper, though our names weren't mentioned. But of course Colleen knew, through Dan, and Gloria had a friend on the Highway Patrol. So as we met the rest of the golf group, hitting the women's room or getting paired into our carts, we took their commiserations but didn't feel a need to elaborate. Nobody asked any questions. Everybody knew the facts, or thought they did. And everyone anticipated a long talk over lunch. Now it was playtime.

We're the Feel Good Golfers, but we do have a few rules, which are designed to get us to lunch in time for a good gossip. First, we start on time. Tee time is tee time. Second, no mulligans. Third, if you've taken two shots above par for the hole and you haven't reached the green, you pick up your ball, walk with ball in hand to the green, putt with the rest of your friends, and give yourself a 9 for the hole. Last, and this is the rule most broken, no conversations while standing. It's fine to talk about the play as long as you don't give unasked-for advice, but talk about the rest of life waits till you're riding in the cart or have arrived at lunch. Once we get going, we're in a trouble-free bubble, where the worst that can happen is you lose your ball. Without the distraction of chatter, you concentrate on the grasses, the slopes, the sea, the breeze, and how to move your ball around efficiently in the moment's conditions.

The sun was out, and it was a perfect day for cheering me up and for showing Angie one of the most beautiful courses in the world. Each point on the course has a dramatically different vista, designed to give stunning views at every turn. One tee looks up to the graceful hills, where we often see deer. Another perches scarily above a long ravine. Hares dart around down there. Three holes nestle against the dunes, just yards from the beach. All the tees have spectacular views of the Pacific Ocean, royal blue in the morning light and studded with rugged black rocks. In the morning, snowy egrets are out, their narrow bills pecking into the grass.

Sure enough, as play began, I felt the tension ease in my back and shoulders, and after a few holes, I was fully absorbed in the rhythm of my swing. However, that feeling of placidity was short lived. We had just teed off at a mound that looks across the harbor to our side of the bay when Angie sparked a conversation that brought me out of my protective bubble.

"Wow!" she said. "That's amazing."

"What?" asked Gloria.

"The view." Her hand was cupped over her eyes and she was looking out toward Bodega Head. "That's exactly what it looks like in *The Birds* the first time you see Bodega Bay. You know, the scene where Tippi Hedren takes a little motorboat across the water to get to Rod Taylor's house on the other shore? That's where it was, wasn't it, somewhere over there?" She pointed to our side of the bay.

"Sure was," said Colleen, nodding in the general direction. "It was called the Brenner house in the movie."

"My mom told me about that," said Gloria. "The set was somewhere out where Angie's pointing."

"Yup," said Colleen. "The old Gaffney place. Too bad it's gone. It would be another landmark for the Hitchcock fans, just like the Potter schoolhouse."

Everyone around here knows about the schoolhouse Hitchcock used for the scene where the frenzied birds attack the children—only there is no schoolhouse in Bodega Bay. The building still sits atop a hill in the separate hamlet of Bodega, a few miles inland from here; even I know that. But I drew a blank when it came to the location of the farmhouse where the main action of the film takes place. It had been a long time since I'd seen the movie. That was before I moved to Bodega Bay.

As I looked out across the harbor, the penny finally dropped. It had taken a few seconds to register, I guess. "Colleen, when you say Gaffney, do you mean Rose Gaffney, the woman who led the protests against the nuclear power plant back in the '60s?" As a real-estate agent, Colleen knows all the local property lore.

"The very same," she answered. "Gaffney owned a dilapidated ranch house out toward the head. They used the house in the movie. Hitchcock fixed it up, of course, added a gazebo and some outbuildings and built a dock. That's where Tippi Hedren ties up her boat, and that was the house you see in the film."

Suddenly my head was spinning—because as I followed Angie's gaze, I thought I could pick out the spot along the distant shore where Dan said Charlie had been killed. How close was it to the site of the Gaffney house that had been used as a set for *The Birds*? And was there a connection?

Gloria, who always keeps us to the rules, cut Colleen short, saying, "Let's save this for the clubhouse. Clare's group is just behind us." It was true. They were already on the hole and would have to wait if we didn't hurry up.

As we scurried to our cart and then rumbled down the golf path, my mind was racing. What did I know for sure? The Brenner house, the main setting for *The Birds*, was on the Gaffney property. Rose Cassini's boyfriend Peter was working on the film when he gave the icon to her, shortly before he died. On his deathbed, Peter started to say something that sounded like a message. "Tell Rose Gaffney . . ." What? He died before he could complete the thought. Did he give the other panels of the triptych to Rose Gaffney? Not likely, since the icons would have shown up in her estate after she died. But what if the movie set was the place where Peter hid the panels? Along with the icon, Charlie had bought some storyboards showing the set of the Brenner house that Peter had drawn. It couldn't be mere coincidence. And then it came to me. Peter's message could have been meant for Rose Cassini, not Rose Gaffney. "Tell Rose . . ." something about the Gaffney house.

My golf bubble had been well and truly pierced. From that moment, I had trouble concentrating on the ball, and as a result, my self-effacing sister had a better game than I did. I lost two balls in the "native coastal ruff" that Robert Trent Jones Jr. proudly designed into the course. And a third ball plopped in among the cattails in a beautiful but treacherous marsh. Angie, on the other hand, shot her ball straight down the middle of the longest fairways and kept herself out of all hazards—including that marsh area, which you have to cross over on a bridge.

After eighteen holes of windy but sunny golf, we were all tired and hungry. Gloria, ever the organizer, directed us to seats at the clubhouse cafe. She wanted the other two foursomes, Clare's and Jan's, to get a chance to talk with Angie over lunch, so Gloria waved Colleen and me to the end of the table, as if to say we'd had our chance to socialize with the newcomer. When we were seated, I turned to Colleen to finish the exchange that we'd started back on the fourth tee.

"Colleen, what ever happened to the Gaffney house? There's nothing out there anymore."

"It burned up, not too long after the filming. They say it wasn't much of a loss for Rose. She wasn't living in it when she rented the property to Hitchcock, and it was already a wreck. She let his people do whatever they needed to the inside for the purposes of filming. She didn't intend to live there again. Good thing. It burned right to the ground."

Oh boy. If the icons were left on the set after the filming, they became ashes, along with the house. I didn't want to think about that. "That's a shame," I said. "I guess if the house were still there, it would be worth a bundle, wouldn't it?"

"No, it wouldn't," Colleen replied. "When the shore road was improved, it was rerouted right over where the Gaffney farmhouse used to be, or close enough. If the house had still been standing, the county would have torn it down."

"You think so?"

"Oh yeah. Our county surveyor is a no-nonsense kind of guy. When he chooses the best site for a road, he gets his right of way." Local knowledge—that's what Colleen has. Her family's lived in Bodega Bay for three generations.

"Do you think you could show me where the Gaffney house stood?" I asked, trying not to sound too insistent.

"Sure, but I can't pinpoint it exactly. From your house, you head west on the shore road out toward Bodega Head. Stop when you see the sign on the right warning people not to drive into the Bodega Marine Laboratory Housing area. There's a group of cypress trees nearby. It was right around there."

"I know where that is. I pass that sign when I go walking."

The arrival of clam chowder broke up the conversation. That opened me up to questions about the car crash and death, Charlie's murder, and the break-ins. Ours had definitely been the most eventful household in the time since our last game. As we talked, I planned my afternoon: an excursion out to the old Gaffney property.

Angie was eager to come along, once I explained what was behind the outing. After showering at home, we changed and waited for Toby to join us. Monday's normally his day off, but he had spent the sunny morning repainting the door to his shop. It had been looking scruffy since the lock was replaced. For Angie, the proposed jaunt was about finding the movie location. Toby wanted to check the crime scene to see whether anything more could be learned from it. And I was interested in the relation between the two sites. On a fine day like this one, we decided to walk.

Our first stop, the crime scene, was easy to locate. There was a ditch behind a stand of Monterey cypresses on the dune side of the road about midway between the Spud Point Marina and the entrance to the Bodega

Marine Laboratory's dorms. The sheriff's department had cordoned off the site with yellow crime-scene tape clearly marked "Do not cross." Within the taped area, the long grass of the ditch had been matted by trampling feet. Looking out to the harbor, I saw the marooned sailboat still tilted on its side. It was in our direct line of sight. According to Dan, the murder had taken place here, and then the killer had rowed Charlie's body out to the boat. Yes, it could have happened that way. The rowboat was gone now. Out on the mudflats, a lonely heron stood on one leg and eyed us impassively.

Toby hunched his shoulders. "I guess Dan's squad went over this ground with a fine-tooth comb. I don't see anything here, do you?"

I didn't. The lab tests might have revealed bloodstains, or fibers or what-not, but nothing of interest was visible now.

"Let's look for traces of the movie set," Angie suggested.

"Or anything that might tell us there was once a house nearby," I added. "A foundation, maybe, or a fireplace or something."

We spread out and meandered up and down the road, along the fringe of land at the water's edge, and back from the shoreline into the dunes. But there was no sign of any remains of a house. "Colleen said she thought the place was near a group of cypress trees," I said. I was standing in front of some.

"The trouble is," said Toby, "from where we're standing, there are groups of cypresses all up and down this road a half mile in either direction, so that's not much help. They all look the same. Anyhow, I think we're too close to town here. Let's go out toward the head a little farther."

We walked on well past the driveway to the marine lab housing, stopping at every promising clump of cypresses, rummaging through the grass and scuffing along the sandy ground, but if there had ever been a movie set here, its traces were long gone. "We'll never get anywhere this way," I grumbled.

Toby was frustrated too. "And even if we did locate the spot where the house once stood, what exactly are we looking for?"

"That's just it, I don't know. It's only a hunch. We know Charlie bought the icon. We know he also bought some storyboards depicting the set for the Brenner house. I'm looking for a thread, a tie-in to the case, but this could be a wild goose chase."

"Don't give up so easily," Angie said. "Why don't we rent the movie and see whether we can figure out where they built the set? You know, use the film as a guide. The house may be gone, but the land is still the same."

"That's not a bad idea," said Toby. "It might help. Besides, I haven't seen *The Birds* since I was a kid." My thoughts exactly.

When we got back home, I started dinner while Toby went out to get the DVD. The Surf Shop in the Pelican Plaza has several racks of DVD rentals. Given Bodega Bay's link to cinematic history, they were sure to carry a copy of the Hitchcock classic.

Dan called while Toby was gone. "I hear that your sister is pretty good at golf," he began. Colleen had given him a full report on our game. We exchanged a few more words of banter. I hesitated reporting that I'd spent the afternoon searching fruitlessly for a movie set. After all, what real new information did I have besides a hunch that there was some connection between Rose Gaffney's place and Charlie's murder? I had no evidence there actually *was* a connection, so I held back.

Meanwhile, Dan had news about the crash. "Looks like you were right about who the driver was. The corpse we recovered from the vehicle was badly burned. But get this—he was a big man and he had a gold front tooth. But that's not all. There was a briefcase in the car that was thrown clear of the fire. We've got a Russian passport, so we've got a name, and some other stuff. I'll know more about him when I hear back from Interpol, I hope tomorrow. His name was Ivan Mikovitch. He's been in the country for about a month."

"Do you think he's the one who killed Charlie?" I asked.

"It's too soon to say."

"But I'm right that he was stalking us."

"Looks like it. I do think he was following you. He's involved in this one way or another. I think he broke into Toby's gallery and searched it, then did the same with your house, and then, when he didn't find what he was looking for, he tailed you up to Fort Ross and back."

"But why try to run us off the road? If he was hoping we'd lead him to the icon, it doesn't make sense that he'd want us dead before he found it."

"Maybe he wasn't trying to kill you. Look, the fog was bad, he didn't want to lose you, he was following too close. Then, bam! He hits the cow. All I'm saying is what looked like an accident may have been an accident. Give me another day or two and I'll know more." Dan promised to call again when he had solid information. He reminded me that Charlie's funeral was tomorrow and confirmed where it would be held. Meanwhile, his advice for us was to try to take our minds off the accident.

Over dinner I relayed Dan's report, and Toby thought it made sense. In any case, watching a film tonight with my husband and sister would be a good distraction. While Angie and I did the dishes, Toby popped the disk into the player and cued the DVD. A short time later, we were sprawled on the L-shaped sofa in our living room, settling in for the show. I even made popcorn.

"Look, there's Hitchcock," Toby pointed out in one of the early scenes in the film when Tippi Hedren, who plays Melanie, goes into a bird shop in San Francisco. "He always gave himself a walk-on. That was his trademark." Sure enough, we spotted the portly director coming out of the shop, leading a couple of dogs on a leash. In the film's setup, Melanie meets Mitch Brenner (Rod Taylor) inside, where he's shopping for a pair of lovebirds as a birthday gift for his kid sister. In a variation of the boy-pursues-girl scenario, Melanie decides to follow Mitch up to Bodega Bay, where his mother and sister live, and to deliver the birds as a surprise. A nice touch, I thought. The only innocent birds in the movie are the caged lovebirds, since all the free birds turn vicious and attack the town.

When she gets to Bodega Bay, Melanie asks the postmaster where she can find the Brenner house. He sends her to the dock at The Tides Restaurant and points straight out across the bay. It's near those "two big trees," he says. Toby paused, reversed, and played the scene again. The postmaster was pointing in the direction of where we had searched that afternoon.

Melanie hires a small boat with an outboard motor and chugs across the harbor (dolled up in a fur coat, for some reason). As she approaches the opposite shore, we get our first good look at the Brenner house, which is close to the water, nestled behind a stand of cypress trees. There's a white fence surrounding the property, which contains several outbuildings, including a red barn. The house backs up against the dunes, and there's a little dock in front of it, where Melanie ties up the boat.

How familiar it looked. Yes, we must have passed the spot this afternoon, but where exactly was it? House, fence, barn, dock, were gone, of course; only the trees remained—but which trees? As Toby had noted, there were multiple stands of trees all along the road, a road that hadn't been there at the time of the filming, and several places where trees stood near the dunes.

The next important scene for our purposes was the birthday party for Cathy (Mitch's little sister). Mitch and Melanie climb one of the dunes and look down at the house from above, watching the kids playing under a grape arbor in the yard. There's a split-second vista looking back toward the marina, and then, as the camera pans, a glimpse of the mudflats in front of the house at what must have been low tide. Toby paused, reversed, and froze the shot. The view was tantalizing but inconclusive. We couldn't match it with any place we'd been in the afternoon.

The children's party is interrupted by a bird attack, and from this point, the pace and violence pick up. The children are attacked at school, and Annie, the schoolteacher, is killed. There's an explosion at a gas pump outside the restaurant, a neighboring farmer has his eyes pecked out, the birds continue to go berserk, and Melanie and the family hole up inside the Brenner house. But the remaining scenes are shot inside, which provides no clues as to the site. The climax occurs when Melanie decides to investigate some sounds coming from the attic. She goes up alone (was she crazy?) and is badly bloodied by the avian zombies. The final frame was probably a shot done in the studio against a painted backdrop. It shows dawn breaking as the survivors drive off surrounded by thousands of perched and gathering birds, massing for the next attack.

By the end of the film, we were no closer to pinpointing a location for the house than we were at the beginning. I enjoyed seeing the movie again, though. Some of the special effects looked cheesy compared to today's computer-generated images, and a few of the birds looked fake. Even so, fifty years later, the film stirred primal fears.

That night I had a disturbing dream. It wasn't about being attacked by birds; it was about Charlie. I was standing in a grassy clearing ringed by a circle of low cypress trees. It was getting dark. Rain was threatening. Out of the trees, something gray and low to the ground started coming toward me. At first I thought it was a wolf. But as it got closer, I saw that it was a human head carved out of stone, like the head of a statue that had fallen off—and it was moving under its own power. It was upright and tipping from side to side, walking, except it had no trunk or legs. It was Charlie, or rather, it had Charlie's face. It advanced to the center of the clearing and then rocked back and forth. When it stopped, the face was looking straight at me. It seemed to be trying to tell me something, but its stone lips couldn't move. Suddenly the gray eyes came to life. They gazed into mine and then looked to the ground.

Then I woke up.

9

LEAVE IT TO TOBY to have a rational explanation for everything. It sometimes bothers me that there's so little room in his makeup for the mysterious side of life. In this instance, though, he probably was right.

"You're going to the cemetery today for Charlie's funeral. The grave will have a headstone. Get it? That's your unconscious dreaming self at work. Head. Stone. You're upset that he's really dead. So am I." Toby spooned out a helping of scrambled eggs and poured another cup of coffee.

Yes, that was it. I was steeling myself for Charlie's funeral.

"And the bit about the headstone walking upright, tipping from side to side? Remember the documentary we saw on *Nova* a few weeks ago about Easter Island? They tested a theory about how those giant stone heads could have been transported from one side of the island to the other."

I did remember. An archaeologist had a theory that teams of men could have moved the statues by beveling the bottoms and attaching ropes to either side. As each team pulled in turn, the big stone moved along in an upright position, tipping from side to side, like an awkward giant walking.

"There you have it," Toby concluded. "And the trees? Well, that's from last night watching the movie and trying to figure out where the house was. Charlie was trying to tell you something, but he couldn't."

It made sense to me, but my mood stayed gloomy. I wasn't going to feel better till the funeral was over. I poured a second cup of coffee. Angie was still asleep. I'd promised to take her out to lunch and shopping when we got back from the service.

Bad funerals are dull and painful. Good ones are original and cathartic. Charlie's friends saw to it that he got a good one. Annie arranged to have the gathering at the Guerneville Tavern, where many of Charlie's friendships had been made and nurtured. She was serving coffee at the bar. The closed casket was right in the front window. From nine to nine-thirty, people poured in the door, paused before Charlie's coffin, and shook hands in the short receiving line—Charlie's brother, Jim Halloran, and his wife, and beside them, Tom Keogh. Tom was standing up as the bereaved partner, in spite of the rift before Charlie's death.

Among the crowd, I recognized the two friends who had been sitting with Tom at the bar at River's End, as well as the owners of art and antiques galleries all around the Russian River Valley. Our friends Ken and Gloria were among them. Some of the staff from River's End were there, along with workers from the Cape Fear Café and the Applewood Inn. The majority were men I didn't know, chatting together in friendly knots. I spotted Dan Ellis in the back of the room. He waved, and I walked over.

"Interesting to see who's here," he observed. "For instance, see that guy over there in the suit? That's Arnold Kohler."

"The gambler Charlie owed money to?"

"The same."

He was a husky, middle-aged man with dark, thinning hair, sideburns, and a mustache. Everyone else was in casual clothes, which made

Kohler conspicuous in his blue pinstripes. He was standing in the back talking to a nervous-looking man who surreptitiously passed him a thick envelope. Kohler rubbed it between his thumb and forefinger, and slipped it inside his jacket. Dan had been watching them. "I haven't been able to tie him to the murder, but it's interesting he's showed up."

"Do killers really go to the funerals of people they murder?" I asked.

"Some do," said Dan. His eyes swept the rest of the room as Tom Keogh stepped forward to speak.

At first Tom sounded frail, but his voice strengthened as he went on. "This is not going to be a formal service. This is just a little bit of time when you can say what you'd like about Charlie, or to Charlie, so that we can say goodbye before we put him in the earth. For myself, I just want to say one thing about Charlie. We had our problems, but he was a lovely man. He was tender toward us all. He loved many things, and many people. And we loved him back. We'll miss him. Terribly." His voice was shaky again, but after a pause he continued. "I'll call on just one person, and then the floor will be open. Jim?"

As Charlie's brother moved up to the front of the room, I turned to Dan and whispered, "Tom isn't still a suspect, is he?"

Dan whispered back, "Like Kohler, he's still in the picture. But Mikovitch is the prime suspect now. We're waiting for final lab reports. I'll call you when they're in."

Charlie's brother, who looked remarkably like him, only older, talked about their youth in Santa Cruz, when they were boys who took crazy risks playing on the docks. It was Charlie's bravery he remembered most. On hot summer nights, Jim would stay on the dock playing lookout, while Charlie jumped from yacht to yacht in the marina, looking for liquor or cigarettes carelessly left out on a deck. Charlie never returned till he found some contraband. He'd hold his heist high in the air, bringing it proudly to the dock to share with his brother. In later years, Jim took the safe route—college, business school, a lifetime job in Santa Cruz city administration. Charlie took the risky route—skipping college, crewing on cruise ships instead, then learning antiques, and finally finding a business and life partner in Tom Keogh, here in Guerneville. Jim thanked Tom for giving Charlie a sense of home and a reason to stop taking risks. He paused and looked up and around the room as if looking for the next volunteer to speak about Charlie.

Nobody jumped in. My guess is that everybody was thinking what I was thinking. First, Charlie had not stopped taking risks. His murder proved that. Second, he no longer was at home with Tom. He had moved out to his own apartment and a new shop.

Annie stepped forward from behind the bar, her girth well swaddled in a white apron. "The awkward truth is," she said, "that Charlie was still adventuring. If you loved Charlie, you had to love him for the scamp he was. He was charming and affectionate and surprising, and that was sometimes the problem. Tom loved him that way, and his friends did too. When Charlie left Tom, some of us wanted to kick him, remember? But we'd be ready to forgive him and understand him, whether he got back together with Tom or not, which I think he would have. I'm just sad that Charlie didn't get a chance to make that decision. His life was cut short by a terrible crime. Already we miss him very much."

Annie's honesty broke the ice, and from there a dozen people spoke movingly in tribute to their friend, Toby among them. "I didn't know Charlie as long as some of you did, but in the short time we worked together he became more than just a business partner. He was a friend. I'd always worked alone, and when Charlie came into the business, I didn't know how I would feel having another person in the shop with me. But in fact, he brightened up the day. Charlie was a fabulous conversationalist, and he knew his stuff. I learned a lot from him. And he was fun to be with. This is a sad day for me. And Tom"—Toby looked directly at Tom Keogh—"I'm sorry for your loss. And yours." He nodded toward Jim Halloran and his wife. "I hope whoever did this will be brought to justice."

Several others added reminiscences. The last turned to the undertaker. I hadn't noticed him standing near the casket at the front of the room. He signaled with his eyes to the men who'd be pallbearers, including Toby and Tom, and they moved into position as he told the crowd to follow the hearse to the cemetery on Woodland Drive, just a few minutes away.

Outside, the dim sky had clouded over and a misty drizzle had begun. Dan had remained inside to talk to Arnold Kohler. Neither arrived at the gravesite. There, once everyone had gathered, the ceremony was brief. Don Carlin, an ex-priest who had come out after leaving the church and was now active in the gay community, spoke the final words. He too had been a friend of Tom and Charlie.

"We now commit Charlie's body to the earth. In our grief, we take consolation from whatever beliefs we hold most dear. For some, those beliefs may be religious; for others, not. Perhaps the important question isn't which beliefs are true, but rather which beliefs help make the world a better place. Since I've left the priesthood, I've come to think that those beliefs that harden the heart are harmful. Yet those that open the heart are blessed. 'By their fruits shall ye know them' (Matthew 7:16). So let us open our hearts in memory of Charlie Halloran. And now let us pray."

We bowed our heads, and the casket was lowered into the ground. Behind me I heard a woman say, "He's gone to a better place." The former priest demurred. "Charlie liked it here just fine."

On the way back, Toby said, "That was good, what the priest said at the funeral."

"Ex-priest," I corrected. "You mean about opening our hearts?"

"That too. But it's what he said afterward to that woman about Charlie. It reminded me of a favorite poem of mine in college. I used to quote it all the time. 'To Ford Madox Ford in Heaven.' Do you know it?"

"I don't think so."

"It's by William Carlos Williams. Williams wrote the poem as a lament for his friend when he died. The gist of it is he asks Ford whether it's any better in heaven than it was in Provence, which was Ford's favorite place."

"And what was the answer?"

"There wasn't one. It's a rhetorical question. Williams is saying that nothing beats being alive. And there's this line I love. He says, 'Provence, the fat assed Ford will never again strain the chairs of your cafés.' Now, that's a great line."

"Did Ford really have a fat ass?"

"Yes, as a matter of fact, and that's part of it. The poem becomes a kind of ode to earthiness."

Earthiness. I thought about that as we drove through the redwoods, then alongside green hills splashed with streaks of yellow broom, with the ocean ahead of us. "Provence is lovely, but I don't think it's any more beautiful than Sonoma County," I said. "We're lucky to live here."

"We're lucky to be alive," said Toby.

I dropped Toby off at his shop and headed home to pick up Angie. She was hunched over the half-completed art puzzle, trying to fill out the green sea around Botticelli's Venus on the half-shell. She invited me to join her. "Good funeral therapy," she said. In the interests of maintaining the illusion that the broken pieces of the world can ultimately be put together, we worked till we finished an hour later.

We then had to hustle, because we were going to Occidental, a craftsy little inland town, where the café renowned for its bison burgers keeps lazy hours and closes in midafternoon. Over lunch, we plotted Angie's shopping mission. Mom was on the top of her list, because her birthday was coming up. But Angie had trouble focusing her search. The gift should be natural and luxurious, but that's all she could say. With that fuzzy goal in mind, we had license to visit every store in town and try on the best of everything: locally made earrings, necklaces from Africa, knitted hats from Argentina, and tie-dyed silk in the form of scarves, skirts, and dresses. We couldn't see any of these on Mom. When there were no shops we hadn't scoured, we wanted to pout over a cup of tea, but the café was closed. So we shared a bottle of ginger ale from the General Store before starting on our way to meet Toby.

When we got to Duncans Mills, instead of heading for his shop in the back, I parked in the front, where there was one store that might have something for Mom. Duncans Mills Textiles showcases local weaving, knitting, sewing, and crocheting. When we'd been there a minute, I knew we'd found the right place. Angie was humming as she picked through sweaters and shawls in Mom's favorite colors. Finally, she chose a luminous weave of purple and blue in the shape of a shawl.

"Try it on for me. You're Mom's size," she said, draping it over my shoulders. It was just the right length to cover the arms on a cold day and yet short enough to wear scarf-style under a coat. And the texture was soft.

"What about cleaning?" I wondered. I drew the shawl off my shoulders and looked for the tag. It was handwritten. On one side were the price and the directions "Hand wash, cold. Block and hang dry." The other side said, "Sonoma lambs wool, hand dyed and woven by Rose Cassini, Cazadero," with her address.

"Something wrong?" asked Angie. "Does it have to be dry-cleaned? Mom hates that."

"No. It's just that I know the person who made this. Toby and I talked to her the other day. She's the woman who originally owned the icon that Charlie bought, the one that was stolen from the shop."

"Yikes. Bad karma?"

"I don't think so. She seems like a really good person. You'd like her."

"Because?"

"She's strong and independent, a weaver living alone in her late sixties. When she was young she was a protester against the nuclear plant on Bodega Head. Then she fell in love, and when her sweetheart died—he's the one who gave her the icon—she retreated to Cazadero. It's a tiny, isolated hamlet way off in the boonies, inland from here. She's spent her whole life making beautiful things there."

"Well, that sounds romantic enough for Mom. I'm buying it." Angie took the shawl from me and headed for the counter. I stayed behind, fingering through the other shawls that Rose had for sale there—beautiful, every one. We soon had the gift package stashed in my car, and we walked around to the back of the complex to Toby's shop. As usual when he's open for business, the front door was ajar. I thought I heard someone talking.

Inside Toby and Andrew Federenco were standing beside the large oak dining-room table. Federenco was rocking back and forth, his left hand cupped atop his right, which pressed down on his cane. Toby's posture was stiff. "We were just talking about the break-in at our house. Mr. Federenco thinks he's being harassed."

Federenco acknowledged our entrance with a nod and turned back to Toby. "So it wasn't you who suggested I be interviewed about it?"

"No, it wasn't."

Angie came over. Toby introduced her, and she drifted away.

"Look, if you're here to complain," Toby continued, but Federenco cut him off.

"That's not why I came. I'm here to warn you. The sheriff knows I'm looking for an icon that by rights belongs to me. Your partner had it. Now he's dead, and someone's broken into your home. You may be in danger."

"From whom?"

"I don't have a name, but someone else has been making inquiries. I've talked to other dealers."

"A Russian? Someone speaking with a Russian accent?"

Federenco's eyes narrowed. "Possibly. Have you met such a person?"

"You might say we had a run-in," Toby observed dryly, "or more precisely, he almost ran into us." Toby paused for effect. "He's dead."

I studied Andrew Federenco's face as he absorbed this news. His shock seemed genuine. "What?"

"He's dead," Toby repeated. "He was following us home from Fort Ross and almost drove us off the road. But he went over the rail instead. It happened Saturday."

"My God!" exclaimed Federenco. "I read about a crash but had no idea you were involved. The paper didn't give names. Who was he?"

"You don't know?" I asked pointedly.

"No, why should I? Do you?"

"According to the deputy sheriff, his name was Ivan Mikovitch. Does that ring a bell?" Again I observed Federenco's reaction, trying to test whether he was hiding something.

He took a moment to reply. "I've heard the name. He's connected to the Russian mafia, a circle of art thieves and extortionists."

"How do you know him?" I pressed.

"I don't know him. I said I've heard the name. When you're a collector and you follow the trade, you hear these things."

"I see." It was hard to read his face.

"Now, may I ask *you* a question?"

"Go ahead," I replied.

"What were you doing in Fort Ross?"

Was there any reason not to tell him? "To be honest, I was interested in finding out more about your family."

"Oh, really?"

I explained how my research into the icon that Charlie bought led me eventually to his ancestor Andreyev Federenco's memoir, which he himself had donated to the Fort Ross Interpretive Association in 1972.

When I finished, his face bore a bemused expression. "Well, that was clever of you. And did you find his life story of interest?"

"Very much so," I said. "I've been wondering how the icon came into the possession of your family."

"It was given to one of my ancestors by a pious monk in the seventeenth century. It was a reward for his work in helping build a cathedral."

"And how did the tradition start of passing the icon down from son to son?"

"It was that way from the beginning."

"Then why was the chain of inheritance broken? As I understand it, the icon was supposed to go to the eldest son of the eldest son."

"That's exactly right."

"So when Andreyev died, the icon passed to his son, Vladimir."

"My grandfather, yes."

"But when Vladimir died, the icon didn't go to Feodor, but rather to Boris."

"My uncle. That's so."

"But your father was the elder brother, so why—?"

"Because my father wavered in his faith. As far as my grandfather was concerned, he was an atheist. That isn't exactly the case. What happened was that my father wanted to go back to Russia after the 1917 revolution, in sympathy with the Communists. Grandfather prevented him, which made him bitter. They fought about it all their lives. But since my father had left the church, my grandfather willed the icon to his younger son, my uncle, breaking the family tradition."

"So that's how your cousin got the icon."

"Yes, my uncle died young, and Peter inherited it. But that never should have happened. So now you understand why my side of the family has a claim to ownership."

"But it wasn't until that story appeared in the newspaper in 1962 that you went after your cousin. That was because the article suggested the triptych might be extremely valuable. Am I right?"

"I never 'went after' Peter, to use your words, but the family did put pressure on me to try to work out a sharing arrangement with Peter. I suppose that was prompted by the publicity. For me, it was never a matter of money. It still isn't. I have no idea what the icon may be worth. Its value for me is its heritage. I don't care if it's not worth ten dollars, I want it back."

This speech was delivered with such passion that I was tempted to believe it. Toby, I noticed out of the corner of my eye, looked dubious.

"You know, I lost my wife two years ago," Andrew Federenco continued. "Since then I've been thinking a lot about what I've done with my life and what I'll be able to leave to my children. I want to succeed where my father failed. It's important to me to recover the triptych or whatever's left of it, and to see that it goes rightfully to

Nicholas, my son, and that his children and theirs have the chance to venerate it. So again, I'm asking for your help."

Toby didn't reply.

"Can you tell me if there have been any developments? Are you any closer to locating what we're both looking for?"

"Not really," said Toby, on his guard.

"As I told you before, I'm prepared to offer a substantial reward for the recovery of that icon. That's another reason why I'm here."

Toby thanked him for the offer. "We'll keep it in mind. By the same token, if you come up with any information that might help us or the sheriff, you'll share it, won't you?"

At the mention of the sheriff, Federenco stiffened. "I'll keep it in mind," he said, echoing Toby's words with his fingers raised and curled in air quotes. He had decided to disengage. "Nice meeting you," he called in Angie's direction. She was sitting at the other end of the gallery, reading.

"You, too," said Angie, looking up from her magazine.

With that, he turned and left.

Obviously, he was fishing for leads," said Toby. "He seemed surprised to find out about the Russian, but that could have been an act. How do we know they weren't working together?"

"Do you think that's likely?"

"I'm not sure what to make of him, to tell you the truth. What's your read?"

"He can be persuasive. But I don't buy that 'I don't care about the money, it's all about the family' line, do you?"

"Not for a minute."

Angie walked over to us, and Toby turned his attention to the oak dining table he was standing next to. "Nora, could you give me a hand with this? I was trying to open it when he came in. It seems to be stuck."

"Sure. Isn't this the table that Charlie brought into the gallery? The one that Tom Keogh claims belongs to him?"

"Yeah, it is. Since the funeral, I've been thinking that I don't want to fight with Tom about Charlie's inventory. If it's so important to him to get the table and desk and a few other things back, then, what the hell. He can have them."

"I'm glad you feel that way."

"Yeah. So I was checking this table out. It has a storage space for leaves in its undercarriage, but I'm having trouble getting it open. It takes two people, so just grab it like this and pull when I tell you to."

"Okay." I followed Toby's example and grasped the underside of my end of the table and gave it a tug when he said to pull. Nothing happened.

"I've opened the release on my side. See if there's another release on your side," he said.

"What am I looking for?"

"A small iron lever underneath. You should be able to feel it with your fingertips."

"Nope, I don't think so."

He came around and checked himself. "You're right." He ducked his head under the table. "There's just the one release on my side and it's open. Let's try again." He resumed his stance at his end. "Ready? Go."

We both tugged, and the table lifted an inch off the floor on Toby's side, but it remained stuck.

"Let me give it a try," said Angie. I yielded my place to her. Angie is seriously buff.

"Hard this time," instructed Toby. "On three. One. Two. Three. Pull!"

There was a loud crack, and the two halves of the table slid apart. "You did it!" I clapped Angie on the back. Then I followed Toby's gaze. He was staring at the open compartment. Nestled between the railings of the undercarriage was a package encased in bubble wrap. That's what had caused the jam. My heart raced. Was it possible?

Toby gently detached the package from its hiding place. One corner of it, where the bubble wrap had torn, had been crushed by the attempt to free the table mechanism. I shuddered to think of the damage done.

"What is it?" asked Angie. "Is it the icon?"

"Let's just see." I took the package from Toby's hands and brought it over to the desk. Carefully I unwound the bubble wrap, which had been folded around the item several times and fastened with Scotch Tape. In another minute, the icon was exposed.

"Oh," exclaimed Angie. "It's the angel Michael!"

The panel was obviously the right wing of a triptych, with a curved top and two straight sides. Grooves on the left side marked the place where hinges would have connected it to the central panel. The angel stood with legs apart, his sword upraised against a background of golden sky, now murky and coated with a layer of grime. A pink cloak billowed around his torso. The white curves of Michael's pinions rose behind his shoulders. His eyes, with their large black irises, looked directly out at us.

Angie was thrilled. "Nora, it's a sign. He's your guardian angel. Now there can't be any doubt about it."

I felt a wave of emotions, but the dominant one was distress, for a deep gouge had been dug into the upper corner of the panel, obliterating the tip of Michael's sword. A web of fine cracks radiated outward from the indentation. "Look what we've done," was all I could say.

"Charlie would have opened the table without hurting it," admitted Toby. "We didn't know."

"Don't feel bad, Nora," Angie said.

"It can be restored," said Toby, "can't it?"

"We've got to call Al and bring it in and see what he says. I hope so."

"Let's call him right away. In fact, let's get this home. We can call him on the way."

As our discovery began to sink in, I felt the first flutters of excitement balancing the wrenching feeling prompted by the damage. We had discovered Charlie's hiding place. The icon had never left the shop. Toby quickly closed up the store and bundled the icon into the trunk of my car alongside Angie's purchases; then we started home. I reached Al on my cell, and he suggested that we lose no time in bringing him the icon. He would assess the damage. We made an appointment for early the next morning, since Al taught in the afternoon.

Now that she had seen the icon, Angie was bursting with questions. On the ride home, I gave her a recap of what we'd gathered from Rose Cassini and the Fort Ross documents. Having just met Andrew Federenco, she declared: "I'm on his side. He cares enough to be looking to get the icon back for his children. And this Peter guy, how much could he have cared about the icon if he split it up into three pieces and gave one of them to a girlfriend?"

"Peter was afraid of Andrew, so he gave the icon to Rose for safekeeping," I explained.

"That old man? He doesn't look scary to me."

"He wasn't old at the time. And according to Dan, he ran with a tough crowd and had some brushes with the law. Besides, if Peter hadn't been killed in that traffic accident, he could have reassembled the triptych."

"Unless the other panels were hidden in the Gaffney house," said Toby, "in which case they burned up a long time ago. Speaking of which, I still haven't returned the DVD. I've got it with me. Mind if we stop at the Surf Shop on the way home?"

"We have to stop anyway," I said. "We don't have anything for dinner."

While Toby went into the Surf Shop, Angie and I went into the attached grocery store and picked up fresh crab cakes and "homemade" coleslaw. I was a little surprised that we got back to the car ahead of Toby.

"What?" I asked when Toby came out of the shop flushed and excited.

"On impulse, I asked the clerk to look up who the last person before me was to check out *The Birds*. Guess."

It took a few seconds to register. "Charlie," I said. "When?"

"He brought it back the day he died."

Now I was certain there was a connection between the movie and the site where Charlie was killed. If we had the storyboards that Peter had drawn for the Hitchcock film, maybe we could work it out.

10

THE NEXT MORNING a bleary-eyed Toby drove us into Berkeley, with the damaged icon cradled in my lap. Angie was off for another session with her angel reader. I hadn't been in touch with Al since our previous visit, so we had some catching up to do. Sitting in his familiar living room over tea in china cups, Toby and I went over everything we had learned about the icon, while he peered at the damage, turned the panel over, and examined its back.

Today Al was wearing a herringbone sports jacket and a bowtie. He was in his teaching outfit. "Well," he said at last, "it can be repaired, but not by me. You need a specialist. I was right about the panel, though. It's much older than the painting on it, at least sixteenth century, probably even fifteenth. The grooves, cleats, condition of the wood all point to its age, so that in itself makes it rare. There's almost certainly an older image under Michael—or several. There's no telling what you might have here."

"Maybe there is," I said, surprising him. "Read this." I handed Al a copy of the *San Francisco Chronicle* article from 1962, the one that recounted the legend of Rublev's lost triptych.

His eyes widened as he read it. "Whew!" he exclaimed when he had finished. "Call me Ishmael." He reached for his cup and took a sip of tea.

"Huh?'

"*Moby-Dick*," he explained. "You've been chasing the white whale of icon-hunting. You're not the first to go running after that legend."

"But is there anything to the legend?" Toby asked. "There actually was a white whale in *Moby-Dick*. Ahab found it."

"And it killed him," noted Al, a twinkle in his eye. He sighed and put down his cup. "About the legend—we all know it. It's been around a long time, but there's never been a reason to take it seriously. No grounds, no real evidence. Every once in a while someone claims to have traced the Rublev triptych through a reference in some arcane document, but it's never turned up. I've always considered it a myth."

"But what if it's more than a myth and someone found it," persisted Toby. "What would it be worth today?"

Al snorted and his tea sloshed dangerously. He steadied the cup and leaned forward. "What if Leonardo had made a small copy of *The Last Supper* to carry around with him on his travels and it showed up after having gone missing all these years. What do you think that would be worth?"

"You'd put Rublev in the same category as Leonardo?"

"In the history of Russian icon painting, he's the equivalent. There are very few examples of his work, aside from a few undisputed masterpieces and fragments. But no one else had a greater influence on the genre. You must know something about him, don't you, Nora?" He reached into his jacket pocket and brought out a meerschaum.

I confessed I knew the name but not much else.

"You should have taken my Russian icon seminar," Al grumbled as he filled and lit the pipe.

"I took your Giotto seminar instead," I reminded him.

"Why not both?" He blew out the match, then smiled. "All right, I'm teasing. Here, let me show you something." Al got up, went to the wall of bookshelves behind him, and returned with a large illustrated tome of Russian icons. His pipe clenched between his teeth, he thumbed through the book and then spread it open on the coffee table to display a full-page, color reproduction of Andrei Rublev's *Old Testament Trinity*. He tapped the illustration with the stem of his pipe. "This is his most famous work, the one that, according to the legend, he duplicated as a small triptych."

The caption identified the icon as a large piece, some 56" × 45", painted in egg tempera between 1422 and 1427 for the Cathedral of the Trinity–St. Sergey Monastery in Zagorsk. "Originally, the panel was part of an iconostasis," said Al, "consisting of several tiers of icons forming a wall between the altar and the main body of the church. They say it's been restored so many times that there are hardly traces left of the original—much like *The Last Supper*, come to think of it, but even so, you can see why it's so revered."

Indeed I could, even though it was only a photograph. Against a gilded background, the work depicts three graceful figures closely grouped around a table. They are angels. Faintly, you can make out their wings and halos. They wear sumptuous cloaks and appear to be seated on an elevated, throne-like dais. The three angels are shown bowing their heads toward one another. Their facial expressions are tender, sorrowful, meditative. The right hand of the central figure, two fingers extended in benediction, is raised above a chalice on the table. In the upper left-hand corner of the icon, there are traces of a building, and above one shoulder of the central figure is the fragment of a tree. These elements are greatly reduced in size. The painting's tones are rich but muted, and the colors are subtle.

"The icon illustrates a story from the Old Testament," Al went on between puffs. "But it's really a visualization of the Trinity. The angel on the left represents God the Father, the angel in the center God the Son, and the angel on the right the Holy Spirit. The scene was inspired by the story of three angels who visited Abraham and Sarah in their tent. The Byzantine artists always included Abraham and Sarah, who served the three angels, but Rublev omits them. Here the angels are alone, conversing about the mystery of the Incarnation."

We stared for a while, not speaking. As I studied the image, I remembered what Vasari, himself an artist and a contemporary of the great Renaissance masters, had said of Raphael. Yes, he had mastered all the technical advances of his day—linear perspective, naturalistic detail, proportion, and the rest—as well as any of his rivals, but there was something special about his work, a new element that set him far above his peers. Vasari called it "a certain pervasive beauty," a mysterious quality akin to serenity that made his paintings not only competent but also spiritually great.

Rublev had that indefinable quality too. Perhaps it was the flowing, rounded contours of his figures, the fluidity of their silhouettes, the lovely colors of their cloaks, their radiant facial expressions and subtle gestures, or the way their delicate, inclined heads bowed toward one another, uniting the three as one. Whatever contributed to the ethereal effect was elusive.

"It's quite beautiful," I said.

"Yes. It's that and more," said Al.

"I've never seen so deep a blue," Toby added, pointing to the central figure's robe.

"That's because he used crushed lapis lazuli in the pigment," Al said. "Nobody else could match his colors. Or his skill in composition. Look closely and you'll see that the three figures are contained within an imaginary circle. And what's more, the three figures, with the central one slightly raised above the others, form a pyramid. So, the compositional rhythms are complex but harmonious."

"What's that little structure in the background?" asked Toby. "It looks like a section of a palace, a portico or balcony supported by pillars. You don't see much in the way of background in most icons, do you?"

"That's true. It's unusual. Everything in this painting is symbolic," Al continued as he pointed to each feature. "Here the building suggests the tent of Abraham. Some think it represents the Church, just as the cup on the table represents the Eucharist, and the tree in the background suggests the Cross."

Then he leaned back, inviting us to take a more encompassing view. "But it's the composition as a whole that makes the most powerful statement. According to the Orthodox creed, the three persons of the Trinity are equal and are parts of an indissoluble unity. That's what Rublev suggests by inscribing them in a circle. It was an important statement for him to make as an artist. Portraying the Trinity as undivided appealed to a yearning for unity at a time when the country was weakened by internal feudal strife."

"I see," I said. "And was the icon well known during Rublev's life?"

"Yes, and its reputation kept growing after he died—so much so that a Church Council held in Moscow ruled that any painter who wanted to represent the Trinity should follow the model of Andrei Rublev."

"All well and good," said Toby. "But if Rublev's work was so famous and he made a smaller copy of it before he died, why would anyone want to paint it over? Wouldn't they want to preserve it?"

"Aha," said Al, pleased by the question. He tapped the ashes from the bowl of his pipe into an ashtray and set the pipe down beside it. "Now you come to the nub of the legend. Let's run a thought experiment. Nora: Say you're the artist and you want to transform the *Old Testament Trinity* into a small triptych in which the side wings fold over the middle panel. Then you'll have a portable work suitable for travel. So, how do you do it? How do you change the composition?"

I considered the question. "Well, besides reducing everything in size, I guess you'd place the central angel in the middle panel and the other two on either side, in the wings, one on the left and one on the right. How else?"

"And what effect would that have on the composition?"

"You would have to break the circle."

"Exactly. And worse, from the perspective of the Russian Orthodox Church, you would divide the unity of the Trinity. Remember, they were rigid about that sort of thing, fanatical. You would separate the Father, Son, and Holy Spirit. And that would be heresy!" With that, he snapped the splayed picture book shut, suggesting with a hint of violence the punishment that might await the creator of such a work.

"But is it likely Rublev would have gone against the Church?" Toby asked.

"You wouldn't think so." Al rose and returned the heavy book to its shelf. "That's just one of the reasons I've never credited the legend. Then again, perhaps the work meant so much to him that even if he had to adjust the composition, he was compelled to make a copy he could keep with him always."

"That was the case with Leonardo," I recalled. "He couldn't bear to part with the *Mona Lisa*, so he took it with him wherever he went. He had it with him when he died in France."

Toby frowned. "But if the Church found out you had a subversive painting in your possession, you'd be in trouble, so you would either have to destroy it or disguise it."

"And that's the genesis of the legend," Al concluded, returning to his seat. "By the end of the sixteenth century, Rublev's *Trinity* had become so iconic—pardon the pun—that whoever owned the heretical triptych at that point would have been in real danger. So the legend goes that its owner, unwilling to destroy it, had the work painted over, and after a few generations, it disappeared into anonymity."

"It sure makes for a good story," said Toby, rubbing his chin.

"And that's all I ever thought it was, a story." Al paused. "Until now." He picked up the damaged icon, which he had laid aside during his discourse, and stared at it thoughtfully. "When did this Federenco fellow say that his family acquired the triptych?"

"Sometime in the seventeenth century. He was vague about it," I replied.

"Hmm. Well, the chronology fits. The age of the panel fits. The dimensions are plausible." He shook his head. "It's hardly likely. But still . . ."

"I was thinking maybe you could clean it, you know, remove the surface layer, to see what's beneath."

"Not me. If there's the slightest chance this could be a Rublev, I'd be afraid to touch it. And in any case, the panel badly needs repair. That's beyond my skill. You need a professional restorer, the best."

"Do you know someone in the area you could recommend?" asked Toby.

Al thought for a moment. "I do know someone, but he's not in the area. He's in Wisconsin. An old friend of mine and colleague. As far as I'm concerned, he has the best hands in the business."

"Oh?"

"His name is George Greeley. We were at Yale together in the art history program, but George lasted only two years and finished with a terminal MA. He came to Yale with an undergraduate degree in art, and that was the problem. He was an artist, not a historian. Didn't give a damn about dates or theories."

"That'll get you tossed out of art history in a hurry," I said.

"Yes, but in this case, it was our loss. When it comes to technical analysis, I've never heard anyone as eloquent as George."

"But now he's doing restoration?" pursued Toby.

"Yes, and that's what he was made for. He has the eye of an art historian and the hands of a painter."

"But, Al," I said worriedly, "wouldn't working with an old Russian icon require special training? This isn't your everyday restoration."

"That's why I thought of George. Not far from Madison, in Iowa, there's an auction house that specializes in Russian icons, old and modern. The university also has its own collection. So George has had a fairly steady stream of local work, and over the years he's been called on by museums and private collectors from around the country. In this case, you couldn't do better."

"Does he teach at the University of Wisconsin?"

"Well, no. And I should tell you that's rather a sore point with him. He's always wanted a permanent position at the university. In fact he did some fill-in teaching in the art department until he ran up against a barrier they have for part-time lecturers. It seems that if you teach the same course for a certain number of semesters, you gain the right to be rehired with permanent benefits, and the dean wouldn't allow that. But he landed on his feet. He teaches art conservation workshops at Madison Area Technical College as well as the occasional art course there, and he still has time for his own practice. Just don't get him started on the university. He's still resentful."

"If you trust him, Al, that's good enough for me," I said. "What about you, Toby? The decision should be yours."

"My worry is the distance," he said. "We've already damaged the panel once. I hate to put it at risk a second time."

Al spoke gently, reluctant to put too much pressure on Toby. "Look at it this way. What you have here might be a valuable icon in need of specialized care, or it may be a banged-up work of little interest. Now if it were mine, and if it turned out to be worth restoring, I'd want George to do the work."

Toby considered the point, and then the businessman in him decided. We had to find out what we had, and the sooner the better. If Greeley would agree to do the work, I'd fly to Madison with the icon solidly packed as carry-on luggage, so it would never be out of my protection. Al was able to reach Greeley on the phone while we were there. His friend was so intrigued that he asked if I could bring the icon to Madison as early as Friday, which was only two days away. I felt a little guilty about leaving Angie, but Toby assured me that he'd be a good host while I was gone.

After we'd settled things with Greeley, Al helped us repack the panel. First he wrapped it in a triple layer of paper, using unprinted newspaper sheets, the kind that professional movers use. They won't smudge ink onto a frame, or worse, onto paint. Then he secured the paper with masking tape, which is easy to unpeel. Next he bundled the icon in a double layer of bubble wrap, again secured with masking tape. Finally, he placed it in a hard-backed briefcase, lined with foam rubber. The well-protected painting was now floating in air, within its case. All ready for the trip, including passage through security.

We took the precious cargo home, and I scrambled to get air reservations at short notice. Using saved miles, I scheduled a flight for early the next day, with a return on Saturday. Now all I had to do was pack and explain my three-day absence to Angie.

By the time she came dancing in the door, my packing was done. But I couldn't get a word out. Angie was babbling irrepressibly about how excited Sophie was to hear we'd found the angel Michael and how obviously Michael was hovering around us, always ready to defend us from danger. I finally had to put a hand up and ask for a chance to talk. "So you told Sophie about how we discovered the icon?"

"You're not mad, are you? Oh, gosh. I'm sorry. I don't think Sophie will tell anyone. She told me our work was confidential. But maybe I should call her and ask her to be sure not to talk about it."

"Would you?"

"Oh, Nora. I feel terrible. Sophie was so happy to hear about the discovery. She asked me to invite you to our session on Friday. She wants you to bring the icon along. We can all work our way to a better understanding of what Michael can do for us, or even learn what he may want from us."

"I'm afraid I can't on Friday." I explained my mission to have the icon examined and, possibly, restored in Madison.

"Well," Angie persisted, "as soon as you get back, will you come with me to see Sophie?"

I gave in. "All right. If you think it will help you, I'll come. Sometime next week. Meanwhile, will you feel okay about being here without me till Saturday?"

"Are you kidding? I'll have a blast. This is the greatest place for just knocking around. After seeing Sophie this morning, I spent hours in Graton at the shops, and I took a super walk in the hills there. Sophie says I need to be alone more and explore what makes me really happy."

"She sounds like a psychotherapist. Is that what angel reading is like?"

"I don't know about that, but Sophie helps me hear what my angels are saying. They think I need a change of course."

"You said that a few days back. Are they any clearer now on what sort of change you need?"

"No, and Sophie said the angels won't tell me directly. I need to look for the answer within myself. So she's recommending that I take a long walk every day and see what surfaces. That's what I can do while you're gone. It'll be like being on a silent retreat."

"Good. I'll only be gone a few days. Then we'll see Sophie together."

"Cool beans! Oh, I almost forgot. Sophie gave me these quartz crystal points, one for each of us." Angie rummaged in her bag and brought out two clear crystal cylinders. Each had a point at the end. "You put this on your night table when you go to bed, with the point facing your head. And while you're sleeping, the crystal helps you open your channel to spiritual receptivity. Will you try it?"

"If you want me to," I said. Why not?

Dan called late that evening, after Angie had gone to bed. I had left a message earlier telling him about our discovery, and he wanted to hear the details. He apologized for the late hour, but he also had major news about the investigation.

"Wait a second. Toby's here too. I'll put you on speaker."

"Hi, Dan."

"Hi, Toby. Well, I think we've got our killer. Mikovitch. The Russian."

"Are you sure?"

"As sure as we can be without a trial. We have a positive ID from Interpol, including dental records and a rap sheet as long as your arm. He had links to the Russian mafia and specialized in art theft. We figure he got wind of the icon through the online auction catalogue but too late to bid on it. What tipped him off that it might be valuable, I don't know. Interpol says the Russian mafia's been on a worldwide watch for old triptychs for some time."

"And you're sure he's the one who killed Charlie?" Toby asked again.

"It's a strong case. We tracked down his motel and searched his room. I sent a batch of stuff for lab analysis. The results came back today. They found traces of Charlie's blood on the rubber soles of a pair of shoes that were in the Russian's closet. The shoes had gunk in the treads that matched the debris in the bottom of the rowboat that was used to transport the body. It was him, all right."

"So, circumstantial evidence."

"We've got more than enough for an indictment. He's the guy. I figure it happened like this. The Russian gets Charlie's number from the auctioneer, tells him he'd like to make an offer on his purchase. They meet, my guess being at your gallery. Charlie gets scared, puts him off, hides the icon—now we know where. The Russian comes back some time later. What happens next I'm not sure, but for some reason they end up out on the bay shore, where the murder takes place. Either he forces Charlie to take him there, or Charlie leads him there unknowingly. Why that particular place, I can't tell you."

"Dan," I interrupted, "I think I have some idea what they were doing out there." I filled in what I now knew about the Gaffney house, the set of *The Birds*, and Peter Federenco's connection to the site. "It could be they were on the trail of the remaining icon panels."

"You think those panels are buried out there somewhere?"

"If they still exist." I hadn't said as much before, but yes, that's what I did think. I remembered the dream I had the night before Charlie's funeral, when he appeared to me as a stone head walking across the grass. He couldn't speak but he was trying to tell me something by casting his eyes downward, toward the ground. I kept the dream to myself but said, "At least it's a possibility." I looked at Toby, and he nodded in agreement.

"Okay, let's work on that assumption," said Dan. "It may explain the crime scene. Nothing else does. But as I said before, I still don't think the murder was premeditated. First of all, the Russian didn't find what he was after. Second, it wasn't a smart place to kill someone. Maybe Charlie bolted, maybe he grabbed for the knife—we can't know—but there was a struggle and the Russian stabbed him. Then he panicked."

"That's when he saw the rowboat tied up nearby and decided to take Charlie out to the sailboat," Toby added.

"That's how I see it. Then Mikovitch searches Charlie's apartment, the gallery, and then your house, but each time he comes up empty. So he puts you under surveillance, follows you, and you know the rest. End of story."

"So it's over," I said.

"It looks that way. We're still investigating. My chief question is whether the Russian was working alone. Now fill me in on how you discovered the icon."

Toby walked Dan through the process.

"Hold on a minute," Dan said. "You're saying that Tom Keogh demanded the table back? Is there any chance he could have known that Charlie hid the icon in the leaf tray?"

"No way that I can think of," Toby said after a pause. That idea hadn't occurred to us.

"Besides, I thought you told us you had the killer," I added. "I hope you still don't think Tom was involved."

"Just asking. I'll talk to Keogh again, anyhow. You were saying that your professor thinks this icon could be worth a bundle?"

"Potentially. I'm planning to take it out of town to have it examined," I explained. "I guess I should have cleared that with you first. Would that be okay?"

"For you to take it out of town? I don't see why not. It never was stolen property in the first place, since Charlie hid it, and now it seems it belongs to you. I think Toby said he had the bill of sale."

"That's right," said Toby.

"Well, good luck then. Let me know how you make out."

We chatted with Dan for a little while longer, then said goodbye. We sat quietly for a few moments. Toby let out a deep sigh.

"What's wrong? Isn't that good news? Dan says the guy who was chasing us was the killer, and now he's dead."

Toby looked dejected, not relieved. "I thought I'd feel closure when the case was solved. I don't."

"You were even there."

"You mean the crash? That's not how I pictured it would end. I wanted justice, not revenge. I wanted a confession or at least a trial and sentencing. It may be over, but it doesn't feel like it."

"I think you need some serious cheering up."

"I guess I do. What have you got in mind?"

Now that Dan thought the murder solved, I felt a weight lifting. I felt freer, even playful. In fact, I felt more relaxed than I'd been since the day Charlie's body was found. Though Toby's better than I am at the impression game, I decided to give it a shot. I rolled my eyes, patted my hair, and stuck out my hip in a saucy Mae West flounce. "Why don't you come up and see me some time?" I purred.

That perked Toby up. He rallied and returned my invitation in his best W. C. Fields drawl. "I shall be there in a trice, my little pigeon. My little chickadee."

I laughed and started down the hall. He followed.

"What's that?" Toby asked a few minutes later as we settled under the covers.

"Oh, that. It's a crystal Angie gave me. You point it at your head at night. It's supposed to heighten your spiritual sensitivity."

"Is that so?" said Toby. "And what happens if you point it at—"

He never finished the sentence because I bashed him with a pillow.

11

MARCH IN MADISON can still be the middle of winter. That was clear from the airplane window: carpets of snow and two frozen lakes framing the isthmus with its gleaming Capitol. But the sky was the bright blue of summer at the sea.

Deceptive. I almost fainted from cold as I waited outside the terminal for my taxi. California-style layers were definitely not adequate for Wisconsin-style cold. But I kept up good spirits, excited to be bringing the icon for expert analysis. It didn't take me long to get the precious cargo to the Campus Inn. My appointment with George Greeley was set for the next morning at his home on the east side of town. That gave me an afternoon and evening for myself. Resisting the temptation to spend the afternoon in my toasty room, I gently placed the briefcase in the closet and proceeded on foot to the university art museum, the Chazen.

The plowed streets and the Library Mall, piled with snow, were thick with students marching swiftly by. The scene reminded me of Berkeley, in spite of the weather. There the kids would be in cut-offs and flip-flops; here they were muffled under hoods and parkas, long scarves trailing behind them. Still, the two schools were about the same size. By contrast, Sonoma College, where I teach, is small and quiet. I wondered briefly what my career would have been like if I'd landed a job at a big university like this one. A higher salary? A lighter teaching load, with more time for research? Perhaps. But I like teaching small classes where I can get to know my students, and I like the feeling of community that comes along with a small campus. Besides, Toby hates winter. "It's all right for the Eskimos," he says, "but then, they don't mind eating blubber, either." Nothing could induce him to leave California, and I guess by now I feel the same way.

A museum like the Chazen would be a nice teaching aid, though. It's surprisingly complete for a campus collection. Two linked modern buildings house a sampling of sculptures, paintings, and prints from the ancient Greeks to the present. I played my usual game of "What would you take home?" and couldn't decide between two paintings in my own field. The first was a glowing moonlight coastal scene by the Norwegian artist Johan Christian Dahl. The other was a sweet little landscape by a minor American painter named Henry Pember Smith, whose work has always appealed to me. It would be great to walk students over here fresh from class to stand in front of delightful works like these.

A special exhibition of Russian icons was, however, my destination. The university owns a small collection, and it isn't often on view. In a space for temporary exhibitions off the main gallery, I found twenty or so icons in typical shapes and subjects, but almost all painted in the nineteenth century to mimic an earlier style. Several older examples were impressive, but more than a few, at least to me, lacked life. Then I came upon a bright little triptych picturing various scenes from the life of a lesser-known saint, and it had the charm of a naïve painting. It was beautiful in its own way but nothing rivaling the delicacy of Rublev's work. According to Al Miller, a great icon radiates spiritual energy. And you don't get that just by layering on the gold paint. I left the room eager to know whether underneath our Michael icon was a work of uncommon power.

A visit to the museum shop was a must, even though closing time was approaching. In a whirlwind, I picked up my swag: earrings for Angie with Frida Kahlo's self-portrait on them, a reproduction of a Roman glass necklace for our mom's upcoming birthday, and for my desk a miniature Russian icon triptych, just over an inch tall. Something faux but appealing for each of the Barnes women. The security guard showed me out into the crystal cold.

With ice crackling underfoot, I joined the parade of students heading out to the bars of State Street. If I had forgotten that it was St. Patrick's Day, the signs advertising green beer and St. Paddy's specials would have set me straight. The cold hustled me into the first appealing restaurant, the Brat House. There I enacted every Wisconsin culinary cliché, devouring a German-style bratwurst slathered in mustard and sauerkraut and washing it down with a locally brewed pilsner. I sampled, but could not finish, the block of caraway-muenster cheese that arrived as an accompaniment to the brat. In Wisconsin, you eat hearty.

By the time I left the Brat House, it was almost dark and the restaurant had become a packed bar scene. I decided to go back to the hotel and check on the booty in Al's briefcase. Though the hotel was only a few minutes' walk away, I found myself anxious by the time I got to the room. I wanted to make sure that the briefcase was still locked and that it contained our icon. All was as it should be.

A phone call to Toby calmed my nerves. He had just reached home after a long day at the shop. I described my visit to the Chazen, and he told me about his day. "No customers. Just as well. I had an idea this morning. Since Charlie hid the icon in one of his pieces of furniture, my guess is that he hid the storyboards as well. I think they're still in the shop. So I spent the afternoon knocking for hollow spots in his other pieces and looking at the backs of things and underneath, all over. Nothing so far, but I'll keep at it. I've got a feeling they must be here. Speaking of which, Tom Keogh called again. He's awfully eager to get his hands on Charlie's stuff. I told him I was thinking about it just to put him off a bit longer while I keep searching."

"Do you know if Dan talked to him about the table?"

"He did. So Tom knows about the icon."

"Do you think he knew about it before?"

"He denied it. But of course, he would, wouldn't he? I just don't know. It's hard to say."

"Well, keep looking for those storyboards. They could be important. I'm seeing George Greeley tomorrow, so maybe by evening we'll have news for each other." After some racy patter about missing me and the power of crystals, I asked him if Angie was there to say hello.

"Hi, Nora. I wanted to tell you Sophie had another insight today while we were calling on the angel Michael to help you on your trip. Sophie says she feels strongly that there are other angels involved with you, and you need to be alert for them."

"Okay, I'm on high alert. But I thought these sessions were about your future, not mine."

"Too proud to accept advice from your little sister?"

"Nope. I promise to keep all channels open."

And so I did. After a little reading, giving time for the beer and brats to settle, I slowly drifted off to sleep with images of painted angels floating before my eyes.

Rutledge Street, just a mile east of the Capitol and downtown Madison, reminded me of my grandparents' working-class neighborhood in Gloucester. The antiquated wooden houses were not quite Victorian, not quite bungalow, but a slapdash mix invented in the 1920s to house workers from the nearby Oscar Mayer meatpacking plant. This I learned from the loquacious taxi driver, who was half-proud and half-sheepish about being in his eighth year of a doctoral program in urban history. Madison, I've been told, has the highest concentration of postgraduate taxi drivers of any city on the planet.

George Greeley's was the tallest home on the block and therefore easy to spot. Greeley himself opened the door before I reached the top snow-covered step of his wooden porch. The packed snow crunched underfoot. Immediately, he reached out with both hands to cushion the progress of my briefcase over the threshold. Here was an expert totally focused on his professional task. He barely looked at me as he took the weight of the case and transferred it to a cushioned chair. Then he turned to greet me.

"You can call me George," he said, offering a hand to shake. The gesture, like his whole body, was firm and graceful. Greeley was as lean as a dancer, or, more likely here, a runner or biker. Perhaps because of that, he looked much younger than his friend Al. Gray hair cut close to the skull contributed to the lithe look. "Let's get to work right away," he suggested. "We'll have to go upstairs." He picked up the briefcase from its bottom and led me briskly up a narrow staircase to the second floor.

"I have my studio up here," he explained. "The light is best on the second floor, and there's running water in my workroom." He led me down a hall into a small room with windows on two sides, a double sink, and deep cabinets above and below spacious counters. "During World War II, the house was converted into a duplex, and this was used as the kitchen for the upstairs apartment. I'm lucky the owner never took out the plumbing." He placed the icon on a high workbench, positioned where the stove must have been in years past. We sat down on two kitchen stools.

"So you can do all your consulting and restoration work from home?"

"Yes, this is my studio. After my wife left, I turned her study, across the hall, into my library and office. So I'm all set." That could have been a neutral statement, but he gritted his teeth when he mentioned his wife, and he sounded less than happy.

"We should talk about your fee before we start, don't you think? Al said you'd be reasonable, but I really don't know what that means."

"Sure. It will be six hundred dollars for today's consultation, if it takes as long as I think it will, that is, the rest of the day. After that, the cost of restoration will depend on what we find. If we're only cleaning the current painting, the total could run you under a thousand, even if I have to do some reconstruction and repainting in the corner. Al tells me that it's got some damage."

"Yes. But what if what we suspect is true? What if there's an older painting underneath and your job is to uncover and restore that?"

Greeley's smile was condescending. "If we find what Al told me could be under here, you won't be worried about the fee, my dear. Let's cross that bridge if we come to it." Suddenly I felt the barrier of decades of professional experience that separated us. I wasn't only Greeley's customer. I was his student, too, as I was Al's. I let the "my dear" pass without challenge.

"Did you bring the key? The briefcase is locked."

I quickly produced the key and moved to insert it, but Greeley put out his hand. "Allow me, please. I was the one who taught Al how to wrap a painting, and I want to do him the courtesy of unwrapping it properly."

Seeing that I was taken aback, he explained, "Everyone's careful when doing the wrapping. Most damage to artwork is done at the unwrapping stage. People get careless because of excitement, greed. Just like at Christmas. It's human nature." He gently lifted the wrapped icon from the case and placed it on a soft towel on his workbench. "Did you have any trouble with it on the plane?"

"No. I went through security without a hitch and kept the briefcase under the seat in front of me."

"Better than in the overhead bin. When did you get in?"

"Yesterday. I had time to visit the Chazen, and I saw their icon exhibit. I've been wondering how a collection like that ended up at a university museum. It seems unusual."

"That's the Davies collection. He was a university alumnus and the U.S. ambassador to Russia just before World War II. Later wrote a book about his time there called *Mission to Moscow*. Ever hear of it?"

I had but hadn't read it.

"It turns out Davies had a mission of his own, which was to buy up all the Russian treasures he could lay his hands on. His pal Stalin arranged some sweetheart deals for him. This was during the time of the purges, which, by the way, he never protested. Maybe that was just a coincidence, but I don't think so. Anyhow, Davies made quite a haul. Later he donated the icons to the university because he was buddies with the governor and with some other bigwig donors. You know how these things work; each one scratches the other's back."

I was unsettled by Greeley's resentful tone. All the while, his slender, delicate fingers flew over the package on his workbench, efficiently unwrapping its protective layers until the icon was exposed. He took a quick, dismissive glimpse at the angel Michael, then flipped the panel over, as Al had done. He studied it. "Al was right," he said. "This panel is much older than the painting on it." He turned the icon face up again and examined the damaged corner, probing the gouged wood with a fingertip.

"Can it be repaired?"

"That won't be a problem. In this case I can rebuild the surface and retouch to match the gilding, if that's what you want. But we're after bigger game than that, aren't we?"

"I hope so. That's what Al thinks."

"Right. I'll start with some photos. That way you'll have a complete photographic record of the process." He picked up the icon and placed it on an easel facing the window. "Natural light is best." Then he brought over a digital camera on a tripod and positioned it between the window and the easel. He took a few shots, checked the display on the back of the camera, and made a satisfied sound.

He returned the icon to his workbench and began laying out his tools and materials. "The first thing we're going to do," he said as he repositioned an extension lamp clamped to the bench, "is remove the darkened drying oil and the top layer of pigment. And while I'm doing that, you're going to tell me the story of the panel, everything you know, just as if Al hadn't briefed me."

Greeley had already prepared his solutions. While he set about the preliminary cleaning, I gave him the broad outline of what I knew so far, beginning with Charlie's murder, my interviews with the auctioneer at Morgan's and with Rose Cassini, our pursuit by a Russian gangster, our discovery of the icon hidden in a table, how we damaged it, and finally Al's account of the legend of the Rublev triptych.

"That's quite a tale," said Greeley. "And what about the other two panels? Do you have any idea where they are?"

"Not really," I had to admit. "But I'm following a lead."

"Then I wish you luck."

He said nothing more but concentrated on his work. Greeley followed the basic procedure Al had demonstrated to us in Berkeley, but he was quicker and more adept at his tasks. He began with balls of sterile cotton on toothpicks (homemade Q-tips), dipped in a light-colored organic oil, which he swabbed across the surface of the icon using circular motions that quickly brought up black gook. Then came the process of paint removal, using a small swatch of absorbent cloth soaked in a darker solvent. The swatch was positioned with tweezers, pressed under a weight, and lifted after a few minutes, followed by additional swipes with clean cotton, until a circle of previously unexposed color stood out from its surroundings like an area lit by a spotlight on a dark stage. He had chosen a small section of Michael's cloak to begin with. What had been dull reddish pigment now was rich ocher.

Without doubt, he said, there was an older version of Michael beneath this one, probably dating from the eighteenth century. As I watched in fascination, he repeated his procedures until the entire surface of the older painting was exposed. "Well," he said, stepping back from his work, "what do you say? Shall I keep going?" Removing the outer layers of darkened oil and pigment had taken about an hour. What was revealed at this stage was an almost identical version of the archangel Michael, but one brighter by far than the surface image. It was evident that the artist who had repainted the angel in the nineteenth century had dutifully copied the outlines and colors used by the previous artist. By then the older image probably had been barely discernible.

"Yes, keep going," I said after a moment's hesitation. I was fighting the urge to call Toby, to share responsibility for this crucial decision.

But he had warned me ahead of time that calling him would be bootless. I was the one on the spot, and it was up to me to make the decisions.

"Good, because I don't think this is the original image, either," said Greeley. "What you have at this point is an unremarkable eighteenth-century painting compared to an unremarkable nineteenth-century painting that covered it, but in terms of value, it isn't worth that much more. I'll do another small test area. If there's a painting underneath, I'll continue, and if there isn't, I can retouch the test area so you won't notice it. How's that sound?"

"Perfect," I said. "Let's do it."

"I'll get a few more photographs first." Greeley placed the icon on the easel again and took several shots. Back at his workbench, he began the cleaning process all over again, choosing a small area toward the top of the panel above the angel's head. First he dissolved and wiped away a portion of the gilded sky, disclosing another layer of darkened varnish under it, to which he reapplied his solvent, glass press, and weight. After another interval, he lifted the soaked flannel cloth, bringing up black smears, and then he swabbed the area clean again with fresh cotton balls. He peered at the treated area, held it up at a slanted angle closer to the light, and said, "That's interesting. There's an inscription under the varnish, but the script is awkward, as if copied by someone unsure of the letters."

"Can you read it?" I ask.

"Yes, I read Russian and I know the old alphabet. The letters are Church Slavonic. But I'll have to enlarge the test area." I nodded, and he proceeded. The work took only a few minutes. "Yes, just as I thought, it says, 'Archangel Michael.' That's not a surprise, but there may be something else."

Greeley went over to a cabinet and brought back a small black microscope. It wasn't anything fancy—it reminded me of the instrument they had us work with in my college biology lab. He delicately balanced the icon on the specimen tray, positioned it, adjusted the focus, and peered into the eyepiece. "There may be traces of another inscription underneath. If the patch I've just exposed is from the seventeenth century, that means there's an even older painting under that. Now, that would be something, wouldn't it?

"I guess it would," I said, my pulse quickening.

"But I can't rush it. This isn't about saving time, it's about saving art."

"Absolutely."

"I need to complete the cleaning of this layer before doing anything else."

"You mean, completely dissolve the painting you've just exposed?"

"I'm afraid so."

"And you're sure there's another painting there?"

"I'd bet on it."

"The question is whether I should bet on it."

"It's your call, but you already know that this isn't the first layer of paint."

"That's true," I agreed. "All right, go ahead."

This time the process took longer. Greeley needed to prepare a more concentrated solution to remove the pigment; the older the painted surface, the stronger the solvent needed to be. The intervals between applications took longer, too. And he needed to use a scalpel to delicately clean away sticky and resistant remnants of loose pigment after the solvent had done its work.

When he was finished, a subtly painted, more commanding figure of the archangel Michael looked out at us below an inscription in Cyrillic letters. The angel's facial features and pinions were more skillfully painted than they had been in later iterations. The colors were denser, and new details emerged, as well. The angel's robe was fastened by a wide belt painted blue and fixed by a golden clasp. His feet bore elaborate sandals, and his upraised sword had a jeweled hilt.

"Mid to late 1600s is my guess," Greeley observed. "A nice example from that period. Worth something, too, but even so, still not what you're after. What now?"

I felt like a roulette player faced with the choice of leaving her chips on the table or walking away with sure but modest winnings. This version of Michael, compared to the others, seemed worth keeping.

"What now?" Greeley repeated, as he photographed the latest result of his work. I hadn't responded, unsure of what to do. "I understand," he continued as I hesitated. "Too many decisions, too fast. Anyhow, it's time to take a break. In fact," he said, checking his watch, "it's past time for lunch. What would you say to a grilled cheese sandwich and a bowl of soup? You can think it over while we're eating."

That sounded great.

We sat at a rickety table in Greeley's old-fashioned kitchen, eating our sandwiches and making conversation, which served to distract me from my upcoming decision. Winter light slanted through the windowpanes, reflected from the bright snow outside. The furnace groaned from the basement, and I caught a faint whiff of oil from the doorway leading to the cellar stairs. I noticed the linoleum floor was peeling. But the soup was tasty: Campbell's Tomato, my favorite.

We chatted, casually at first, about our respective workplaces, shop talk mostly. He wanted to compare teaching loads, benefits, and so on. But as we went on, Greeley began to seethe. He was furious at Scott Walker, the newly elected governor of Wisconsin, who was trying to ram a bill through the state legislature ending collective bargaining for public employees. The protests at Madison's Capitol Square had made national news, and earlier in the day I had noticed people with signs at the far end of State Street. Even to an outside observer like me who knew nothing about Wisconsin politics, the actions of the governor looked heavy handed.

But for Greeley the issue was bitterly personal. Madison Area Technical College, where he taught, belonged to a state teachers' union. "For the first time in my life I'm making a decent salary, and now this son of a bitch is going to cut our compensation package, take away our benefits, and pile on more work, and we won't be able to do a damn thing about it. And that's just the beginning!" He actually pounded the table, rattling the plates. "Next he's going to privatize the retirement system, which I finally got vested in. It's the best one in the country—fully funded, good benefits, pension guaranteed by the state. If he has his way, that'll be gone too, just like that." He snapped his fingers.

"Why would he want to do that if the system is fully funded?" I asked.

"Because he's got big donors in the financial and investment sector. Think of the commissions they'll make if the system goes to private retirement accounts. Plus the payouts will never match the returns that the state system provides now. Which means the taxpayers will be asked to cover the difference. Which they won't do. Which means the whole system will eventually collapse. And that will be fine with him, since he doesn't believe in decent benefits for state workers in the first place. I was counting on retiring in a couple of years. Now . . ."

His voice trailed off and he stared at his empty bowl for a moment. "Al's at the top of the heap," he went on. "Berkeley. Big salary. Prestige. Cushy retirement package. But me?" He waved at the refrigerator. It and all the other appliances in the kitchen looked like they dated from the fifties. "I was living from hand to mouth until I got this job. And even now, it's tough making ends meet. I have a mortgage that's under water . . ." He made a dismissive gesture of disgust with his hand.

I didn't know what to say, so I just mumbled, "I'm sorry."

He shrugged. "There's no point my laying this on you. Forget it. Sorry I brought the whole thing up. Well, what about the icon? Have you decided?"

"Yes. We keep going." I hadn't come all the way to Madison to stop halfway.

He sprang to his feet. "Let's get back to work."

By now each step of the process was familiar. The result of the latest cleaning, however, was dramatic. Greeley was right. Underneath the previous image, there was an older inscription that read "Archangel Michael," in lettering more elegant than the overpainting. This version of Michael was more gracefully painted and posed differently. Now Michael was in profile, facing left, whereas in the other versions, he faced the viewer. Here he gripped the hilt of his sword with both hands, with the blade resting on his shoulder, as if poised to strike. His wings, unfurled behind him, were impressive, and the colors were brighter than any we'd seen so far. This painting was older and much finer than the previous painting, which I'd been hesitant to destroy. But now that I was determined to press on, it was Greeley who was cautious.

"Maybe it's time to stop. The style and calligraphy date from the Renaissance. At this point I can't say if the panel is any older than the painting."

"But it's not Rublev. Couldn't there still be another painting beneath it?"

"Possibly. But taking off more paint could be risky."

I recalled Al Miller's warning of overdoing a cleaning and ending up not with a work of art but with a blank layer of gesso, the white ground used to prepare the wood for painting. That was a stomach-churning prospect. "Couldn't you do another small test area like the last time?"

"I could, but remember, original paint that's removed can't be restored. It can be retouched, but that isn't the same thing."

"I understand. I'd like you to try."

"It's your call. I'll start near the damaged corner then, where I'll have to do some retouching anyway."

"Wait. Let me take a picture of this one on my cell phone," I said. Just in case, I thought. Greeley stepped aside obligingly and then resumed his work. I felt the tension mounting as the restorer methodically swabbed a small area with cotton wool and applied his solvent, waited, lifted the soaked piece of cloth with tweezers, and dabbed again with clean cotton wool. The softened-up paint came off as expected on the cotton, but this time, instead of dark varnish underneath, or even another layer of paint, there was nothing but a plain white surface. Gesso!

"Let's not panic," he said quietly. "It's possible the gesso was exposed when you gouged the icon and the damage caused some paint loss in the area. The gouge is deep enough. I'll try a different spot."

This time Greeley chose a test area at the bottom of the panel. The result was the same. He tried a third time in the center, wiping away—forever—a small patch of the archangel's robe. Everywhere he applied the solvent, paint gave way to empty white spaces: dreadful spaces, accusing spaces. I felt a pain at my waistline, the tug of despair.

"There's one last thing I can try," Greeley said. "It's a long shot, but at this point you have nothing to lose." He placed the icon on the tray of the microscope again and focused on the damaged corner. "I see tiny traces of pigment ground into the gesso where it meets the wood, which could mean a painted surface." He placed the icon back on its towel on the bench and took up his scalpel. "I'm going to chip off some gesso." He slanted the scalpel sideways at a low angle and inserted it into the gesso that had been exposed near the damaged corner. "Hand me that hammer, please." He pointed to a small hammer that was out of his reach. I did as I was told. He gave a light tap on the scalpel and knocked away a tiny chunk of brittle gesso.

There was gilding underneath.

My heart took a leap. "Is there another painting?"

"I think so. And if there is, it would square with the legend. Usually an icon was repainted only when it darkened naturally over time and you could barely see the image. But if you wanted to cover up a painting to hide it, one way would be to add a new coat of gesso and then paint something different on it."

I gulped. "Can you remove the gesso without damaging what's under it?"

"I can, using my secret solution."

I gave him a questioning look.

"Water. Normally old gesso was made of chalk or calcium carbonate mixed with water and rabbit-skin glue. Warm water will dissolve the glue, but it's got to be done slowly."

Greeley was as good as his word. What followed was a painstaking process that began with the complete removal of the last Michael painting until nothing remained but a smooth, blank, ivory-colored surface. Then he set to work with a fresh supply of raw sterile cotton balls on toothpicks. Each was dipped in warm water, then applied to the gesso using a rhythmic circular motion, with light pressure. When the cotton was saturated, it would be replaced. The work went in stages. He would stop periodically to check his progress using the microscope. He had decided to concentrate on the top of the panel, working his way down.

Outside, the afternoon light waned. Greeley signaled me to move so that I didn't block light from the window. I pulled my stool into a corner of the room and sat, stifling the impulse to peer over his shoulder as he worked. Finally he said, "Come look."

Just the top portion of the new painting was revealed. It was magnificent. Against a muted gold background, the serenely beautiful head of a graceful feminine figure inclined downward and toward the left. A halo encircled her thick, braided hair, and a blue robe draped her shoulders—a blue so vibrant that it could have been painted only with lapis lazuli. The angel's face was infinitely expressive, tragic. Her downcast eyes directed the viewer's gaze toward what I knew would be a chalice on a table—but of course there was no chalice visible, nor table, nor any other detail, for no other part of the painting had been exposed. Nevertheless, I knew the object of her gaze, because I recognized her as one of the three angels from Andrei Rublev's great *Old Testament Trinity*. My mind's eye filled in the rest. The chalice, the table, and the majestic angel seated next to her belonged to another painting, still missing: the central panel of the triptych.

"She's . . ." I searched for the right word.

"Sublime," said Greeley. His eyes were shining.

12

TOBY SHOULD HAVE BEEN THERE. He deserved to share my joy at seeing the long-lost image emerge from under the crust of ancient gesso. I snapped a dozen shots for him, using my cell-phone camera. Now the question was how long we would have to wait to view the fully cleaned panel. I put that to Greeley.

"After I finish the cleaning, the corner will have to be rebuilt and retouched. If things go smoothly, the icon could be ready to transport in about a week. It may take longer if there's additional restoration to consider. In any case, if you want to go home as planned tomorrow, I can give you regular progress reports. Do you use Skype?"

I said I did. "Good. Then you can watch the work as I go along."

That sounded like a reasonable plan. I didn't want to spend a week or more away from home, especially when I had a houseguest. "I'll have to come back to Madison to pick it up. I wouldn't want to rely on a shipping service."

"Of course you wouldn't," he snapped back. "And neither would I. Or you can take it with you in its present state and have someone else complete the work, if you'd prefer. That's up to you."

Now he was insulted. Al had warned that Greeley could be testy. I didn't want to alienate either of these allies, so I hastened to set things right. I expressed my admiration for his skill and my gratitude for his taking on the project at short notice. Al had the highest confidence in Greeley's expertise, and everything I had seen so far confirmed Al's judgment.

Mollified, Greeley wrote out a receipt for the painting and proceeded to clean and put away his materials, as he gave me directions for taking the bus back to my campus hotel. He insisted that Madison's bus system was a model for the nation, and there was no reason to call a taxi, now that I wouldn't be carrying a precious work of art.

As I waited at the stop at the end of Greeley's block, I wished for a pair of long johns and a down coat. Freezing there, I berated myself for letting Greeley's prickliness intimidate me into a decision I wouldn't have made on my own. Right then, I would have given my wallet's entire contents for the warmth of a taxi and a chat with another PhD candidate.

The bus came quickly enough, though, and it gave me a pretty tour of the town at evening's fall. Icy sidewalks were being trampled by boots heading home from school or work. White lights decorated the trees around the Capitol Square, intensifying the midwinter feeling. Small groups of protestors still clustered around the Capitol, stamping their feet to keep warm. When we turned onto State Street, the crowds surprised me, until I remembered that it was Friday night, the start of the weekend. I'd better find a restaurant and grab a seat before they were all taken. That's how I wandered into Humal Chuli, which I now declare to be the best Nepalese restaurant on either coast. I ended the meal feeling supremely pleased with Madison and the choices I had made there.

Still ahead was the happy chore of notifying Toby and Al of my discovery. Toby of course was jubilant, exulting over the photos I'd sent to his cell phone. "I wonder what a third of a famous triptych could be worth? Plenty, I bet. We could be rich!"

"Don't go overboard," I laughed. "We'll have to see about that. The icon still needs to be authenticated."

"Sure, I know that, but just think!"

Al was so thrilled at the news, you would think he'd just become a grandfather. He'd already received an e-mail from George with photos attached documenting the cleaning process. Al congratulated me on having the courage to go the distance. "What a crime it would have been to leave a work of genius undiscovered."

"Thanks," I said, but I was thinking what a crime it would have been to erase a seventeenth-century painting and find nothing underneath.

At home Toby and Angie gave me a hero's welcome. No Russian caviar, but Russian River champagne and a spread prepared by Angie with fresh crab she'd bought right off the boat moored down the block from our house. The bubbly loosened my tongue. In reporting the various stages of the icon's cleaning, I discovered just how anxious I had been, step by step. Fatigue and relief hit me at the same time. I was exhausted, and by early evening I was ready for bed.

On Sunday morning, Angie and I messed up the kitchen trying to make our Irish grandmother's typical breakfast—crisp bacon, fried eggs, and puppy toes (quarter-size dabs of biscuit dough, cooked in bacon fat in a covered frying pan). When Toby didn't wake up in time, we ate everything up, laughing greedily. As penance, when we heard Toby stirring, we started all over again, ostensibly to get his opinion of Irish American breakfasts, but actually to get another helping of puppy toes.

Since Charlie's death, Toby had missed the freedom of being able to staff the shop with a partner. He'd gotten used to not showing up till noon and staying later than Charlie, till six or the last sign of patronage. Lately, he'd adopted new open hours for the shop, noon to sundown. He might lose some morning customers, but he'd gain others by being the last business in the complex to close down. Today he could hardly wait to get there to resume his search for the storyboards. Maybe they'd lead us to another missing panel. He was hoping to double our luck.

As our main activity for the day, Angie and I had planned an afternoon of hiking. I never tire of walking Bodega Head, but after nearly slipping off the cliff one windy, wet morning, I've decided not to do it alone. The day was sunny and warm, and I'm protective enough of Angie that I kept us both from that dangerous last foot of perimeter. Angie exclaimed over the ice plants that bordered our route. These low-lying succulents bear pink daisy-like flowers, and they cluster tightly together, forming a cheerful edging for the perilous pathway. At the height of the head, we stopped to take in fabulous views of the bay and the harbor. Coming back down to the car park, we joined a dozen whale-watchers for a half hour and were rewarded by a sighting of several pods pushing north toward their summer waters. Then, for real exercise, we walked away from the head, over the trails between sand dunes to Salmon Creek Beach.

Along the way there and back, Angie brought me up to speed on her angel therapy. She'd seen Sophie on Friday, and they had concluded I'd be essential to their Monday session. Angie reminded me of my promise. "I want you there tomorrow. There's something important I want to discuss, but with Sophie there to help me."

"This is starting to sound serious. Is everything all right? You're not sick, are you?"

Angie laughed, but it was a short, scratchy laugh. "No, it's nothing like that. But it is sort of serious."

"And you can't tell me now?"

"If you'll come with me tomorrow, I'd rather wait till then. Will you do it?"

"Yes, of course. If it's serious to you, I care about it."

"Then let's go home and make spaghetti. I'm seriously starved."

I'd been curious about Sophie from the beginning, and I decided to look forward to meeting her.

The Graton Bakery was closed Mondays so that Sophie Redmond could have one lie-in a week. But she didn't spend the whole day resting. Monday was her busiest day for angel readings.

The steep staircase to the second floor lay to the right of the bakery entrance. At the top landing, Angie rang the buzzer and opened the unlocked door, ushering us into a living room that doubled as a waiting room. Angie cued me to sit with her on the couch that faced the window, so that the client ahead of us wouldn't have to meet us on the way out. Sure enough, within moments, we heard two women's soft voices and the sound of one escorting the other to the door. In a moment, Sophie was standing before us, offering her hand in greeting. I rose to take it.

With all the talk about angels, I'd assumed that Sophie would look ethereal—tall, blond, and willowy. Instead, she was a tiny woman, no more than five foot one, and squat. Her short, curly hair was mostly gray. But her handshake was warm and firm, and she did have a beatific gaze—head tilted up, blue eyes inquiring amiably, a generous smile offering welcome. It was difficult to guess her age. I understood why Angie had spoken of her protectively. This woman radiated innocence. You'd never want to see that aura broken.

"Thank you so much for coming, Nora," Sophie huskily whispered. "It means so much to your sister." She turned her benevolent smile on Angie. And she placed her right hand on Angie's cheek and held it there, like a mother appreciating her child's perfect face. Angie accepted the gesture without embarrassment.

We followed Sophie into her consulting room, which was obviously a repurposed bedroom. Aside from bookshelves, the only furniture was a small round table surrounded by four dining chairs. The focus of the room was a yard-square poster of Botticelli's Annunciation, with its resplendent Angel Gabriel and its sweetly receptive Mary.

"It's about good news," Sophie said happily, in response to my glance. "And that's what we're here to discuss with you, today, Nora." She straightened the folds of her loose blue dress as she sat down. "By the way, have you been using the crystal Angie gave you?"

"Um, yes, I have," I said. But I didn't say what for.

"Good. People say it prepares them to be receptive."

What was coming? I ventured a smile.

"And I only mean by that, receptive to significant conversation, not just superficial talk."

As I used to do in Catholic school, I folded my hands on the tabletop and adopted a pleasant mien with eyebrows raised expectantly. That word actually came to mind, and then it morphed to "expecting," and my heart clutched. I might have gasped. The women looked at me, puzzled.

"Angie, you're not pregnant?" I asked, with a choke in my voice, in spite of myself.

"No, no, nothing like that," Angie assured me.

"Sorry."

Sophie cut in. "You need a little background first. Angela has been struggling with her life's purpose."

Angela? Nobody had called Angie that since the day she was baptized in my arms.

"Yes, she told me." I could hear myself sounding defensive, as if Sophie had accused me of not really knowing my own sister.

"But, Nora," Angie half-pleaded, "you don't really get it."

That stung a little. I waited for her to continue.

"You've always known what you wanted to do. You were teaching art to me when I was still in diapers. You don't know what it feels like to be working at something that just feels wrong."

"You mean cutting hair?"

"It's not the cutting hair. I like cutting hair and coloring it and everything. Barb is the best boss in the world, and Carol cracks me up. But I feel unsatisfied. I feel there are other things I could be doing that would make me feel better about myself at the end of the day."

"So you want to go to school for something else?"

"No, and I know what you're thinking. I just spent Grandpa's trust money on a season's training at a top salon in London. Big waste."

"Do you really think so?" asked Sophie.

Angie looked determined. "Actually, no. It showed me I didn't fit in there, not because it was the best in the business and I'm not, but because it's not the business I belong in. However good at it I may be."

"And you are good," I said. "So what's next?"

"That's the part I want your blessing for," Angie admitted softly. Then she murmured, shaking her head, "Mom and Dad are going to have a cow."

"They will if you don't tell them more quickly than you're telling me! What is it you want to do?"

"Go into the convent."

"Jesus, Mary, and Joseph!" That was the first time I'd actually said that in twenty years.

"Yeah, that's what Grammy Molly's going to say, for sure." Angie sighed.

I was flabbergasted. "But nobody does that anymore."

"Not many. But some. Anyhow, this would be a trial. I would join as what they call a 'sojourner,' for a year. Then we'd consider whether I want to take vows."

"Wow, Angie," I said. "Wow. That's a lot to take in."

"Of course it is. That's why now would be a good time to listen to your angels," Sophie prompted, with calm assurance. "Nora, would you be willing to help your sister go through an exercise for that purpose?"

Do with me what you will. For the moment I was speechless.

Sophie reached across the table toward my clasped hands. She gently opened them into a cup-like receptacle. Then she reached over to Angie, who offered her right hand, from which Sophie removed a silver ring. Angie knew the routine, from here. She turned to me and said, "Nora, please accept my ring as a sign that as we call on my angels, we are one. You may speak for me, and I may speak for you. Will you accept my ring as a sign of our unity?"

When I said yes, Sophie dropped the ring into my hands, and I instinctively closed one hand over the other, as if to warm it.

"Angela doesn't need protection, Nora. She needs openness. So please open your hands, and let Angela's ring rest in your left hand." Sophie's firm but gentle voice induced me to comply.

With her eyes closed, Angie began her invocation. "Archangel Michael, please use your powers to help me and my sister, Nora, discover my life's purpose."

That seemed to me a tall order, so I tried to be more practical when it was my turn to contact the beyond. "Um, Angel Michael, please help us to discover the kind of work that will bring happiness to my sister, Angie."

"We will wait with open minds and hearts," Sophie intoned.

We were supposed to keep our eyes shut during the meditation. I have to admit, I cheated and looked at my watch after what seemed a long time. My mind had been dancing about between visions of Angie cutting hair in a nun's habit, Angie teaching a modeling class, and Angie inventorying a rack of expensive-looking wool suits. I also tried calling to mind the faces of Angie's old boyfriends, but that inventory was way too extensive.

Trying to get back on task, I focused my mind on the image of Michael from Charlie's icon, an image that was now erased. I was hoping that Michael, if he was tuning in, wouldn't take offense. Gradually, the image in my mind changed into a picture of Angie seated, her blond hair shimmering around her head like a halo, with the angel Michael standing behind her, one hand on her shoulder, the other on his sword. Whoa! Was that my imagination playing tricks?

I was so startled that my eyes popped open. There was Angie, just as in my "vision," sitting up straight in her chair, but of course with no angel behind her. I turned to Sophie, who shook her head slightly as if to say not to disturb Angie. We waited a while, and then Angie's eyes opened.

"I heard him," she said, looking at Sophie. Then, turning to me, she asked, "Did you?"

"Hear him? No," I said, with some uncertainty. I may have seen something, but I didn't hear anything. "What did you hear?"

"I felt something, too," Angie said. "I felt as if I was being supported by someone standing right at my back. I heard him saying, 'The first step takes courage.'"

I gulped. "What do you think that means?" I asked.

"It means I need to tell the mother superior that I want to be a sojourner. Then we'll work out the details—whether I need to quit my job, or if she has work I can do for the convent, and what sort of spiritual program I should follow."

Sophie turned to me with a question. "Did your meditation help you to prepare a response for your sister?"

In a strange way it had. I didn't mention what I'd visualized, but I said, "I think my instinct is telling me to accept my sister's judgment. I know we'll talk more about this decision, but it's Angie's life. It's going to be up to her." It came as a natural gesture to take Angie's ring out of my palm and give it back to her. Angie slipped the ring on her finger and smiled back at me.

"You two work well together," Sophie said.

I returned the compliment. "It seems you've helped Angie clarify what she wants to do." I added to myself: that's a sign of good counseling, whatever its underpinnings. "Tell me, how did you get started with this angel work?"

"At a very painful time, a painting of an angel was a comfort to me. My fiancé died after I discovered I was expecting his baby. The last time I saw him, he gave me a lovely little icon of the angel Gabriel. After I heard the awful news, every night I prayed to Gabriel, asking that our child would fill the hole in the world I felt after Peter died. I named my son Gabriel after the angel in the painting."

Angie and I both started. The name Peter rang loudly in our ears. It couldn't possibly be a coincidence. "Do you still have the painting?" I asked, trying to contain my shock.

"Of course. It hangs in my son's bedroom. It's all he's ever had of his father."

I asked if we could possibly see it, fearing she would think it a rude request, but she seemed pleased.

"Oh, yes. I thought you might want to look at it. Angela told me you're a professor of art history. And you've had a similar experience, haven't you—finding an icon of Archangel Michael around the time of a friend's death? That's why I was sure you could help Angie in her process of discovery. It was a sign from above, wasn't it?"

Sophie had turned away from Angie and was facing me. Angie brought a finger to her lips in warning. I nodded in acknowledgment, a gesture that Sophie took as confirmation of her spiritual insight. My mind was racing. A glance at Sophie's painting would tell whether we were talking about the same Peter and another panel of the triptych. But I already knew the answer.

"It's quite small," Sophie almost apologized as she led us down the hall to the room her son occupied as a boy. It was now a more generic guest room. Over the dresser, where most people have a mirror, hung the twin to our icon. It was obviously the left side of a triptych, just the same size and shape as our panel, but in reverse. The figure in the icon was an angel the same size as our Michael, but with feminine hair and figure. She held a long-stemmed lily. The halo was copper, not gold, and the palette of the rest of the painting was in harmony—a pale orange robe and ocher background. There was no doubt in my mind.

"Did your fiancé tell you anything else about the painting?" I asked.

"No. He just asked me to keep it always near me. I think he must have had a premonition of his death. This was what he could leave me of himself."

"It's a Russian icon, isn't it?"

"Yes. Peter's name was Russian, and he told me it had been in his family a long time. I've always believed it to be a sign that the archangel Gabriel was watching over us, my son and me, even though Peter was gone."

"And that's what started your interest in angels?"

"Yes, I've been grateful to Gabriel and the angels ever since."

Angie was bursting to say something but it was clear that she didn't want Sophie to hear it. We thanked Sophie and hastily got ready to go. While Angie arranged another meeting, I pondered Sophie's faith in the goodness of her life and how devastating it would be for her to learn the truth.

As soon as we were at the bottom of Sophie's long white stairwell, Angie grabbed my arm, and insisted, "We've got to talk."

"I know we do. On the way home, or here?" I pointed toward the café next door.

"Let's eat, right now." When Angie has a problem, her metabolism races, and she gets awfully hungry.

The Willow Wood Café's turkey club took care of the hunger, but Angie couldn't constrain her emotion. Between bites, she implored: "Promise me you won't tell Sophie about the icon her boyfriend gave to that other woman. What a rat. He was two-timing her while she was pregnant! How is Sophie going to feel if she finds out about that?"

"I know. But we can't pretend it didn't happen, can we?"

"Have a heart, Nora. Sophie's spent her whole life being a single mother, going through everything a mother and child go through together, hanging on because of her faith in her fiancé who lovingly left her in the protection of the angel Gabriel. It would be cruel to take that away from her."

We were in a pickle. It would be no small thing for Sophie to be faced with Peter's infidelity. I was torn between two choices. Revealing what I knew to Sophie would destroy her innocence. But stifling that knowledge would destroy the prospect of ever restoring a lost masterpiece. Even if Sophie learned the truth, would she ever agree to let her icon be cleaned if it meant losing the image of Gabriel? Of course, we still didn't have the third panel. But discovering the second panel so close at hand now raised my hopes of finding the remaining one. Maybe there was a third girlfriend still keeping it safe for her lost darling Peter.

"We can't keep this quiet forever, Angie. It doesn't work that way."

"What doesn't work that way?"

"The truth. Sooner or later it will come out."

"But you don't have to say anything about the other woman, do you? Couldn't you just say you found your icon in the table but you don't know how it got there?"

"What good would that do? Once the discovery of the second panel gets out, Rose Cassini will hear about it. There's no way of preventing that."

"Couldn't you talk to Rose and ask her to keep quiet for Sophie's sake?"

"I don't know how Rose would feel about that," I said. I remembered she told me that Peter had been the love of her life. The truth would be a blow for her, as well. "I need time to think this through. I need to talk to Toby."

At Toby's name, the man at the table in front of us twisted around to look. Until then I hadn't paid the least attention to any of the other patrons in the café. I did now. The man whose back I had been facing was Arnold Kohler, the gambler. Dan had said Charlie owed him money. Kohler quickly turned back to his soup and his companion. I recognized the other man as one of the two pals who had taken care of Tom Keogh when Tom was drunk at the River's End. Sonoma County is a very small world. How much had they overheard?

"We should leave," I said, lowering my voice.

13

THE HOUSE PHONE was ringing as we walked in the door. It was Al Miller.

"Hi, Al."

"Hi, Nora. I was just talking to George on Skype. He's finished the cleaning. It looks magnificent. Have you seen it yet? He's been trying to reach you."

"Not yet. I've been out. I just this minute got home."

"Well, wait till you see what it looks like now. I'm sure it's Rublev. I feel it in my bones."

"Oh, Al, that's fantastic. And something else just happened, something amazing. I think I may have located the other wing of the triptych."

"No!"

"Believe it or not, it's at the Graton Bakery." It sounded unreal, even to me.

Al was beside himself at this news.

"But I have a dilemma." I didn't give him all the details, but enough to explain my concerns.

"Nora, if you're right, this is a major discovery for the art world. You can't just let it drop. It's too important."

"I know it is, but things are happening so fast. I'm not sure what to do."

"Then you'd better slow down. You'll talk it over with Toby, won't you?"

"Of course."

As if on cue, my cell phone rang. Caller ID said Toby. I told Al I had to ring off; he understood.

"Hi, it's me."

"Toby, wait till you hear what just happened."

"You can tell me in a minute. Federenco was in again just now, with his son. He wanted to introduce me to him, like he thought I'd be happy to sell them the icon if I had it, just because I met another member of the family. It made me very uncomfortable."

"Oh? What's he like, the son?"

"A bruiser. Didn't say much, just stood around looking sulky. I felt threatened. They just left a minute ago. I can tell you, I was glad to see the back of them. Okay, so what just happened that you wanted to tell me about?"

"Oh, nothing much, I guess, compared with your news." I played him on my hook. "It's just that I found a second panel of the triptych."

There was silence on the line. "You did?" Toby finally managed to blurt out. "How? Where?"

I reeled him in. "At the angel reader's. It's hanging in one of Sophie Redmond's bedrooms, although she doesn't realize what she has. It's the left wing of the triptych, same style and size as ours, with an image of the angel Gabriel on it. Peter Federenco gave it to her around the same time he gave the other one to Rose Cassini. He was sleeping with both of them. How do you like that?"

"I can hardly believe it."

"It's true, though."

"What did you tell her?"

"Nothing. At least not yet. Angie is desperate to keep Sophie from finding out about Rose. She's worried that Sophie will be devastated when she learns that Peter was unfaithful to her, and she wants us to keep it all a secret."

"We can't do that," said Toby. "We have to tell her. In fact, it wouldn't be fair to Sophie not to tell her. First of all, she may own an extremely valuable work of art. It's in her interest to be aware of that, even if it means finding out about her boyfriend."

I hadn't considered that. I'd been too locked in to the emotional matrix of the love triangle to give money any thought.

"And by the way," Toby went on, "what about Rose? Does she know about Sophie?"

"I don't think so. She certainly doesn't know about the other icon, or she would have mentioned it."

"Right. So Rose doesn't know. Well, she'll have to find out about it, too."

"I'm afraid so. But Angie will have a fit."

"That can't be helped."

I told Toby about the two men in the café who could have been eavesdropping on my conversation with Angie, and then we continued talking about Sophie. Finally, Toby said, "Let's finish this conversation over dinner. Maybe I can bring Angie around."

But Angie was adamant about keeping our discovery a secret, and the discussion during dinner was heated. I made a roasted chicken, served with fresh asparagus and polenta, with ice cream for dessert. I let Toby do most of the talking since Angie already knew my position. Still, she stuck to her guns.

"I guess I'll just have to let you two work this out," said Toby when the meal was over, rising from his chair and clearing his place. "I've said my piece. If you'll excuse me, there's something I need to look up on the Internet." He went into the other room. I knew what he was up to. Yesterday I'd caught him checking out the website for Mercedes-Benz. Tonight it might be BMW or Lexus. Toby was counting his eggs and hatching luxury cars.

Angie remained at the table with her arms folded, looking cross. "Okay, truce," I said to her. "I think we've talked enough about Sophie for one day."

"Promise you won't say anything to her until we've talked some more?"

I sighed. "All right, but it's not a promise forever. I'll make some tea." I put the kettle on and laid out cups and honey. "Now, do you mind if I change the subject?"

"Let me guess," she huffed. "The convent, right?"

"Um-hmm. May I be blunt?"

Angie unwound her arms and tapped her spoon on her saucer. "Go right ahead."

"Men. Are you sure you want to give that up?"

"Am I sure? Well, no," she admitted, and even cracked a smile. "But isn't that what a trial is for? Anyhow, look at my track record. It's nothing to write home about."

"Maybe so, but you could fill up quite a few pages." I grinned.

That brought a giggle. "Don't rub it in."

"Seriously, I can't see you being celibate for the rest of your life."

"I don't know. Sophie and I discussed it. She's managed quite well herself all these years without a husband."

"She's not you. Plus she has a son, and it sounds like they have a close relationship. By the way, where does he live? Do you know?"

"He's been in London for the last couple of years. He's an architect. She's very proud of him."

"Think about it. If you take vows, you'd be giving up the chance to have a son like that. Don't you even promise to give up your parents and siblings and make the other nuns your new family?"

"Not at Grace Quarry. Remember, they've broken away from the church hierarchy. They're part of a new movement. They say they want to reclaim the church for the people."

"I don't quite get what being a nun means in those circumstances."

"That's what the sisters are defining right now. I'll have a chance to be part of their experiment."

"But what would you be promising? And what would you be doing every day? And how does it work financially?"

"The sisters and I will talk about all those things. When we work it all out, we'll write up a plan, a kind of contract, and I'll have time to think about it."

"Will you let other people see it before you sign it? Like me?"

"I'm not hiding anything, and neither are the sisters. It's just that I'm only at the beginning of thinking about this." I could hear the unspoken plea to cut her some slack. And, a bit late, I remembered my intention to let Angie lead her own life.

"I'm sorry, Angie. I'm sure you've thought through these questions, and more. I'm still just getting used to the idea."

"Does that mean you're not completely against it?"

"I'm not. As you say, a trial is a trial. At the end of it, you'll know."

Angie narrowed her eyelids. "You think I'll give up on the idea after I've tried it for a year, don't you?"

"We'll see, won't we? You know, Oscar Wilde once said that the best way to get rid of a temptation is to give in to it. He was talking about vice. You're talking about virtue, but it's the same principle."

"So, you'll help me talk to Mom and Dad?"

"If that's what you really want." The tea was ready. I poured.

The next morning, I slept in. Angie kept to her room. After lunch, she put on her walking shoes and said she was going out for a long walk. "I've got a lot to think about."

"I know you do." I waved goodbye. A long, meditative walk would do her good.

At about one-thirty, Toby called from the gallery, almost breathless. This time he was the one who had big news, and he didn't tease me about it. "Guess what? I found them. I finally found the storyboards!"

"What? Honey, that's wonderful. Tell me!" Immediately, I was as excited as he was. We'd been waiting for this break since first talking with Rose.

"They were hidden in two secret compartments behind the half-column pilasters of Charlie's desk."

"Say again?"

Toby was eager to share the details, but it was difficult for me to picture what he was describing until he slowed down and patiently explained how he had made the discovery.

"Okay. Picture the big oak desk from the front. There are two carved columns, one on each side of the opening where you put your feet. They look like pedestals, but they're hollow."

"Yes, I remember them."

"Behind each one is a vertical compartment, each almost as tall as the desk is high. And they're deep, too, as deep as the space extending to the back."

"How did you find them?"

"Well, 50 percent stubbornness and 50 percent luck. It turns out there are tiny release catches behind the back of the front drawer. I just kept looking over every inch of that damned desk because I knew it had to be Charlie's hiding place—had to be, by the process of elimination. I'd looked everywhere else. It just took me a while to figure it out."

"Toby, you're amazing."

"I don't know about that. I should have worked it out sooner. I've seen plenty of desks with hidden compartments but never one like this. Anyhow, I've got the storyboards, all three of them, and all in good shape. Now maybe we can figure out what Charlie saw in them. I'm closing the shop and coming home."

Twenty minutes later, Toby rushed into the house with the storyboards under his arm and went straight to the dining room, where he laid them out on the table. I felt we were closing in on the Rublev triptych. We now had located two of the panels. Could Peter's sketches provide the last piece of the puzzle and lead us to the third?

The drawings were done in black watercolor and ink on heavy illustration boards, each about 12" × 20". They were simple in composition. They depicted the exterior of the farmhouse in the Hitchcock film, shown from different angles, partially hidden by trees. Time and again I had looked at the tiny illustration of one of the drawings that had been reproduced in the auction catalog, but with no clue as to its import. Surely, I'd thought, if we could find the actual storyboards, the result would be different; then I could penetrate their meaning. But now, with the originals in front of me, I was no closer to an answer than before. I stared and stared. There had to be more, something about them that had led Charlie to return for the second day of the auction, when he bought the icon. For that was the sequence of events, Toby reminded me. The sale receipts were clearly dated. Charlie bought the storyboards on day 1 of the auction and the icon on day 2. It wasn't by chance that he went back for the icon. But nothing I could see here suggested the connection.

One of the drawings showed the Brenner farmhouse from the front, surrounded by trees and set back behind a split-rail fence. Another showed part of the house from a different angle, closer up, next to the corrugated trunks of some trees. The third showed a side of the house sheltered by an arbor, with a group of trees off to the right. In the film, the children's birthday party takes place under that arbor and spills out onto the lawn. But the drawing looked a little different from the way I remembered the scene. In fact, something seemed to be slightly amiss in all of them. I looked at the drawings close up. I stepped back from the table and looked at them from a distance. I looked at them from the side. Something was definitely odd, but I couldn't say what.

We must have spent hours at it. Finally, Toby said, "We're not getting anywhere. We need a break. Then maybe we can look again with fresh eyes."

"Agreed."

Toby went to the fridge and popped open a can of soda, which he brought back to the couch. "Tell me about Sophie again. Peter was seeing her and Rose Cassini at the same time."

"Yes."

"Okay. He gave each one a side panel of the triptych. And did what with the central panel?"

"My guess is that he kept it himself. When he dismantled the triptych, he split up his holdings, so to speak. Of the three, the central panel was the most important, so my bet is that he hid it where he thought no one else could find it, somewhere in or around the Brenner house. That was the message he was trying to give Rose when he died. And I was hoping the storyboards could tell us where."

"That makes sense to me. When the coast was clear, he was planning to retrieve the central panel and collect the sides from his two girlfriends, who didn't know about each other."

"Yes."

"I wonder. Do you think he ever had any intention of marrying Sophie?"

"Maybe he didn't know himself. Maybe he wanted to marry Rose. But he didn't live long enough to make a choice."

"But Sophie thinks he would have married her."

"Of course she does, and that's why Angie doesn't want us to say anything to her about the icon."

Toby sighed. "Oh, jeez. And now you tell me Angie wants to go into a convent?"

"Uh-huh." By now Toby knew all about the other bombshell resulting from our visit to the angel reader.

"If you ask me, she has way too much spirit to be a nun, not to mention flesh and blood." He scratched the back of his neck. "My stomach's rumbling. I'll find a snack. Too late in the afternoon for lunch."

While Toby went back into the kitchen and rummaged in the cupboards, I considered our next move. Toby was thinking about money, but my professional curiosity was engaged. I wanted to see the triptych restored and to participate in its recovery. That meant I needed to level with Sophie, despite Angie's reservations. I reasoned that Sophie would be more likely to let her own panel be cleaned if the triptych could be restored in its entirety, so my priority was to find the central panel. I stood in the kitchen door and explained my thinking to Toby as he wolfed squares of Sonoma cheddar on Wheat Thins. He nodded and munched.

I kept talking. "The storyboards must hold the key. So far we've missed the clue. We're going to have to try something else."

"I'm with you," said Toby.

"Let's watch *The Birds* one more time now that we have the storyboards and see if we can match any of them with the film. Maybe we can find a shot or an angle that can direct us to the exact site where the house stood."

"It's worth another try." Toby got up and went for his coat.

"I'm coming too. While you rent the DVD, I'll pick up dinner fixings. Give me a second to leave a note for Angie." We were soon out the door.

Angie still wasn't home when we returned. We'd had our eye out for her as we drove to the stores and back. I decided not to worry. Either she was on a very long walk, or she'd stopped for coffee at the surfers' café or the fishermen's café, or the golfers' café. You don't lack for cafés around here.

This time we didn't watch *The Birds* from start to finish. Instead, over and over, we stop-started the scenes that gave us a view of the Brenner house and the surrounding trees. With every replay, we became more frustrated. As far as I could see, no single shot in the film precisely matched any of the storyboard views. In a moment of pique, I said, "Hitchcock seems to have ignored these storyboards." I felt like throwing them on the floor.

Toby admonished me. "It doesn't matter whether Hitchcock used the storyboards for the film. It only matters whether Peter used the storyboards to encode a message."

Of course, he was right.

As I was absorbing this point, the phone rang. It was George Greeley. He had tried to reach me earlier to let me know he had sent a prompt to set up our Skype connection. Would this be a good time to connect, he asked? It meant an interruption, but I assured him it would be fine. Toby was right here with me, I said. Of course, we'd be thrilled to see the uncovered Rublev. "George, just give me a minute to boot up my computer, and I'll see you online."

In a few moments, Greeley was on screen, looking proud and ready to display his handiwork. On our side Toby stuck his head into the picture, and I made the necessary introductions.

"Here's what it looks like," said Greeley. "Don't mind the damaged corner; I haven't started on that yet. But I've removed all the gesso and finished the cleaning." He brought the icon up to the camera and positioned it until it filled the screen.

The result took my breath away. Toby whistled. "It's gorgeous. It's much more impressive than I imagined," he said. "You've done a fantastic job."

The deep, rich blue of the angel's robe looked even more intense on her full, extended arm compared to the partial section I'd seen exposed in Madison. A thinner robe of sienna brown with yellow highlights was draped atop the blue. It fell from the angel's right shoulder, crossed under her left arm, and billowed down to her ankles. The plumes of the angel's heart-shaped wings were visible behind her shoulders—details that hadn't been clear before the cleaning. One hand rested placidly on her knee; the other was poised above her lap. She was seated facing left but slightly turned toward the viewer, giving us a three-quarters frontal view. Her shape was gracefully elongated, but what held the eye was her sweet, delicate face, with its solemn expression and downcast eyes.

"Yes, it's wonderful," I said, echoing Toby's praise.

"I'm glad you're pleased with the work. Now, it'll take a few more days for me to finish up," said Greeley. "I've got to rebuild the support, fill in the wood losses, and restore the gilding in the damaged part. But it might be ready by next weekend. I'll let you know."

"That would be great," I said.

"There's something else I should tell you, though," said Greeley. "I had a disturbing call yesterday from someone with an accent, unmistakably Russian. He was asking a lot of questions about your icon. He was specific about that. He mentioned your name, Nora Barnes. He wanted to know when the cleaning would be finished. When I asked him to identify himself, he hung up. That didn't seem right. Do you have any idea who it was?"

I looked at Toby. "No, I certainly don't. Nobody besides Al knew that I was bringing it to you."

"Then that's very strange," said Greeley.

"I'll let the sheriff here know about the call," I said.

"I think you should be careful," Toby warned Greeley. "Make sure you lock your house at night. And I'd feel better if you didn't let the icon out of your sight until we can get out there to pick it up."

"All right. I'll do that. I'll call as soon as it's ready."

"Be careful," Toby said again.

"I will. You, too," said Greeley.

As soon as we disconnected, I tried calling Dan, but he didn't pick up.

"Damn," Toby said.

I didn't like it either. A man with a Russian accent. Did Mikovitch have an accomplice who was still out there somewhere? If so, how did he know that I had taken Charlie's icon to Madison? Toby covered his chin with his hand and scowled. "What are you thinking?" I asked.

"Try Dan again."

I did. Still no answer. I left a message, asking him to get back to us. In addition to this new worry, I was growing uncomfortable about Angie being gone so long. The sun was sinking in the west, shooting orange filaments across the harbor waters. I felt relieved ten minutes later when I heard her at the door. "You look exhausted," I said before I could censor the motherly remark. I instinctively helped her off with her jacket. She seemed done in.

"Yeah, I got lost on a path in the dunes."

"Those paths can be confusing. How did you get back?"

Angie looked evasive, and I concluded I had overstepped the bounds with my protectiveness. But she had an answer. "I spotted the surfers' coffee shack and headed for that. I hung out there for a while, and a nice guy gave me a ride back." She said this without meeting my eyes.

"Rest up then," I said. "How about some water for hydration and some wine for relaxation, and I'll start some dinner?"

"I'm too beat. I'll make a cup of tea and take a bath and go to bed." She turned away and went into the kitchen, as if she didn't want to interact. I left her alone in there and heard her tinkering around. Soon she went into her room without saying goodnight. Maybe, I thought, she'd emerge after her bath, to make nice. But she didn't.

Later, sharing a chicken salad and cornbread, Toby and I ruminated over George Greeley's message and what it might mean. Dan still hadn't called back. The thought that another Russian mafioso might be stalking us made my stomach turn over. How could anyone know about my trip to Madison? Al certainly wouldn't have said anything about it to a stranger, and no one else knew. On top of everything else, I was really worried about Angie. She seemed more than just tired. She seemed distraught. Maybe during her walk she had been brooding about her decision to become a nun. "It's totally unlike her to skip a meal," I said.

"That's true. Tell me more about what happened at the angel reading yesterday."

This time I gave Toby a fuller account of our session with Sophie, complete with that moment during the meditation period when I'd pictured Angie with her supporting angel behind her.

"Oh, come on, after all these years, you're not telling me you're having visions of angels," Toby protested.

"It was a very strange experience," I said. His eyes widened. "It's a matter of semantics," I continued. "The images I remember from parochial school are stored away up here," I said, tapping my temple, "the same way phrases are from all those classes I took in French and Spanish."

Toby continued looking at me as if I had changed into a witch before his eyes.

I didn't let that bother me. "So for example," I said, "since I know

French, if I were meditating on French history, I might hear '*Plus ça change, plus c'est la même chose*' in my head."

"Go on," he replied.

"And since I know Catholic iconography, I saw in my mind's eye an image of St. Michael protecting Angie. Just as if it were a message spoken in French, that image was telling me whether Angie is up to figuring out what her own life's purpose is. The message was: Yes, it's as if she has the protection of the archangel Michael, who helps people sort out their purpose in life."

"So you don't really believe an angel flew into the room and stood there behind Angie."

"You don't have to be so literal about it. The experience I had was powerful. It helped me come to a decision about Angie. You might say it reinforced my faith in her. That's what faith is, anyhow."

"You've lost me there."

"All I'm saying is that faith is choosing to believe what your heart tells you, what your inner spirit intuits as true."

"Why call it faith, then? How is that different from woman's intuition?"

"Don't tell me you're belittling woman's intuition," I said.

Toby smiled. "Perish the thought. How about applying your woman's intuition to the storyboards? Are you ready for another try?"

"As ready as I'll ever be."

14

WE CLEARED THE TABLE and laid out the storyboards again. This time it seemed to me that one felt thicker to the touch than the others. I ran my fingernail along the edge and felt a slight indentation, like a tiny groove. "Look at this, will you? Am I right that this one's thicker than the others?"

Toby held a corner of the board between his fingers, rubbed them, squinted at the edge, and confirmed my guess. "I think these may be two illustration boards pasted together. If so, I may be able to pry them apart." He fetched his toolbox and came up with a box cutter. Inserting the sharp edge of the razor blade into the groove, he exerted pressure in a smooth downward-slicing motion. To my surprise, the two sides separated easily, as if they had been pried apart recently and then squeezed back together. Yellow gobs of hardened old paste dotted the exposed interior surfaces. Sticking to one of the sides was a newspaper article clipped from the *San Francisco Chronicle*. It was dated April 16, 1962. The headline read: "Hidden Treasures of Russian California."

I'd seen it before on microfilm in the Santa Rosa library. It was the story that outlined the legend of a lost Andrei Rublev triptych and encouraged descendants of Russian immigrants to search their attics for forgotten heirlooms. It was the story that had spurred Andrew Federenco to renew his campaign to get the family triptych back from his cousin. And that was when Peter took the triptych apart, gave each of his girlfriends a panel, and hid the remaining one.

"Okay, I think I know what happened. Peter must have pasted this story between the illustration boards, and Charlie must have found it when he got the boards home from the auction. The story about a valuable long-lost icon sparked his curiosity. He went back to the auction catalog and noticed that a Russian icon was for sale the next day and guessed it was from the same consignor. He figured there was a connection, so he bid on it and then confirmed the connection when he spoke to Rose Cassini on the phone."

"That sounds right," said Toby.

"Then this Russian thug shows up and pressures Charlie to sell him the icon, probably threatens him and scares him into hiding it, along with the storyboards. Meanwhile Charlie was trying to work out the relationship between the icon and the Hitchcock set, just the way we are. He checked out the DVD of *The Birds* on the day before he was killed."

Toby agreed. "That explains why Charlie was at the site of the old Gaffney house on the night of the murder. Either the Russian forced the story out of him and made him go there, or he followed Charlie to the site. I think Dan figured that part correctly. A fight broke out, Charlie was stabbed, and the killer stowed his body on the abandoned boat in the harbor. It all fits."

"Which brings us back to the storyboards," I said. "They hold the answer to the missing panel, but we just can't see it. Yet it's there right before our eyes."

"You said earlier that we have to find another way of looking," said Toby. "How else can we look?"

Yes, I thought, how else? Already I had looked at the drawings every which way—up close, from a few steps back, from each side—every which way except one, I realized. Now I walked around the table and looked at them upside down. It was a trick I'd learned in graduate school while studying art composition. If you're trying to analyze the formal construction of a work, it sometimes helps to disorient yourself from your normal point of view. Seen upside down, the abstract forms and volumes become more obvious. That's because the eye isn't distracted by the subject matter. And that was the case now. Something I hadn't seen before became obvious.

There's a principle of composition known as "the rule of thirds." The artist or photographer who wants to use it is told to imagine a tick-tack-toe board imposed over his picture. Where the lines cross to establish the middle box is the center of interest. That's where the subject goes. It's called "the rule of thirds" because that focal point will be about a third of the way from the top or bottom and left or right.

I'd assumed the subject of the storyboards was the Brenner house. But in none of them, seen upside down, was the house at the center of interest. Instead, in each, what occupied the center was the same cluster of trees. That's why the storyboards didn't match the film. Hitchcock never would have put a subject without interest at the center of his frame—it would have made for a confusing shot. No, Peter had made these drawings for himself. They were a way of fixing a location in his memory. They pointed to a hiding place, of that I was sure. I explained all this to Toby.

The same three trees were centered in each drawing, and in each drawing they were configured as a triangle. If you were looking toward the front of the house, the three trees were off to the right. It didn't matter that the house was gone now, because that triangle of trees must still be there. If you stood at the right spot, looking toward the dunes, you'd be facing the top point of the triangle, which was marked by the largest tree.

"Run that by me again," said Toby.

"Say you're standing on Westshore Road facing the dunes near where the Brenner house used to be. Now imagine a triangle laid out on the ground and you're standing midway along its base."

"Okay."

"Now look straight ahead." Toby stood, looking straight ahead.

"Directly in front of you, say eight or ten feet, is a large tree, larger than any of the others nearby. Imagine that's the apex of the triangle. Remember, you're standing at the midpoint of the triangle's base."

"Got it," said Toby.

"Now look to your left. You see a smaller tree."

Obediently, he looked left.

"Now look to your right." He did. "You see another tree about the same size and the same distance away as the one on your left. Those two trees mark the corners of the triangle's base. That's the cluster we're looking for. Now do you follow?"

"I'll say I do. What you're telling me is, we've got a treasure map. That's where he buried the panel." Toby tapped the triangle of trees on one of the storyboards. "X marks the spot!"

We were up at first light, ready to go. Toby went out to the garage to find a shovel and spade. I headed to the kitchen, to make us a quick breakfast. But I was stopped in my tracks by Angie, who was sitting disconsolately at the kitchen table, red-eyed and nursing a cup of coffee.

"Angie, what are you doing up so early?"

"I couldn't sleep. I've done something stupid. It might be really bad."

"How much harm could you do at this hour?" Angie looked pained, so I dropped my teasing tone and waited.

"It was yesterday," she said. "I didn't go for a walk like I told you. Instead, I went to see Rose Cassini."

"What? I thought we agreed to wait before talking with her."

"I know, but it was really upsetting me. I've been so worried about how Sophie will feel when she finds out that Peter had another girlfriend."

"Sophie's a grown woman, Angie. She can face the truth."

"You don't know what it's like. I do. I've had more than one guy make a fool of me. When you find out you've been betrayed like that, it's horrible." Angie was starting to cry. "You don't know. You think that someone really loves you, and then you find out you meant nothing to him. It's humiliating. I wouldn't wish that on my worst enemy, never mind a sweetheart like Sophie." Now the tears were flowing freely.

I sat down facing her and pushed a box of tissues within her reach. When she was quieter, I said, "Okay, let's not argue about whether you should have gone. Tell me what happened."

About then, Toby came back into the house. He started to say something, but I signaled to him not to and instead to join us. He came over and sat down at the table quietly. I popped some slices in the toaster and poured us coffee as Angie told her story.

"I know it was wrong of me, but I didn't know what else to do. I could tell that you and Toby had made up your minds to tell Sophie everything so you could get her to restore the icon, but I didn't want you to."

"I know, we've been over that. So you took it upon yourself to visit Rose Cassini to try to persuade her in advance not to say anything about Peter once the story came out, is that it?"

"Yes." She looked down at her hands in her lap.

"How did you know where to find her?"

"Her name and address were on the tag on that shawl we bought for Mom, remember?"

Of course.

"So I only pretended to go out walking. I took the car instead and drove up to Cazadero. I rang the bell, and when she came to the door, I told her that I had bought the shawl she made and I wanted to talk to her about weaving, so she invited me in." She paused, sniffling.

"Then what?"

"Well, we talked a little, and then I told her who I was and why I'd really come. At first she was shocked to hear that Peter had given another person one of his icons. In fact, she didn't believe me, but eventually, after I described it, she did. And then I told her about Sophie, and—oh, Nora, it was awful. She got really mad."

"Did she?" I wasn't surprised. Angie had been so obsessed with Sophie's reaction to learning about a rival that she'd failed to anticipate that Rose would have a reaction of her own.

Angie reached for another tissue, wiped her nose, and continued. "I should never have told her that Peter was Sophie's fiancé. She just lost it when I said that. And then when I told her he was the father of Sophie's child, she flew into a rage. She wanted to know how old the son was, when had he been born? I didn't know the answers, and that made things worse. I tried telling her about Sophie's relationship with her son and why it would be really good of her if she didn't let Sophie know about her own relationship with Peter, but at that point she threw me out of the house."

"Physically?" asked Toby.

"No, not physically, but she told me to get out. She said it was all a lie. That some other man had gotten Sophie pregnant, not Peter, and that Sophie must have claimed Peter as the father because he couldn't defend himself. She said that Sophie wouldn't get away with lying about a dead man and that she'd get the truth out of her one way or the other."

"That's not good," I replied. "Did she say anything else? Did you?"

"I asked her to wait to talk with you. I said you knew more about it than I did. I just wanted to slow her down and get her to cool off. But she didn't cool off. She got angrier and angrier. So I left."

"When are we supposed to talk?"

"Today. I told her we'd call. But now I'm getting worried. I don't think she'll wait for us. She knows who Sophie is. She knows where Sophie works. I'm afraid she'll go over there on her own."

Toby said, "You'd better call to warn Sophie about this."

"That's what I'm worried about," Angie replied. "I just tried the bakery. That's where she'd be at this hour. She'd just be finished baking. But she's not answering. Maybe she doesn't answer till the bakery is open, but I don't remember when that is."

"Try again," I urged. We waited the call out, and there was no answer.

"Did you try her apartment?"

"Yes. No answer there either." Angie stood up. "I'm going over there. I have a bad feeling about this. If anything's happened, it'll be my fault."

I said to Toby, "We better go with her. If we arrive and everything is okay, we'll figure out a way to tell Sophie about Rose. If not . . ."

We all piled into Toby's car. There was little traffic on the coastal road at this hour, but early morning mists and drizzle slowed us down. It was almost seven-thirty when we arrived at the Graton Bakery. The front door yielded to a push, but there were no lights on at the counter, and the shelves held no bread or pastries. I took that as a bad sign. But light was shining through the round window in the door to the baking room.

I held up a palm to stop Angie from barging through. I knocked and called Sophie's name. No response. We opened the door and walked into the hot baking room, with its bright lights, large ovens, and long working tables. It took a second's sweep of the eyes to spot Sophie, slumped on the floor, in her baker's whites, with flour spilled all around her. Near her head, the flour was smeared with blood. We started toward her, calling her name, but again I blocked Angie.

"Watch out. There are footprints in the flour on the floor—don't step on them. I'll check if she's alive." I made my way carefully over to Sophie and reached toward her neck to take a pulse. She stirred and moaned. I didn't see a wound, but the gray hair on the back of her head was darkly matted and there were abrasions on her neck, face, and hands. I knew better than to move her.

"Toby! We need you! Call 911. Then call Dan."

The ambulance arrived first. By the time Dan pulled up, the paramedics had Sophie on a stretcher, and they were sliding it into the back of the ambulance. She was unconscious but her vital signs were good, one of the paramedics said. She had suffered an obvious blow to the head. If there were other serious injuries, they would be discovered in the emergency room. Angie was tormented by self-blame and insisted on riding along in the ambulance, but that wasn't permitted. Besides, Dan needed to question her.

After checking the scene, he led us back into the front room of the bakery. On the phone, Toby had given Dan only the briefest information. Now we brought him up to date, starting with my discovery of Sophie's icon and ending with the unanswered phone call this morning that had brought us here.

When the ambulance, its blue light twirling and siren sounding, left with Sophie for Palm Drive Hospital in Sebastopol, Angie burst into tears. I put my arm around her shoulders. Dan needed Angie to be lucid. To her credit, she was calm again in a few moments and provided a thorough account of her conversation with Rose, repeating what she'd told us at breakfast, omitting nothing.

"What was the last thing she said to you again?" Dan asked, going over the same ground a second time.

"That she'd get the truth out of Sophie. She sounded pretty mad."

"What do you think she meant? What truth?"

"Whether Peter Federenco was the father of her baby."

"And those were her exact words?"

Angie hesitated. Dan waited.

"She said she'd get the truth out of Sophie one way or the other."

Dan jotted down those words. Angie looked dejected.

"Nora," Dan said, "you were the first one to find Sophie injured this morning, right?"

"Yes."

"You didn't move her, did you? Or touch anything?"

"I touched her neck to check her pulse. Otherwise, no one's touched anything. We tried to be pretty careful about that. Like the footprints in the spilled flour. We walked around them."

"Smart. Put these on now." He handed each of us a pair of paper shoe covers.

"Those are fairly small shoe prints in there," Dan said. "They could be a woman's." I knew they weren't Sophie's, since the footsteps led away from where she was lying on the floor. Sophie was short, so she could easily have been hit from behind by a woman.

"How well do you know Rose Cassini?" Dan asked me.

"We interviewed her just that one time. You've read my notes."

"Yes." He thought for a moment. "I'm sending a car out to Cazadero to pick her up." Dan dialed a number and gave the order over the phone.

"You're not arresting her, are you?" Angie said in consternation.

"I'm bringing her in for questioning. I have to, don't I, based on what you've told me?"

"I suppose so," Angie conceded in a meek voice.

Dan put his notepad in his shirt pocket and looked around the room. "Is anything missing, do you know?"

We glanced around the bakery shop. Everything looked untouched. The cash register hadn't been opened. Dan gave the buttons a push and found them unresponsive.

"There's probably a key for that," he said. "We'll check later to make sure the register wasn't tampered with. Step back into the baking room with me, and tell me if you see anything amiss."

I told him that none of us had been inside it before this morning. "But if you just want other eyes on the room, let's do it. Toby, why don't you wait here?"

"Sure," he said. "I'll man the shop."

Angie and I stepped in, just a few feet, so as to leave the site clean. I remarked to Dan that the scene told us something about the timing of the attack. The ovens were on. Bread loaves were cooling on a back shelf. On the counter in front of where Sophie had lain was the mess made when she was disturbed rolling out some pastry, maybe dough for croissants. A bin of flour—probably open for dusting the pastry while rolling it—had overturned and spilled over the counter and onto the floor. The rolling pin still lay on the floor where Sophie had dropped it. With no pastry yet in the oven, Sophie must have been interrupted before 5 a.m.

I looked at the white footprints, which led away from the counter toward the back of the room. Dan's eyes were following mine. The prints pointed in the direction of a stairwell. That must be the inner stairway toward Sophie's apartment.

I don't know why I hadn't thought of it before. "There's nothing of value down here, but what about the icon? Sophie lives upstairs. Her icon was hanging in one of the bedrooms."

"You better show me," said Dan. He motioned to Angie and me. We walked awkwardly upstairs, slowed by the paper shoe covers.

When we entered the apartment, everything was orderly. Nothing seemed different from the way it had looked the day before. But above the dresser in the second bedroom where the icon once hung, a naked picture hook on the wall confirmed my fear. "Oh, no," I cried. "It was here yesterday. We both saw it."

"Rose must have taken it," said Angie.

Dan looked at me inquiringly.

"She couldn't have known its value," I said. "Otherwise she wouldn't have put hers up for auction. She still doesn't know what we know about the triptych, unless you told her about it, Angie."

"You mean about the other painting underneath St. Michael? I never said a word. But that wasn't why she wanted the icon. It was jealousy. She wanted it because Peter gave it to Sophie. She took it from Sophie to get even."

But Rose wasn't the only person who might have wanted the icon. I now told Dan about the suspicious phone call George Greeley had received from a caller with a Russian accent. "I tried to reach you yesterday to tell you about it."

"I got your message. I was going to call you today. That changes things," Dan agreed. "I'll get in touch with Interpol to see what leads they have on other Russian mafia in the United States."

"But that's not all." I reported seeing Arnold Kohler with a friend of Tom Keogh's at the Willow Wood Café while Angie and I were talking about Sophie's icon. "They may have overheard us."

"I'll get on that, as well," said Dan. "But right now I need a search warrant for Rose Cassini's place." We stood by while he made the arrangements by phone.

Angie shifted impatiently from one foot to the other, waiting until he finished. "Can we go?" she asked. "I want to get to the hospital." Dan nodded yes. He stayed behind to wait for his crime scene team to arrive.

We drove to Sebastopol through the rain, which now was coming down in sheets. By the time we made it inside the hospital, we were soaked. We sat in our wet clothes in the waiting room while Angie paced the halls searching for a doctor who could inform us of Sophie's condition. When she finally found one, the news was guarded. Sophie had a concussion, a serious one. She was still unconscious, but her life wasn't in danger, in the young doctor's opinion. At this point no visitors were allowed.

"We can't do much good here right now," I said to Angie, "so let's go home, dry off, and have some lunch." She started to protest, but I continued. "Then you can come back in your own car and stay all day if you want. Would that be okay?"

Reluctantly, Angie agreed. The news about Sophie's prognosis had relieved some of her anguish, and keeping vigil at the hospital would give her a purpose.

When we got home, I made lunch and bagged some nuts and raisins for Angie to take with her. "Sophie will pull through," I said. "She's going to be all right."

She nodded silently, her chin on her chest.

"Now I understand why you slunk home yesterday like a guilty dog with her tail between her legs."

"I should have told you about it last night, but I was too ashamed," she admitted.

"But you told us this morning, and that's what's important. We got there in time to help."

"I hope so."

"We did, Angie."

She managed a weak smile.

After lunch, Angie gathered what she needed for a long stint in the waiting room. She took a thermos, the snacks I'd bagged, a poncho, a blanket, and some magazines. I followed her out to her car. "Are you coming home for dinner, or will you get something in Sebastopol?"

"I guess I'll decide later. I'll call from the hospital." She gave a distracted wave and drove off.

15

TOBY CAME OUT OF THE HOUSE and walked up beside me as I stood on the curb. "Poor Angie."

"She'll be okay."

"Are you still up for our treasure hunt after all that?" He pointed to the gardening tools he'd fetched from the garage this morning and had left leaning against the side of the house.

"I think so. There's no reason to put it off." The rain had stopped an hour ago, but the sky remained threatening. The ground underfoot was soggy, which might even help with the digging.

"All right, then," said Toby, "let's go." We loaded everything into the car—Peter's storyboards, two shovels, a hand fork and spade, and a tarpaulin that Toby had found in the back of the garage. That was optimistic. He was hoping to find the missing panel to wrap up.

This time we drove all the way out to the end of Westshore Road and worked our way back toward the marina, using the storyboards as our guide, searching for just the right cluster of trees. According to what Colleen had told me on the golf course, the Brenner house had stood somewhere near today's entrance to the dormitories for the marine lab employees. It turned out we weren't far from their driveway when we found the most promising area. In fact, we parked right in front of a sign that said "Restricted Access." That brought up the question of digging on the marine lab's land. This was UC–Davis property. It was something we hadn't considered, but now we realized we'd better ask for permission. We rang Dan again and asked him if he would call the marine lab office and request authorization for us to proceed. He warned us they might require a search warrant, and that could take time. We told him we'd wait to hear back.

Meanwhile, we felt safe enough to scout around with the storyboards in hand. There were clumps of Monterey cypresses at the shoreline just opposite the housing entrance, as well as to the right of the entrance and to its left. The ones on the shore were too close together and too small to match those on the storyboards. The cypresses to the right of the entrance were all in a line, following the contours of a ditch. We needed to concentrate on the grove to the left of the entrance.

A light fence, made of two thin cables stretching between posts, defined the entrance to the housing area and ran the west length of the road for a quarter of a mile or more. The top wire was chest high. As I waited, I saw that we could do some of our analysis from this side of the fence without ducking under the lower wire. There were fifteen to twenty trees in the shallow grove, about half of them very large and obviously old. The grandfather of them, toward the back of the space, had started to fall apart with age. Its trunk was so thick that it might have started with two or three trunks that had grown together. Half of its crown had fallen in some recent storm. It looked like our landmark tree. I pointed that out to Toby.

We took another look at the storyboards and the triangular composition they delineated. "So now we need to look for two cypresses that are up here near the road and are more or less equidistant from the big old guy," Toby said.

And there they were, only two yards in from the fence and about three yards apart from each other. Without crossing the barrier, it was hard to tell if the big tree was set at the correct distance to be the apex of a triangle that was approximately three yards on each side. But it seemed about right.

We looked around for other candidates to match the storyboards, but with every passing moment I became more confident. We were anxious to dig, but where exactly to begin? "The area inside the triangle isn't that huge, but it's too big to dig the whole thing up," I said. And something else was nagging at me, too. "How deep do we have to dig before we decide we're at the wrong spot?"

Toby replied, "I thought about that problem last night, and just as I was falling asleep, the answer came to me."

"Don't tell me you had a vision too."

"No, it's just logic. If Peter buried the icon out here during the filming, he wouldn't have had much time to do it. There'd be people around. He'd have to come out at night and dig in the dark, using a flashlight. And he wouldn't want to leave a big pile of dirt nearby or leave the ground looking obviously torn up. Ergo, he didn't dig too deep a hole."

"I hope you're right." I was losing heart, standing in the damp with a storyboard in one hand.

"Besides," Toby continued, "I'm beginning to see the way this guy's mind worked. On top of everything else, he was superstitious. There was a pattern to everything he did. He was obsessed with the number three."

That struck a chord. I sensed that Toby was on to something. "Go on," I said.

"Three panels. Three hiding places. Three trees," Toby ticked off on his fingers.

I saw he was right. "Three storyboards. The rule of thirds. The Holy Trinity," I added.

"There you go. Everything comes up three. It was like a magic number for him, some kind of good luck charm."

"But how does that help us now?" I asked.

"We start at the center of the triangle and dig three feet down. The center, I admit, is a guess."

"It's worth a shot. Let's call Dan and see if he's getting permission for us to dig."

Toby phoned and found Dan in the middle of a call with the security officer at the marine lab. Toby asked Dan to tell the security man that we hoped to limit our digging to a couple of holes no more than three feet deep. Of course, we would fill in any dirt we removed when we were through. Dan put Toby on hold and came back shortly with the needed permission. "This is your lucky day," Dan said. "The guy I talked to was a drinking buddy of your partner. He said if this was related to Charlie's murder, he wanted to be of help."

"So we can go ahead."

"Yes. Go ahead and get started. But the security guy—Joe's his name—will be coming down to check you out. Be nice to him. He's doing you a big favor."

We bent down and crawled under the fence's lower cable. Then together we mapped out the triangular area between the trees. Toby walked toward the center of the triangle, while I checked around from different positions to see if it looked like the center from every side. Finally I gave a nod, and Toby made his first thrust with the big shovel. The rain had indeed softened the earth, and the work went rapidly once we were working together, Toby with his shovel, me with my smaller one.

By the time the security man pulled up in a pickup truck, we had a hole about two feet deep and wide. He rolled down his window and rested a beefy hand on the side-view mirror. We had a friendly chat with Joe, who wanted to talk about Charlie and the good times they used to have with a poker group at the Guerneville Tavern. Joe was the outgoing sort, in his midthirties, with a ruddy complexion and an easy smile.

"So you used to play poker with Charlie," said Toby. "Was Arnold Kohler running that game? We heard Charlie was in debt to him."

"I heard the same thing. But no, those stakes are too rich for my blood. Kohler is one of the big boys. The guys at my table play for dollars and change. Why do you ask? You think Kohler had anything to do with Charlie's murder?"

"The sheriff's still looking into that," I said. "What we're hoping to do is find out what Charlie was doing out here the night he was killed."

"Yeah, Dan told me about it. Well, you go ahead. As long as the sheriff's okay with it, it's all right with me." For Charlie's sake, Joe was prepared to go out on a limb with his bosses, letting us dig for whatever Charlie might have been looking for when he was killed. Joe took our names, address, and phone number as well as our car license and advised us that if anyone stopped and questioned us to have them call him in the security office. We thanked him, and he gave me his card. We promised to call him when we were through digging. He wished us luck, returned to his truck, and drove back up the road toward the lab.

Digging was harder now that we were deeper into the earth. Thankfully, this was well-mulched earth, thick with the loose debris of a grove undisturbed for decades. We ran into tendrils of root, but they were tender enough to cut through with the smaller shovel, which had sharp edges. When the hole was three feet deep and no box had turned up, Toby moved over a little and started again—with the same result. Next he moved over in a different direction and tried once more. Again, nothing but dirt. He continued, gopher-like, in this vein while I labored with my shovel and the hand spade, trying to widen the girth of the several holes. By now both of us had worked up a sweat. I took out a handkerchief and mopped my brow. The gray light of the afternoon was growing dimmer. It was going to rain again.

"Too bad, Toby. It was a great idea."

"It still is," he said. "Let's try a variation on the theme." This time he marched over to the big, gnarled Monterey cypress that was the storyboards' most prominent landmark. It stood at the apex of the imaginary triangle that connected the three trees. Toby leaned his back against it, facing the harbor and the two smaller trees that stood at the triangle's remaining corners. With ceremony, he paced off three steps and started to dig. At two feet, with a thwack, his shovel struck something solid.

"Could be a root," I said.

"O ye of little faith!" Toby shouted, grinning. "Come over here and give me a hand."

Kneeling over the hole, I poked with the spade and felt a thump that seemed promising. Moving around, I poked again, this time feeling just the same thump at the right depth. "Feels like you've hit a box," I said triumphantly.

"Then we need to be careful not to punch the shovel through it."

Working carefully, we finally dislodged the box from the surrounding earth. It was covered in plastic, so it was somewhat slippery, though the dirt on it, as well as the effects of long-term burial, gave it just enough texture to allow for a grip. We knelt facing each other. We dug our knees and toes into the ground, dropping our heads and arms down into the hole. I got a purchase on my two corners, and we gave it a heave-ho. Up it came, and we moved over to place it on the ground. The box wasn't heavy, but my shoulders, arms, legs, and back were going to ache tomorrow.

We had before us a rectangular shape, maybe 24" × 14". It was still thick with dirt, but a little scraping showed that the outer surface was a black plastic bag, tightly wrapped over the box. I had been working in gardening gloves, but I took them off to untangle the wire closure. Sometimes a woman's fingernails come in handy. Toby was watching expectantly, and as soon as I had the tie undone, he began pulling at the bag from the bottom. All this revealed was another layer of plastic bagging, also tightly tied. But once we had struggled to get both bags off, we were looking at an extraordinarily well-preserved box, really a small trunk.

Top, bottom, and edges were strapped with metal, while the body of the trunk was painted wood. All surfaces of the rust-red paint were stenciled in white and blue with bands of flowers, vines, and fruit. The front of the box bore a keyhole and, above it, a small ring for lifting the top. It was probably a foolish thing to do, but I gave a tug on the ring. Nothing budged, which was just as well, since we should get the box into a safe environment before we looked for the treasure we hoped would be inside.

Intent on our task, we paid no attention to a car driving by until it slowed to a crawl and left us with the uneasy impression that we were being spied on. By the time I looked up, it had passed us, heading in the direction of town. All I could see of the driver was the back of his head. I had a glimpse of gray hair. The car sped up and disappeared around a bend.

"Who was that?" asked Toby.

"I think it was Andrew Federenco."

"Uh-oh," said Toby.

But I couldn't be sure.

We stayed on the site until it was nearly dark. First we wrapped the box in our tarpaulin and set it in the front seat so that I could carry it in my lap. Then, as promised, we were dutiful about filling in the dirt holes and restoring the area to something like its previous state. It was certainly easier moving the earth back into the holes than it had been getting it out, but still it took some time to do it right. Finally, we called Joe and thanked him again for allowing us to search, and yes, we told him, we had found what we were looking for.

Back at our house, we tried to brush off the creepy feeling of being under surveillance. Really, I couldn't tell who'd been in that car. It could have been Federenco, but it could also have been a curious passerby. Instead of worrying about it, we bent our efforts toward breaking open the box, at the same time taking care not to break its contents. We were mindful of the damage we'd caused in extricating Charlie's icon from its hiding place. Toby worked for a while with a hammer and chisel on the lock. When that approach failed, he tried using the chisel to pry the lock away from its wooden support. Eventually the wood creaked and splintered, and with a little more force, the base of the lock came away from the trunk. Toby opened the lid and we peered inside.

The object in the box had been wrapped carefully in a soft cloth and cushioned by fistfuls of balled up newspaper. Toby flattened out a page and read the story's date: April 20, 1962. Gingerly, he reached inside the box again and lifted the small bundle from its resting place. He carefully unwrapped it.

Immediately I knew it was the central panel by its shape and by the side hinges, to which the wings had been attached. This panel was slightly larger than the other two. It bore a rather commonplace painting of the Virgin and Child, in a style similar to that of the angel Michael we had removed from Charlie's panel. And it matched the description in Andreyev Federenco's memoir. That's how the triptych had been disguised: the Mother of God occupied the central panel, the angel Gabriel on her left, and the angel Michael on her right. The iconography was conventional. But I knew that underneath its surface appearance, the hidden work was highly unconventional. Layers beneath this image, waiting to be revealed, was a work of genius that some might call heretical.

I was so lost in thought that for a time I didn't realize the house phone was ringing. When I picked it up, I froze. The voice on the other end was guttural and spoke haltingly in heavily accented syllables.

"We have your sister. Is pretty girl. You do what I say or I cut off ear. With no ear, not so pretty."

Angie!

Toby, alarmed at the twisted look on my face, sprang to the phone and punched the speaker button. "Who is this?"

"We have your sister," the man repeated. "Is pretty girl."

"What do you want?" Toby demanded.

The voice continued with calm menace. "What you have."

"If you mean the icon," said Toby, "we don't have it." He was thinking quickly. "We sent it out of town for restoration."

"Is other one. You found today."

So it wasn't just our imagination that we'd been under surveillance. The voice said "we." Whoever these people were, they knew where Charlie's icon was, and they knew about the one we had in front of us.

"Bring it tonight. Come alone. No police. If you call police, I feel sorry for sister."

I was terrified. I let Toby take over the conversation, while I wrote down the directions. We were to bring the panel to a cabin on the outskirts of Monte Rio, a small village on the Russian River. We were to come at nine o'clock, and no police—or else. If we followed the instructions, Angie would be safe and we could bring her back home with us. The man hung up, leaving us fraught.

"What should we do?" I asked Toby. "Should we call Dan?"

"No. For Angie's sake, we better do just what he said."

"My God! If anything happens to Angie . . ."

"I know. We'll get her out of this, I promise. But we can't call Dan, not yet."

What I could do was to try to call Angie. Maybe the threat was a bluff. Maybe she was safe. But she didn't pick up. "She could still be at the hospital. You're supposed to turn off your cell phone inside."

"It's almost seven o'clock already," said Toby. "We would have heard from her by now if she wasn't coming home for dinner." That was true. "But I need something to eat, myself. I'm feeling weak with hunger from all that exertion. Then we'll go."

I had no appetite at all, but Toby was right. We both needed food, something fast and easy. I threw some fish sticks in the oven and microwaved a bag of frozen peas. It made for a grim meal.

I could see that in spite of the adrenaline rush, Toby was still dog-tired from the day's digging, so I offered to drive. It would give me something to concentrate on besides Angie's danger. But I was surprised that he agreed. That meant he must really be exhausted, and we'd need all our strength and wits once we got there.

We started out before eight. Monte Rio is a few miles inland from Duncans Mills and Toby's shop. We knew the road but wanted extra time to find the cabin and to allow for driving conditions. The night was wet and black. There would be no starlight or moonlight to aid our drive.

As we made the turn onto Highway 1, I remembered with regret that there isn't a single street lamp on the winding coast road. I prayed that my generally good night vision would help me hold to the center line, avoiding deep ditches on the right where the road has no shoulders. I was relieved when the lights of an occasional house set close to the road offered a moment of clarity. I felt safe enough on those stretches where moors on the left led to cliffs down to the sea, but when there was nothing on my left but a steep drop to the ocean, I just gritted my teeth. Thankfully, we encountered few cars, so I drove with the brights on most of the way. But I was keenly aware of potential crash sites.

"A little slower on the curves," Toby advised. He takes this drive daily, so I wasn't about to doubt his judgment. I braked down to a safer pace.

In the deep dark, with nothing illuminated but the immediate road ahead, it was hard to gauge how fast we were covering ground. I asked Toby the time—I didn't want to take my eyes off the road to look at the dashboard clock. The landmarks familiar to me were invisible in the dark.

Finally we approached the lighted windows of the Indian restaurant that guards the bridge over the Russian River, just before Jenner. Once over the bridge, we turned in from the coast, to follow the river to Duncans Mills and Monte Rio. We had hardly spoken on the coast road, but now we began talking again. Who would be waiting for us in Monte Rio? Russian gangsters? Arnold Kohler? Or maybe Andrew Federenco and his bruiser son? How were we going to handle this?

As we reached the wide lanes and bright lights of Duncans Mills, we developed our strategy. Of course we would turn over the central panel in exchange for Angie. We could promise to give them Charlie's icon as well, as soon as we had it back from the restorer. What else could we do? What if they had no intention of letting us go? One step at a time. Right now the focus was on saving Angie.

The road narrowed at the bridge over Austin Creek, and after that the huge redwoods that bordered the road threw us into even darker obscurity. I concentrated on my driving. Soon enough we were at the Monte Rio crossroads. We took a hairpin turn to the right, followed the sign toward the center of the village, and crossed the metal bridge that spans the Russian River.

The caller's directions were to take a left just after the bridge, onto River Boulevard. That seemed a grandiose name for the narrow lane, which was posted with a sign reading "No Outlet." But it must have been a thoroughfare in the old days when Monte Rio was a popular summer residence for San Franciscans. On either side, the road was jammed with vacation cottages, most of them weather-beaten. However, only a few of the buildings we passed had lights on. After a good half-mile drive, we reached the final block, where we had been instructed to seek the last house on the left.

There it was: a log cabin, tucked back farther from the street than any of the other houses. The cabin presented its side to the road, with the one window lit but curtained. The door would be to the right of the house, down the driveway. We didn't pull in there, though. We decided to turn around at the cul-de-sac and park our car on the road, facing out, headed toward home. We might want a quick escape.

"Are you ready?" I asked, glancing over at Toby, who sat with the icon cradled in his lap. It was wrapped in the cloth that had covered it in the box, which we'd left at home.

"Let's go," he replied. "They've seen our headlights. They already know we're here."

We closed our car door without locking it. We walked up the driveway and stood for a second in front of the doorstep. We could see a car parked on the grass behind the house. We mounted the wooden steps and knocked.

"Good. Right on time," a voice that I recognized said as the door opened.

"You!" I exclaimed.

"Yes, me," said George Greeley. He was holding a gun.

I stammered, "But I just talked to you. In Madison."

"We talked on Skype. From here. I had a hunch you'd lead me to the other panels, and I was right. I just didn't know it would happen so soon." He stepped aside to let us in. I stood there, not moving, dumbfounded, until he waved us inside with his gun. I entered first, then Toby, with our treasure in his hands.

"Where's Angie?" I demanded. I scanned the large living/dining room but didn't see her.

"Don't worry. She's all right." He went toward the back of the room and unlocked the door that led into the single bedroom. "They're here," he said. "You can come out."

Angie staggered into the main room of the cabin, calling my name. I rushed over to comfort her, then realized when she didn't return my hug but stood with her arms squeezed together that her hands were taped tightly at the wrists.

"Over there," Greeley commanded, pointing to where he wanted her to sit, at the table. "And you two over there." He gestured toward a wicker couch. "Sit." We obeyed.

"So you were lying. You never got any suspicious phone call," Toby said accusingly. "The business about a second Russian gangster was a ruse."

"*Da*," said Greeley, imitating the voice I'd heard on the phone. "Is pretty girl, your sister. Too bad I cut off ear." He laughed at his own impersonation.

The pieces fell into place. "You're the one who attacked Sophie," I said. I remembered Greeley's delicate hands. I checked out his feet: small for a man's, like the shoe prints left in the flour.

He shrugged. "When Al Miller told me on Monday about the icon you discovered at the Graton Bakery, I couldn't pass up the chance. I took the red-eye and flew in yesterday."

"You monster!" shouted Angie. "You nearly killed her."

"That was regrettable. I'm afraid I hit her harder than I meant to. But now I have both panels. And you are about to give me the third. Hand it over, please. Slowly." Toby had it balanced on his knees. He started to stand up. "No. Stay as you are. Just hold it out to me." Toby did as he was told. Greeley took the package with one hand and shook the cloth aside. His other hand held the gun, pointing at Toby. He looked at the icon, front, back, and sides, careful not to takes his eyes off us for more than a second at a time. He walked back a few steps and placed the icon on top of a cabinet.

Toby said, "And let me guess. You were the one who drove by today while we were digging up the box."

Greeley smirked. "I've been following you since this morning. I couldn't believe my luck."

Angie, who had been fretting throughout this interchange, burst out, "It's my fault, Nora, I couldn't help it. He grabbed me as I was coming out of the hospital. I tried to get away but he had a gun."

"It's not your fault, sweetie."

Greeley was talking freely, so I pressed him. "How did you know where to find my sister?"

"I already told you. I was watching your house. I overheard you talking with her as she was getting in her car to go to the hospital. I figured taking her would give me the leverage I needed, and I was right." Greeley laughed once more. "I improvised. All right, I've answered enough of your questions. Now you're going to do exactly as I say. I don't like violence, but you know I'll use it if I have to."

"It won't do any good to steal the triptych," I argued. "You'll never be able to sell it. It'll be too well known. No one will touch it."

"You don't know Russia," said Greeley. "There are new billionaires who won't care whether anyone else ever sees it again as long as it's theirs. As long as they have it all to themselves or to show off to friends in their private hideaway. Not to mention the real Russian mafia, which would pay a fortune to lock it in a safe as collateral for future drug deals. It won't be in any museum or well-known collection or ever be seen at auction. As far as the world is concerned, it will disappear again just as it disappeared five hundred years ago. But someone will own it. And I'll be a rich man."

"It's not too late to stop before you make things worse," said Toby.

"Isn't it? Armed robbery, assault with a deadly weapon, kidnapping—I don't think they'll let me off with a warning, do you?"

"You'll regret this," said Toby, playing a weak card.

"Oh, please. I'll tell you what I'd regret—I'd regret spending what's left of my pathetic life in Wisconsin, where everyone I know is a professor and I'm still an instructor. I'd regret having a crummy old age trying to live on a pittance from Social Security and whatever's left of my lousy pension after that beady-eyed bugger of a governor gets through wrecking the system, that's what I'd regret. And guess what? I won't regret for a minute living in a fancy villa on the Black Sea, sipping vodka and eating caviar for the rest of my days."

"Fine," said Angie defiantly. "Go live in Russia and see how you like it. It stinks over there. But you've got what you want. Now let us go."

"Ah," said Greeley. "I'm afraid I can't do that. Not just yet. You see, someone might tattle before I can get clear of here."

That sounded ominous. "Then what are you planning to do with us?" Toby demanded. "You said if we brought you the icon, no one would get hurt."

"And no one will, unless you try something foolish." He went to the refrigerator and brought out a bottle of white wine, already uncorked. "This won't be too unpleasant. You're all going to enjoy a nice glass of wine and then take a nap. And while you're snoozing, I'll quietly take my leave." I now noticed three wine glasses on the table. Greeley poured the wine and dropped a small, white tablet into each glass.

"What are you putting in there?" I asked.

"A harmless drug called Rohypnol. You'll sleep until tomorrow and maybe feel a little woozy when you wake up. But otherwise, you'll be fine. You might not remember everything about tonight, which is a plus. And even if you do, I'll be long gone."

"Rohypnol," said Toby. "The 'date rape' drug."

"Some people call it that," Greeley acknowledged.

"Date rape!" cried Angie. "That's the last straw." And with that, she suddenly launched herself across the room and caught Greeley, just as he was pivoting toward her, with a deadly kick that landed where it hurt the most. "That's what happened to the last guy who tried that on me," she said. He let out a howl and sank to his knees, clutching himself with his left hand, while managing to hold on feebly to the gun in his right. "And this one's for Sophie," she added, stepping back to deliver the coup de grâce. The second kick landed in the same place, or rather, on the cupped hand that fruitlessly shielded his squashed privates. Toby cringed. Greeley crumpled like a newspaper, and his gun went clattering across the floor, stopping a few feet in front of me. I picked it up.

By then Toby was on top of him. He hauled Greeley up by his shirt collar and pushed him roughly down into a chair. With his free hand, Toby reached out for the gun, which I gave him. Greeley was whimpering. "I bet that smarts," said Toby, with grim satisfaction. "All right, Nora. Now we call Dan."

But first I ran over to Angie and embraced her. I gave her a fierce hug. I was laughing and crying at the same time. "Who needs Michael," I said, "when I've got you?" I covered her cheek with kisses. "Angie, my warrior angel!"

Epilogue

SIX MONTHS LATER, we were all standing in the lobby of the UC–Berkeley Museum, attending the reception for the world debut of Andrei Rublev's restored masterpiece, *The Old Testament Trinity Triptych*. Al Miller had organized the exhibition. The place was packed, as the publicity had been tremendous.

Angie had taken a vacation from her "sojourn" to join us for the big event. She looked a little different, with her hair cut short and her face without makeup. But Angie could never be anything but beautiful. She wore roomy black pants topped by a white embroidered blouse. I was surprised she was allowed embroidery.

Observing me looking over her clothes, she winked and said, "I haven't taken the plunge yet. But even the nuns wear street clothes, you know."

"You look happy," I said. "I'm glad you could be here for the opening."

"I am happy," she replied. "And I wouldn't miss this for the world."

The museum was only a temporary home for the newly acclaimed artwork, pending resolution of the multiple lawsuits that already had been filed. Let me see if I can get this right. As the holders of two of the panels, Toby and I were being sued by Andrew Federenco, Tom Keogh, Charlie's brother, the University of California–Davis, and the Russian government. Of course, each had a different claim. Federenco wanted the entire triptych, which he claimed had been stolen by his cousin. That meant he was also suing Sophie for the panel that Peter had given her. Tom Keogh argued that Charlie had bought the Michael panel for purposes of resale while legally still his business partner, so Keogh was entitled to half the proceeds from any sale. Charlie's brother claimed ownership of the same panel, citing Charlie's will, which named him as the heir. The University of California–Davis had dibs on the central panel, which, they pointed out, had been dug up on their land. And the Russian government was suing everybody, including the museum, on grounds that the triptych was a national treasure that had been spirited out of the country illegally. It was shaping up to be another epic case like *Jarndyce v. Jarndyce* in that Dickens novel, a dispute that dragged on for generations until everything had been eaten up by legal costs.

"All I want out of this," said Toby, "is a finder's fee, a modest finder's fee, that's all I want. They can have the icons." The problem was, "they" was an indefinite pronoun. Toby was talking to a lawyer. I told him not to.

There had been other developments. Rose and Sophie, who had recovered nicely from her attack, did meet, shortly after Sophie got out of the hospital. By counting months on her fingers, Rose deduced that Peter had fallen in love with her after he unwittingly had gotten Sophie pregnant. She was convinced that Peter, had he lived, would have broken off with Sophie, whose only claim on him was guilt, and that in the end he surely would have married *her*. Hence, Rose was disposed to behave magnanimously toward Sophie, extending a victor's olive branch. She went so far as to allow Sophie to believe the contrary scenario—that Peter had met Rose first and that he surely would have left her for the woman who was carrying his child, but for his fatal accident. I'll say this for Peter, he certainly was a charmer. The very thought of him fifty years later could make each woman believe what she wanted to.

It worked out well enough for Sophie. It seems her opinion of the angel Gabriel had lost its luster as a result of Peter's affair with Rose. In any event, she was persuaded to let her icon be cleaned for the exhibition, even if that meant expunging Gabriel forever. Her son had something to do with persuading her. The potential value of the restored Rublev was a factor in his enlistment in that cause. He had come over from London to attend the opening.

Joe the security guard was fired by the marine lab for giving us the go-ahead to dig up their property without first checking with his superiors. We were sorry for his trouble, but he too landed on his feet. He and Tom Keogh were now an item, and he was learning the antiques business.

George Greeley, needless to say, did not get to complete the restoration work. He was in custody and awaiting trial. Al Miller was appalled to learn of George's treachery and fell all over himself apologizing for recommending him. None of it, of course, was Al's fault. I kept having to reassure him of that.

But the most surprising development was the unexpected budding of an autumnal romance between two lonely people of a certain age: Rose Cassini and Andrew Federenco. It's true, they had a lot in common. Rose confided to me that her new beau reminded her of Peter in many ways. Andrew had looked her up, and well, as she said, you never knew. I hadn't yet heard Andrew's take on things, but then, he was communicating with us only through his lawyer.

Dan had closed the file on Charlie's murder, satisfied that Mikovitch had acted alone without an accomplice. At least, no evidence had turned up to suggest otherwise. We accepted that conclusion. And Toby accepted that he'd done what he could for his partner, Charlie, living up to Bogie's example in *The Maltese Falcon*. Today's opening marked the end of our journey of discovery—of crime, of art.

I had mingled and greeted and paid my respects, and now, since it was growing late, I decided to slip out of the reception to revisit the Rublev gallery one last time. I wanted to stand before the icon by myself, before the museum closed. Food and drink weren't allowed inside the galleries, so I set my empty wine glass down on a nearby table and headed for the stairs.

The Rublev display had a room to itself. At this hour only a handful of visitors lingered. Aside from a few couples and the guards, I had my privacy. In the center of the room, on a pedestal, under glass, on a cushion of black velvet, the celebrated and much litigated triptych stood folded open, lit from above by spotlights. How tiny it seemed compared to the original that Rublev had painted for the Cathedral of the St. Sergey Monastery. That huge version of *The Old Testament Trinity*, now at the Tretyakov Gallery in Moscow, was referenced by a life-sized, high-resolution photograph mounted on one wall.

Compared to it, everything in the smaller version seemed compressed. Even so, the lines were just as delicate, the jewel-like colors just as radiant. The noble faces of the miniature angels were as lovely as their larger counterparts, and the subtle interplay of their glances was intact. But inevitably, as Al predicted, the composition had been altered to meet the dictates of a different format. In the larger version, the three feminine angels representing the Father, the Son, and the Holy Spirit were seated around a communal table and conjoined in an imaginary circle, an arrangement that proclaimed their unity. Here each figure occupied her separate space. Each angel was seated on her own dais; and the little table bearing a chalice appeared only in the central panel. Critics or perhaps theologians could debate the symbolism.

There was another aspect of the triptych that intrigued me. As displayed, the outer wings were tilted forward, leading the eye inward toward the central angel, who symbolized the Son. Was that an accident, or was it possible that Rublev was experimenting with perspective? That would have been a revolutionary development for Russian art. I noticed that the platform on which each angel rested her feet was dramatically foreshortened, compared to the larger version. Also foreshortened was the forward pitch of the table on which the central angel rested her arm. That arm appeared to interrupt the line of the chair she was sitting on, so as to convince the eye that she was in front of it. Giotto had used a similar ploy in posing his *Madonna Enthroned*. Art historians would have a field day.

Beyond the technical advances of the painting, I was moved by the sheer beauty of it. That was the magic of art. Beauty was mysterious, after all. It was worth contemplating, like truth. Maybe Keats had it right and it's as much of truth as we can know.

Standing there quietly, I let my mind wander. I thought of the moment when Al Miller first lifted the film of varnish from that icon at his home to reveal the painting underneath it. Isn't that what mystics tell us about the world, that illusion veils some hidden truth? Through a glass darkly—that's what the Bible says is the best we can do at seeing things as they really are. Yet from Plato on down, philosophers have grappled with whether we see anything at all beyond the tip of our nose. I've wondered about that since I was a child.

When I was little, we lived in a big house, and there was a long corridor to walk down at night to get to the bathroom. All I had to show my way was the feeble glow of a tiny nightlight. Halfway to the bathroom was a scary closet that I wasn't supposed to disturb. Who knows what, I worried, was hiding behind that door? I'd tiptoe down the corridor, sneak past the door, use the bathroom, and run back to my bed as fast as I could. Then I'd pull the covers over my head and listen.

I'm still listening.

Sometimes I think the universe is like that closet of secrets. Every once in a while, a great prophet, or saint, or artist, or scientist comes along and pries open the door just a crack to let in a sliver of light. But the hallway is dim, the light is weak, and the closet is deep.

"There you are," said Toby, coming up behind me with Angie in tow. "We've been looking for you. The reception's over. Time to go."

"I'm ready," I replied.

They paused for one last look at the triptych. In silence, we gazed at it for another minute. Then Angie said, "Those are the most beautiful little angels I've ever seen. And you discovered them. Just think, if it hadn't been for everything that's happened, the world would never know they existed. Do you think it was all part of God's plan?"

"Including Charlie's murder? I doubt that very much," Toby scoffed. "Life isn't planned. It just happens."

"Is that so? What do you think, Nora?" Angie appealed to me for support.

I inhaled a long breath and let it out slowly.

Angie said, "Well?"

I smiled at her. "Nobody knows, sweetie." I reached for Toby's hand. He was rolling his eyes. "I mean, really. Who does?"

Acknowledgments

Andrei Rublev is an important figure in Russian art, but the triptych on which our plot depends is fictitious, as are the characters and events in this novel. However, even a work of fiction depends on facts, and we are grateful to the generous people who provided us with information and assistance.

We want to thank Barry Bauman, art conservator, for patiently answering e-mail queries regarding icon conservation and restoration, even taking time out from his vacation to do so. James Jackson of Jackson's International Auctions in Cedar Falls, Iowa, was generous in sharing with us some of his vast knowledge on the subject of Russian icons and their history in the United States. We are grateful to Susie Silverek, formerly of the Sonoma County District Attorney's office, who informed us about jurisdiction and procedures for criminal investigations in the county and particularly in Bodega Bay. Jonathan Davis, of the Links at Bodega Harbour, was kind enough to answer questions about that marvelous golf course. Many thanks to Caitlin Woodbury for enjoyable conversations that yielded facts and color regarding life in Sonoma County. Thanks, too, to Barbara Flaherty, whose salon, The Premiere of Windsor, Wisconsin, is the model for Angie's hair emporium in Gloucester, Massachusetts.

Our research took us to several local libraries. David Dodd, Reference Librarian at the Sonoma County Library, Santa Rosa, helped us find back issues of the *San Francisco Chronicle* using the library's files on microfilm. Katherine J. Rinehart, Library Associate, History and Genealogy Library of Sonoma County, Santa Rosa, assisted us with locating information on Rose Gaffney, the "Hole in the Head" protests at Bodega Bay, and the filming of *The Birds* in Bodega Bay. Thanks to guide Lisa Gurian for her informative tour of Fort Ross and to the staff at the Fort Ross library.

We also relied on a number of books and articles for information. An invaluable source was *Searching for Icons in Russia* by Vladimir Soloukhin, translated by P. S. Falla (New York: Harvill Press, 1971), which served as our model for describing the process of removing darkened drying oil from the surface of old icons. On the subject of Russian icons, we also consulted, among other works: John Stuart, *Ikons* (London: Faber, 1975); Kate Cook, trans., *A History of Icon Paintings: Sources, Traditions, Present Day* (Moscow: Grand Holding, 2005); Robert C. Williams, *Russian Art and American Money, 1900–1940* (Cambridge, Mass.: Harvard University Press, 1980); Susan Wiley Hardwick, *Russian Refuge: Religion, Migration, and Settlement on the Northwestern Pacific Rim* (Chicago: University of Chicago Press, 1993).

We learned about the practice of angel reading through the works of Doreen Virtue, notably *The Angel Therapy Handbook* (Carlsbad, Calif.: Hay House, 2011). Thanks to Zebunissa Collier, an angel reader and speech language pathologist in Petaluma, California, for pointing us in her direction. Much gratitude also to Zebbie's sister Rebecca Printen, yoga instructor extraordinaire, for introducing us to Zebbie. We also consulted David Albert Jones's *Angels: A History* (New York: Oxford University Press, 2010).

Readers who found the cosmological table talk in chapter 6 of interest might want to try Jim Holt's *Why Does the World Exist?* (New York: Norton, Liveright, 2012) for a deeper treatment of the subject.

On Hitchcock and Bodega Bay, we thank Michael Draine, who sent us Kyle B. Counts's "The Making of Alfred Hitchcock's *The Birds*," *Cinefantastique* 10 (Fall 1980): 14–35, which proved very useful. We also benefited from "*The Birds* by Hitchcock," *Sonoma Coast Guide*, no. 25 (April 2005), a special issue devoted to the film; and Jeff Kraft and Aaron Leventhal's *Footsteps in the Fog: Alfred Hitchcock's San Francisco* (Santa Monica, Calif.: Santa Monica Press, 2002).

We should add that any misstatements or errors of fact in this novel are inadvertent and solely our responsibility, not that of our sources or informants.

We are grateful to Jerry Peterson, for his advice on how to improve the manuscript, and to our editor, Raphael Kadushin, for his steadfast support. Finally, heartfelt thanks to friends and family for encouraging us and for sharing our pleasure in the adventures of Toby and Nora.